A Power So Great

Stories of Magic and Love Gone Awry

William Wilkin

Bell Street Publishing, LLC

Bell Street Publishing, LLC

Published by Bell Street Publishing, LLC,
7360 Middlebrook Circle
Nashville, TN 37221-6545

Copyright © 2020 by Bell Street Publishing, LLC

ISBN: 978-0-9600387-0-1

First Published in the United States, 2020

Cover Art:
Digital Painting: James W. Wilkin
Graphic Design: Matthew A. Stone

i

Contents

Acknowledgments

I owe an immense debt of gratitude to several people who have contributed substantially to this book's artistic integrity.

There are my two sons, James and Matthew Stone.

James contributed the digital painting on the cover which captures as I never could my vision of the sense of the book. He also made a number of graphic design suggestions that are incorporated in the cover design and interior of the book.

Matthew Stone made manTy suggestions for the layout and design of the interior as well as completing the cover layout.

My wife, Lou, contributed in both obvious and subtle ways to the completion of the book. She is a Spanish teacher and has extensive experience editing and correcting texts—both student and professional. Any remaining grammatical and spelling errors must not be accounted to her. They proceed from my eccentric ideas about the value of deviating from standards occasionally to accurately portray a state of mind or emotional content. A subtle way that she supported the completion of this book was her endless patience with those eccentric ideas.

In addition, she was willing to endure the many, many times that I worked into the early morning hours pursued by my characters who insisted on telling their stories at the most inconvenient hours.

She has always been emotionally constant in the shifting winds of our lives throughout the long thankless years of the struggle to bring these stories to print. Bravo Lou!

v

Prelude

For those of you who have not read any of the preceding books, I will warn you that this preface contains spoilers. If you want to learn about the story line to the point where this book begins, you could read the stories in sequence—*In the Realm of the Blind, The Chessmaster, The Spare Wizard, The Ministry Witch and other Tales of Perfidy, Wandering With Wizards, The Boy Genius, The Squib's Apprentice, In the Land of the Ghosts,* and *The Legacey.* However, reading the first book by itself would give you a good grounding in the Realm of the Blind.

This story takes place in the universe of the Realm of the Blind where Hogwarts School for Witchcraft and Wizardry exists. It is a residential finishing school for magical youth.

The main character, James Wendt, is an English Literature Professor and muggle (non-magical). He has been hired by the Headmaster Albus Dumbledore to bring diversity to the school and the slightest touch of liberal arts education to an institution that is basically a vocational school. Dumbledore has been assassinated by Severus Snape who became the Headmaster of Hogwarts.

Wendt was "volun-told" to aid the muggle government struggle against Tom Riddle a.k.a. Valdemort. The would-be despot Valdemort had a gang of followers who call themselves Deatheaters. He and his followers were determined to enslave the muggle population. Thus, muggles like Professor Wendt were on their *persona non grata* list.

Wendt and the Assistant Headmistress Minerva McGonagall were "an item." However, the astronomy Professor Aurora Sinestra seemed to have designs on Wendt.

Harry Potter was now a wanted man—the number one undesirable. Every relative of Potter was now in danger. They would be used by the Deatheaters to reach Potter. These relatives included his cousin Dudley Dursley, his aunt Petunia Dursley, and his uncle Vernon Dursley. They fled their home and eventually fled England. After the defeat of Riddle, they returned to England.

Meanwhile in England, Wendt was organizing a resistance to Riddle by both muggles and Wizards. He organized an attack on Azkaban that resulted in supporters of Potter being released and taken to a refuge. Among his muggle allies were a technical guru that everyone called the "Boy Genius" and his personal assistant, Sally Harker.

After the Dursleys returned to England, Wendt discovered that Dudley Dursley had magical powers. Dudley was hired by Hogwarts to assist the janitor, Mr. Filch.

Later, there was an invasion of Earth by a race that called themselves "Souls". Other called them "Ghosts". They "possessed" people by overwhelming the nervous system of their victims. The wizarding community resisted this invasion and, with the participation of Wendt and a few other muggles such as the Boy Genius, defeated the invasion.

Immediately before the current story, Sally Harker became the personal assistant of the Headmistress of Hogwarts, and the Boy Genius had set up his internet security business in the Shrieking Shack. They were all involved in a strange incident that puzzled American law enforcement. It concerned an international gang that was executing a plan that involved hundreds of millions of dollars but seemed to have no clear objective.

Other staff at Hogwarts include Rubeus Haggrid (Professor of Magical Creatures), and Professor Flitwick (Professor of Charms), the Librarian, Ms. Pinz; and the Nurse, Madame Pomfrey.

Boys Night Out

The school year began as it usually did. The Head gave a brief greeting to the assembled teachers, staff, and students. I missed most of it because I was lost in reverie. It had occurred to me that there was not a year that I'd taught here that something dangerous wasn't afoot—except, that is, for the year before last year. Somehow, we'd gotten through the whole year without tragedy. If it weren't Riddle and the Deatheaters, it was the brother of Charity Burbage, the muggle Studies professor. If it weren't he, the Souls were taking over the world. If it weren't the Souls, what would it be?

I awoke from my reverie while the First Years were being sorted into houses. As I listened, I was struck that almost all students were sorted into every house but Slytherin. I wondered how long it would be before Slytherin house would be redeemed. Now that there was no descendant of Salazar Slytherin still alive, would the curse that seemed to hang over that house finally end?

Minerva gave the announcements for the year. Thankfully, they were all boring—no corridors to be avoided, no tri-wizard tournament, no Ministry hag to oversee the school. I wondered what announcements that Snape had delivered the one year that he'd been headmaster. Someday I would have to ask Minerva.

As usual, following the opening banquet, the teachers and staff met in the Teacher's Lounge. As usual, Filch and I found seats at the back of the lounge and kept our heads down. Filch had eventually forgiven me for leaving the school that year when Riddle was defeated. It wasn't that he ever objected to a drink in my quarters, but he just didn't invite me down to his office. Of course, Dursley shared his office now, but I know that Dursley's presence was not an inhibition to Filch's various inclinations. They included drinking, abuse of students, and frequently spoken assertions that he was the force that kept the old school floating along on the uncharted sea of time.

Filch whispered in my ear, "Now that you and the Head are sharing . . . uh . . . sleeping arrangements, you'll be wanting a safe place to have a boy's night out, won't ye?"

I didn't deign to answer that question. I knew that Filch knew the answer that he wanted, and no inconvenient facts such as my denial would stand in his way.

□

The next day nothing happened. I don't mean that it was a day when I stayed in bed all day long. I mean that nothing happened that was a consequence of Filch deciding that I needed a safe haven for nights out with "the boys".

It was a normal day. I went to classes. I gave my usual beginning of term speech. It went something like this:

"Most of you are familiar with me and my idiosyncrasies. Just to review them, I'll mention that it should not have escaped you attention that I am a muggle. I suggest that you think about the fact that I've survived quite nicely here at Hogwarts for over ten years.

"No wand work is necessary in this class. I know that most of you would feel somewhat naked without your wand, so you may certainly carry your wand. However, there is absolutely no need to have your wand in your hand. I don't object to your holding it, if it gives you a sense of control, but if you do anything with your wand in this class, you will be subject to discipline. The discipline may be something as simple as 'detention and lines' with me. You should consult older brothers or sisters as to whether they liked that form of discipline.

"For more severe infractions, I refer you to the Headmistress. I give you fair warning that she is also my wife and has a very low opinion of students who take advantage of me.

"For the most severe breaches, I refer you to Mr. Filch. He is a close buddy and takes particular pleasure in dealing out penalties to students who overstep the bounds. I suppose that now I have to mention that he may subcontract some of that work to his apprentice, Mr. Dudley Dursley. Mr. Dursley was tormented as a child by another wizard, Mr. Harry Potter. He may still harbor some resentment toward unruly students".

I then point out the information that I write on the chalkboard in the upper right hand corner—my proper name, my office number, and office hours.

4

I proceed with the objective of the class—to read good, age-appropriate literature of the English language, to practice writing literate essays, and to learn about the history of English literature. I point out that the balance between those goals depends on the age of the students.

□□

As the days passed, I began to wonder if I'd misjudged Filch. So, as I was finishing supper in the Great Hall and preparing to head for my office to polish off a little grading from the previous day, I was surprised by a bony hand that clapped me on the back. I looked around and discovered Mr. Filch and Mr. Dursley.

"Well, if it isn't my two favorite groundskeepers right here before me!" With some trepidation I asked, "What can I do for you?"

Filch smiled broadly and said, "It's what WE can do for You! We're kidnapping you for a little smoozing away from 'She Who Must. . .'"

I opened my mouth to protest but Dursley cut in forcefully, "No need to thank us."

Filch added, "Though you should. Come on down to my. . . " He hesitated and went on, "Our office for a little nightcap, eh."

I could hardly refuse such a gracious offer, so I counted my blessings that it hadn't happened on day one and followed them down into the dungeon.

We arrived. I discovered that Dursley kept his desk quite neat. It was a study in orderliness compared with Filch's. It was hard to believe that they shared the same office, and nothing had rubbed off from one to the other.

Filch opened the bottom left drawer of his desk and was reaching in when Dursley said, "No, no. I've got something special here for this occasion."

He reached into his lower left drawer and pulled out a bottle that turned out to be Johnny Walker Blue Label. I almost gagged. When I regained control of my throat, I said, "That stuff is not cheap. This must be some occasion."

Dursley just smiled a sly smile and said, "You surely haven't forgotten that Professor Slughorn and I have published a book. The revenues haven't been quite what he hoped, but they've been quite respectable. I can afford this once in a while."

He had set the bottle on his desk and pulled three shot glasses from the desk drawer. They looked pristine to me, but he took out his wand and said, "Scurgio." The glasses that were sitting on the table seemed to have a thin coat of liquid golden fire on the inside. Then, he materialized spherical ice

5

cubes into the glasses. Finally, he poured a generous portion of the Blue Label into each.

Filch picked up his glass and gazed at it for a moment. He commented, "It's almost too good to drink." Then he took a deep sip—not a gulp. He seemed to be swishing it around in his mouth and then swallowed. The sigh that escaped his lips spoke of deep appreciation. Nothing further was needed to complement Dursley on his liquor.

We both took smaller sips and agreed thoroughly with Filch's sigh of appreciation.

I looked at both of them and said, "Well, it's been a good while since we had time for this kind of celebration. Please tell me what's been going on with you two."

The two of them looked from one to the other. No one seemed to want to start, so I took the initiative. "OK. What's happened with Ms. Myers? I haven't seen her in a long time. Did something bad happen?"

Dursley smiled. 'No. No. Nothing like. After she'd recovered from her poisoning, she applied for jobs—you know, the Ministry, a few manufacturing concerns, AND *The Prophet*."

I interrupted. "You mean the same *Prophet* that we all know and hate? The one that has published so many . . ." I was stuck for words. Luckily, Dursley provided some.

"Yeh. So many inauthentic stories that turned out to be fabricated in some editor's head rather than researched by reporters?" He smiled as he said that. It was not typical of him. Was he quoting something that he'd read somewhere or maybe heard someone say? I guessed that it must have shown on my face because he answered my unspoken question, 'Yeh. I didn't make that up myself. When Pam took the job, I was a little surprised because most of the people around here don't seem to like *The Prophet* very much. She said that *The Prophet* was under new management.

"It was no longer a place where the norm would be inauthentic stories . . . Well, you heard the rest. She was excited. But there was a catch."

I nodded wisely. "There always is."

Dursley smiled again. "The catch was that she would have to start at the bottom. The bottom was being a foreign correspondent. She was excited. . ."

□
□□

Pam was sitting across the table from me in a restaurant with a view of the Seine not far from the Tower. Her eyes were wide as she described this new job. "I'm going to be in on the ground floor. *The Prophet* is all new!" She gazed up and vaguely off to the right as though she were looking at something in the distance. "There's a new managing editor who comes from the Washington Wizarding World. They were on top of the Riddle thing from the beginning. I interviewed with that editor. She is going to have real reporters on real stories."

She paused for breath, and I was trying to ask a question when she wound up again. "She wants me to take Canada! I mean, the whole of Canada! Do you know how big Canada is?"

I opened my mouth, and the first thing that came out was, "Well, as a matter of fact, yes. I crossed most of it by train with my family. There's lots of empty space out there. Also, lots of snow."

She looked at me with eyes even wider if anything. "You've been to Canada?"

"Yeh, we spent maybe about eight months there in various places."

Her mouth dropped open. "When in the world was that? I thought that you went straight from muggle school to Hogwarts."

I kind of lowered my eyes and said, "Well, there was this year when my family and I were on the run . . . and . . ."

I had managed to raise my eyes to hers again. It was a work of tremendous effort. She asked, "Who would you have been on the run from?" Then it hit her, "You don't mean that Riddle was after you?"

I smiled, relieved that it wasn't anybody like Riddle after us, "Oh, no. no. It was just a couple of Deatheaters."

She nodded her head slowly. Then she said, "Sure, you were Potter's cousin, and your parents were the Aunt and Uncle, right?"

I nodded. She went on, "How did you ever escape the Deatheaters?"

I shrugged. "Well, we had help. There was this couple who the Order of the Phoenix had assigned to protect us and hide us out."

Her eyes dropped and took on a look that I could have sworn I'd seen on kids who were getting ready to steal the lunch money from some smaller kid. She asked in a sort of a slow drawl, "Just how did that work? Why don't you tell me all about it?"

She reached into her purse and brought out a small notebook and a quill. Was she interviewing me for a story? I thought about what to say. Then I began, picking my way through the story, trying to find the important parts, and the parts that were not too embarrassing.

Potter was being a real pill trying to convince my Dad and Mum to get us to leave our home and friends and everything we knew because this Valdemort bloke wanted to kidnap us or something.

My Dad would get convinced, and then he'd change his mind. Anyway, THE day came when the wizard and his wife, the Dingles, came for us. We either had to go with them or just wait for Valdemort to come for us. We left with them. Really, it was they who left with us. We drove off in our Ford. I thought that my world had come to an end.

Actually, it had come to an end. Everything that I believed about the world disappeared like a puff of smoke on the breeze. It took us most of the day to get to their home on the North Sea. The first week, I was convinced that I'd die of boredom. Then, I began to get into a rhythm and began to fit in. I did lots of work. I helped around the house and in the garden. I also spent lots of time jogging.

I was really getting to the point of liking staying with the Dingles. Then something happened. The Deatheaters showed up. They attacked the Dingles house. I guess they were sure that we'd be taken by surprise.

The Dingles weren't. Somebody in the Order of the Phoenix warned them. They got away with my Mum and Dad. I was out on the beach jogging. The Deatheaters had pretty much trashed the house but hadn't waited to see if anyone came back. I did, and my parents and the Dingles did.

Dad made a big decision then. He decided that wizard protection was not worth the added danger of being with Order members. He decided that he would take our family off and try to find a place to hide.

That started our great migration. We started by pulling our cash out of the bank and buying tickets on a boat headed for the Caribbean. We were sure that we were being pursued, but somehow, we always seemed to stay a step or two ahead of them.

We boarded the boat and pretty much hid out in our cabin. We had a little run in with the Captain when we sort of broke into another passenger's cabin, but by the end of the cruise we had all that cleared up. We parted on good terms.

I stopped and thought about the cruise ship and the purser we had met. Pam noticed and asked what I was thinking about.

"Oh, we ran into someone whom we'd never met, but whom Professor Wendt knew."

Pam laughed. "Talk about your long-shot coincidences!"

I was still thinking of Jennifer. She was at least ten years older than I was ... but ... Pam picked up on my abstraction. She waved a hand in front of my face and said, "Earth calling Dursley."

I returned my attention to Pam, but she wasn't satisfied with my lame excuse that I was thinking about the coincidence. She can be pretty intense when she has her curiosity up. "Just who was this acquaintance of Professor Wendt?"

"Oh, no one. We met her on the ship and never saw her again."

Pam was a natural reporter. She insisted, "There must be more to the story than that! Now! Give!"

I remembered Professor Wendt's rule of thumb. If you're going to tell a big lie, include as much of the truth in it as you possibly can. So, I did.

Here's the deal.

This friend of Professor Wendt was named Jennifer. He'd met her even before he met Professor, well, Minerva. It sure seemed like she, that is Jennifer, had a thing for Wendt and that it had maybe only gotten stronger across the years.

Anyway, there was a Professor Wendt on the ship's passenger roster. He was in a cabin near us. Jennifer was sure that he must be the same Wendt. She sort of recruited us to help her discover who this Wendt was. We tried various things and finally broke into his cabin.

I don't know if you've ever been in Wendt's office, but his office was never half as neat as his registered cabin. We eventually found out that it was all a ruse to cause the Deatheaters to follow a wild goose. I think that's how they got on our trail.

Anyway, the Captain didn't take it kindly that we broke into a fellow passenger's cabin. We were on the Captain's black list for most of the rest of the cruise, although we eventually got back on his white list.

Pam began to smell a rat. She started asking me a series of pointed questions. "Just what did THIS Jennifer look like?"

"Oh, she had long brown hair that she always wore in a tight bun at the nape of her neck."

"Just how did you know how long it was?"

That had me stumped for more than a few minutes. Then I remembered, "There was a squall that swept over the ship at one point. Everyone was drenched, including Jennifer. Her hair just sort of came down and . . ."

Pam said, "It sort of seems like a wet teeshirt contest."

I opened my mouth, took a deep breath, and didn't have anything come out of it.

"Just how pretty would you say this Jennifer was?"

I took another deep breath, but this time, I had something come out. "Well, on a one to ten scale where you are a ten, Jennifer would be . . . oh . . . a six, maybe a seven on a good day."

"Just how many good days did she have?"

I sort of looked backward in time trying to conjure Jennifer's appearance. Actually, there were an awful lot of good days, now that I thought about it. "Oh, you know. Pretty much average." I delivered that opinion with a hopeful smile.

I hastened on to make one point very clear. "But, you're barking up the wrong tree. Jennifer was Wendt's property through and through." I was pretty sure that was true.

She "hmmmed" reflectively. "Do you suppose that she'd be willing to be interviewed for an article on the last days of the Deatheaters?"

I smiled. "I don't know. She was always pretty willing to talk about Wendt."

Pam eyed me suspiciously. "Yes, willing to talk to YOU about Wendt." She hesitated and said, "I'd like to get in touch with her and see if she'd give me an interview. How would I get in touch with her?"

At least, I didn't have the slightest idea. "I'm sorry. I've never heard from her since. It must be possible to track her down through the cruise line."

She seemed to accept that.

"We spent a few days in the States but had to change plans and take ship on a freighter. It was pretty boring except when we went through the Canal. Of course, we were put off ship in SoCal when there was this little superstition thingee."

She stared at me and asked, "Superstition thingee? And what's this SoCal—a state of Mexico?"

I had to laugh. "I guess that's what everyone on the West coast of the United States calls Southern California. Get it? So Cal?"

Pam nodded, but she'd not entirely given up on Jennifer. "Is that what Jennifer called it?"

"I have no idea if Jennifer has ever heard of SoCal or been there."

She returned to superstition. "Who was superstitious and why?"

"The freighter that we were on had a pretty much international crew. One member of the crew had been picked up in Haiti. He seemed to think that my Mum and Dad and me were being followed by some bad types. Of course, he was right. I was sure that we'd lost the Deatheaters in Galveston, Texas, but who knew?

"We traveled up to the Northern border of the States by train. We thought that we'd found a permanent place to stay. We'd not had a hint of the Deatheaters who we thought were following us for a while, but we just couldn't make a go of it in Seattle.

"Dad decided that we'd do better in Canada anyway, so we crossed the border. It wasn't too long before we all had jobs. Yes, I was an assistant janitor at a muggle high school. That was working out OK, but we were looking for better jobs all the time."

Pam stared at me. "You mean that Hogwarts was not the only job you had as an assistant janitor?"

I shrugged. "Sure. Dad found a job that we could all do and that paid pretty well. The only thing was that we had to travel to Manitoba and be the caretakers of a fishing resort over the winter. That was a really strange job. We got along fine—at first.

"But . . . the Deatheaters finally caught up with us there. We were all trapped together at the resort. I don't want to talk about what happened with the Deatheaters. Maybe sometime else.

"Anyway, the winter ended, and we began to wonder if the big war was still going on with Riddle. You'd think it would be easy to find out, but we didn't have any wizard contacts in Canada. That was part of the reason we ended up there. Without Wizard contacts, no one could trace us, but of course, we couldn't find out what was going on in the "real" world.

"We started another trek to try to find Wizarding news from England. We went to Toronto first. It's a beautiful city. After a while we gave up there and crossed into the States again. That was our third time. It turned out to be the charm. We found Professor Wendt's family there and discovered that the great war had just ended.

"You'd have thought that that was the end of our adventures, but it wasn't. We traveled home through New York City. It turned out that we weren't even finished with Deatheaters. Some of the few who were still on the loose somehow found us there, and we felt lucky to get out with our lives.

"We did get home, but it turned out that our unoccupied home was not as unoccupied as we thought. We spent a night in jail before we were sprung by my Aunt Marge.

"So, we did see a lot of Canada.

Pam gaped at me and asked, "You're not shitting me?"

I had never heard that expression cross her lips before, but after all, she'd been hanging out with newspaper types. What was I to expect. "No. I didn't include all the details, but it's pretty much true."

Her eyes bugged open, and she stared at me in what I guess must have been disbelief. "But you never mentioned any of this to me."

I hadn't thought about it, but now that I was thinking about it, I realized that it maybe was a little more interesting than I'd thought when I was first at Hogwarts. "Well, you know, 95% of the time, it was pretty boring. As a matter of fact it was really boring. There were those couple of incidents, though."

Pam continued to stare at me. "You didn't think that being attacked by Deatheaters—twice—was exciting!"

"Well, you guys were fighting Riddle, the Deatheaters, Dementors, and who-knew-what-all all the time. It just didn't seem that a run-in or two with a couple of Deatheaters was all that unusual."

Pam threw her head back and stared at the clear, blue sky over the Seine as the sun set, and the lights started to come on in the city, "We were not fighting Deatheaters every day. I was in Hogwarts. The Deatheaters were running the school, but they never did anything really bad. Oh, somebody like Longbottom—a real fire-brand—would get a bad detention every now and then, but it wasn't any worse than when that biddy, Umbrage, was running the school."

She stared at me for a minute and then asked, "But you actually killed Deatheaters?"

I thought about that bitterly cold day when we were trapped outside the only cabin within fifty miles with Mum captured inside with three Deatheaters. What we did didn't seem heroic at all. What we did seemed cowardly now, looking back on it. It was just what we had to do.

Pam poked me in the ribs. "Earth to Dudley. What's going on in there?" She tapped my skull as she asked that.

I dropped my eyes again. "Nothing. I was just remembering. Yeh, I guess Dad and I did kill a couple."

She leaned back and laughed. I would have taken offense most of the time except that in my feeling of embarrassment, it seemed like I didn't have the right to be offended by anything. She stopped, shaking her head, "You probably know more about Canada than I will after spending a year there. They should send you, not me."

I came back to my normal self. I realized that I was sitting there with the only woman that I'd ever loved, and she had just told me that she was going to Canada for a long time. It was stupid not to enjoy her presence while I had her with me. "I don't know anything about writing. You will be much better than I would be. *The Prophet* is really lucky to get you to be their reporter in Canada."

I think my earnestness shown through my eyes. She nodded slowly and took my hand, sort of playing with it. "Do you know what? I think that we need to celebrate my new job, and the fact that we're in Paris, and that you've got a new book, and the fact that I'm crazy mad in love with you."

I couldn't believe that my smile could get any wider, but it did. "Just what did you have in mind?"

With an absolutely dead-pan face she said, "Skinny-dipping in the Seine."

I gagged. It was not exactly what I'd hoped for.

She smiled,. "Not exactly what you expected?"

The stunned look on my face told the story. She went on, "Well, if the Seine isn't to your taste, perhaps we could find a little pension and go skinny-dipping in the *chambre, peut-etre*."

At that point, I knew that there would be at least one little advantage to having a foreign correspondent for a lover. That was, of course, that she would be a lover.

"Well, modesty forces me to comment no further on that incident. However, she had to be prepared to leave quickly. We made arrangements on how to communicate.

"She bought a cell phone in Canada. I bought one here. We arranged to talk twice a week. Saturday night, which would be around lunch time in Canada, and Wednesday morning early here. That would be around midnight in Canada Tuesday.

"I would disapparate to somewhere like Inverness. She would be sure to be away from magical interference wherever she was. It was expensive. There wasn't anything too trivial to talk about. Especially on Saturdays, she would walk around wherever she was and describe the scene. Her parents complained that I spoke a lot more with Pam than they did. That didn't move either of us in the least."

"It was a sort of fool's paradise. As you both know, the war with the Soul's started shortly after our separation. Or maybe it had been going on for a while before that. Anyway, after it started, I hadn't heard a word from her for weeks. Then an owl showed up.

"It was from Pam. She had been drafted into the Aurors in Canada. It seemed that they needed liaison officers to keep people informed about what was going on. They tapped her and some other journalists. It was a while before she was able to get an owl off.

"At first, her work had been so hush-hush that she couldn't communicate with anyone about anything. They loosened that up, and she'd got the note off. I remember word for word what it said,

"Darling Dudders don't despair. I'm safe. I'm working with the Aurors over here. I can't tell you anything more now. Who knows when I will be able to? With all love, your Pammy."

After a silent interval, I asked, "Well, it's been the summer since the war was completely over and well into last Fall since it was effectively over. Have you seen her since?"

Dudley seemed to come out of a haze. "Oh, yes. We get together once every month or two depending on her and my schedules. I've learned everything there is to know about port keys.

"I keep trying to convince her to threaten to leave *The Prophet* if they don't bring her back to England, at least. No soap. If she were at least here, we could get married. We could both get a house and commute to work by floo.

"She's determined to establish herself as an independent woman before marrying. It drives me crazy. That would be all right if she weren't assigned outside England."

Filch, who had seemed to be absorbed by the story asked for a refill, and said, "That's women for you. You can't live with them."

Both Dudley and I seemed confused. He said, "Don't you mean, 'You can't live with them; you can't live without them?'"

Filch shook his head, "I meant what I said. You just can't figure a way to live with them. Look at me as an example."

We waited for the example, but Filch didn't say anything. We stared at him, but he didn't say anything. Finally he caught on that we expected him to say something. He said, "Just what more do you wan?. I just can't figure out a way to get a woman to live with me."

Filch took a long pull on his drink and then said, "Now, you take young Wendt here. Hardly a more desirable catch in the sea, and how long does it take him to snare our good Head? Eh? Eh? Case closed. Full stop."

I asked him, "What about you? Aren't you making any headway on the Ms. Pinz front?"

"Well, it all depends on what you mean by head way, don't it? Now, I could tell you stories about our little trysts-like, but I'm a man of honorableness, don't you see. I don't tell tales out of school." He stopped a minute, seeming to consider what he'd just said, and then said, "Or in school for the matter of that."

Dudley punched him in the shoulder and said, "You old dog, you."

Filch smiled at that.

I stood and said, "The Building Maintenance job may run from dawn to dusk, but the teacher's job is never done. I have to go do some lesson plans before I go to bed."

Filch said, "Lesson plans, eh? What are you planning to teach the Head this evening?"

I frowned at the old scoundrel and left the two scoundrels—the young and the old to work on the bottle of Blue Label.

Halloween Redux

It was a few weeks after the boys' night out that I was in my office during my usual office hours. I was pretty well caught up with my home work and was reading an article in *Scientific American* about cosmic inflation.

A knock sounded on my door. I invited the knocker in, fully expecting it to be a sixth or seventh year with a question on my most recent assignment. The door opened, and the person who walked in the door reminded me so much of one of my students that I started to say, "Well, Rebecca, I didn't . . ."

I immediately amended my question to, "Well Aurora, I wasn't expecting you."

She laughed. "I suppose not. Apparently, you were expecting that pretty seventh year, Rebecca Boltzmann."

Becoming exasperated with Aurora is an occupational hazard here at Hogwarts. Minerva has often remarked on it. I tried not to show my exasperation when I said, "I wasn't expecting her. It's just that she has an almost uncanny resemblance to you."

She smiled prettily and said, "Why Professor Wendt, how nice of you to say so."

I simply asked, "Why are you not pestering your infinitely patient husband, hmmmm?"

She stepped forward and planted herself in my red leather chair, pouted, and said, "Is married life not agreeing with you? You used to be. . . oh, , , so courteous."

Then it occurred to me. It was only a few weeks from Halloween. I then made a simple statement, "You are a happily married woman. You have a husband to involve in your crazy Halloween imposture schemes. Go get him to impersonate Lucius Malfoy or Donald Trump or Bobby Fisher, and leave me alone."

She seemed to turn introspective. "Yes, that is a good idea. I wonder where I could find Bobby Fisher?"

"Yes, it is a good idea. Go find him, get a sample of his hair, and while you're at it, you can get some of Boris Spasky's hair, and you and the Boy Genius can go to the Halloween party as the great Match of the Century. So, just run along."

She leaned back in my chair, stretching all four of her limbs. She then said, "Not a bad idea, but it involves a lot of work. Surely, you can think of something easier for us."

I got up and walked to the door, pointedly opening it. "I assume that when you say, 'us', you mean YOU and Brahms. Now, move along smartly, and I can get back to lesson planning."

She rose languidly and said, "I suppose that the *Scienteriffic American* has become great English literature?"

I grimaced and gestured at the open door. She walked past me to get to it, turning as she did so that she could look in my eyes and say, "You can be such a boor at times. I can't see how Minerva abides you."

However, she did leave.

□

From that day forward, I was caution itself in my office. I'd experienced far too many occasions when a slip of the tongue had gotten me enmeshed in one of Aurora's schemes. That wasn't going to happen this time.

After a week had passed without much more than a "hello" when we were at meals or passing in the halls, I had begun to think that she just didn't have the old determination to get me into trouble. I hadn't given up vigilance. I just had begun to believe that I might be safe for once.

By the week of Halloween, I was feeling fairly safe, but I remembered the last minute attacks of the past and began to find new places to do my work. Of course, there were the quarters that Minerva and I used—the Headmaster's quarters. That was as safe as you could get. I couldn't just hide out there, though. Minerva would have begun to suspect something was afoot if I did that too much.

I had to be in my office for office hours. I could reasonably insist that only students visit me during office hours. I was just following my duty to give students every reasonable opportunity to seek help in my classes. So, I posted a sign outside my door: "If you're not one of my students, you don't have business in my office during my office hours."

That stratagem seemed to be working. But there were still times when I

17

wasn't in classes and not office hours and when I couldn't be in the Headmaster's office. I began to haunt everyone's office who ever owed me a favor. I spent time with Professor Slughorn talking about his book sales. They weren't flying off the shelves, but the volume was picking up respectably.

I visited Filch and Dursley, of course. However, there were actually times when they actually did work around the castle, and their office wasn't available. As a matter of fact, they started avoiding their offices.

I even spent time in Madame Pomfrey's hospital wing. I knew that I couldn't deceive her with some phony claim of illness. If she were in a foul mood, she might actually prescribe some noxious medicine for me, like Skelegrow. So, I was honest with her.

The first time I visited her office, she asked me what my ailment was. My answer was, "Aurora."

"Beg your pardon. I thought you said, 'Aurora.' What could you possibly mean by that?"

I smiled the most ingratiating smile I could muster. By this time, my supply of ingratiating smiles was pretty low, and a lot of the time I could only manage a pleading smile. "Well, you see, Madame Pomfrey, the thing is that I'm trying to avoid Aurora Brahms. You may remember that in past years, she's always managed to involve me in some stupid, embarrassing scheme for me to impersonate someone. Those incidents almost always end badly for me. I think that if I can only hold out two more days, I'll be free!"

Pomfrey is a no-nonsense sort of Healer. Her answer was, "Oh, Wendt, just go up to your office and take your medicine. How hard can it be to just say 'NO'? I'm sure that I have no trouble saying 'NO' just like I'm doing right now."

I grumbled. "You just don't know Aurora. She has an amazing ability to make the craziest schemes seem to have just enough sense that they might work and just crazy enough to be funny."

She growled. "You are just altogether too kind. You should put a little wand up your backbone and disappoint that trouble-maker."

I was amazed to hear those words come from her mouth. "You agree that Aurora's a trouble-maker?"

In exasperation, Pomfrey said, "Yes, of course, I've had to treat you enough times after these escapades to know how much trouble she makes."

I was confused. "Well, why then don't you help me out, if you agree with me?"

"Oh, Wendt. The only way that you're going to be free of her is to do it on your own. You won't always have me here to stiffen your spine."

I considered that. "You know, I almost agree with you. I think I'll be on my way back to my office. I'll stay in there and beard the Lioness in my den. I'll see you as myself on Halloween."

Pomfrey had already turned to her medicine cabinet before I left. I suppose that she was inventorying or something like that.

□□

The day of Halloween itself, I was sitting in my office. It was a Friday.

That did not augur well for me. When Halloween happens on a weekend night, it seems like things go even worse than on other days. Friday was the worst because students and teachers have the most time to recover from their misdeeds and are willing to try crazier stunts than at other times.

On the other hand. Aurora had not so much as knocked on my door since that first visit. I hadn't given up on vigilance, but I had begun to hope that I might have bypassed the curse of Halloween for once.

I went to dinner as usual. The students were in high spirits for the very same reasons that I was extra cautious. The house elves had done their usual impressive job providing 5 star cuisine. I was beginning to feel free.

A last minute idea had occurred to me during dinner. I was sitting on the dais and noticed that no student approached it. The staff and teachers were on their best behavior during the evening meal. What would happen if I just stayed on the dais until the party started?

The more I thought about it, the more I liked the idea. I wouldn't be in anyone's way. The tables were all moved back to the walls of the Great Hall, but normally the tables on the dais were left in place. It's true that there is frequently a band, and they normally set up on the dais. Even then, the tables aren't moved. I could just stay up in my seat and be free of anyone's bothering me.

I had plan. It was good plan. I decided to stick with it.

As I sat at my place, I watched the party committee move the tables back magically. I watched the house elves set up the refreshments. I watched the band arrive and set up on the dais. Everything was going like clockwork. Minerva returned after changing into party robes. I complimented her and held my breath hoping that it really was Minerva.

She immediately told me something that assured me that it was Minerva. She said, "Oh, I'm sorry Wendt. I forgot to mention that the School Board of Governors are coming tonight. It's a real bother. I'll have to give them a tour of the school and stay with them during the party.

"I'm sorry. You'll have to hang around with your drinking buddies I suppose. You seem to have no trouble finding like-minded associates."

I nodded. That seemed safe. I wouldn't entirely put it beyond Aurora to impersonate one of them, but there is safety in numbers. She couldn't impersonate more than one at a time—I hoped.

The band had finished setting up and doing sound checks to make sure that the sound was at the ear-drum bursting level. All of the refreshments were set up. I thanked God that the Weasley family was all out of Hogwarts! You never could entirely trust the refreshments while they were around. There were a few students and a teacher or two beginning to show up. I remained seated on the dais feeling myself to be king of all that I surveyed.

Then the Board of Governors started to arrive. They were apparently all coming in through the floo connection of the fireplace of the Great Hall. They seemed to be coming in groups of two and three. Minerva had been standing there, and after they had all arrived, they walked out of the Great Hall, apparently on their tour of the school.

By this time, there were a lot of teachers and students who had arrived. The band plunged into a song that would have done any heavy metal band credit—with someone, not me. I scanned the room for a sight of any of my "drinking" buddies such as Slughorn, Dursley, Filch, or even Flitwick. I didn't see any of them. I was just getting up when . . .

"Hello, hello, hello. Who have we here?"

The voice was familiar but I just couldn't quite place it. It was accompanied by a hand on my shoulder. Could it have been Hermione? I turned wondering who it was. I saw the all too familiar face and said, "Oh, it's you."

She replied, "No need to be grumpy. Yes, it's me. I'm here for the tour."

"I didn't know you were on the Board."

She smiled. "You didn't know that the Minister of Magic is an ex-officio member of Hogwarts Board? What has Minerva been teaching you in her spare time?"

"Well, in the first place, she has hardly any spare time. And in the second place, I really don't have a need to know that Pam Moertl is on the Board. I'll try to forget it as soon as I can. Now, what can I refuse to do for you?"

She pursed her lips. "Oh, we are in a foul mood tonight. Why the glum outlook?"

"Well, you are probably unaware that there are staff members who take a certain perverse pleasure in playing practical jokes on me at Halloween. And then, on top of that, you show up. Why aren't you off getting the grand tour of the old school?"

She smiled again. "Well, I'm only here for show. I know everything I need to know about the 'old school'. The whole board invited itself, and I'm part of the board.

"But, you know, you could make the evening less dull for me if you only would."

I tried to appraise her. She really wasn't bad, and I suppose having a friendly face on the Board wasn't a bad thing. I shrugged. "Well, if you want someone to talk to, I'll do as well as the next, I suppose."

She walked to the edge of the dais and made to descend there rather than take the stairs at either end. She lifted a hand toward me and asked, "Uh. Do you mind?"

I nodded and took her hand. The additional balance allowed her to alight fairly gracefully. She was wearing flats. I hate to think about what it would be like if she were wearing heels. She looked up and asked, "Would you like a hand?"

I grimaced. "No thanks." I then knelt, took the edge of the dais in a hand and sort of jumped down.

She smiled and nodded, "Nicely done."

By this time the band had switched to a slow dance. Pam turned to me and asked, "How about a dance?"

"Why?"

She frowned. "We're at a dance. I'm unaccompanied. I like dancing."

I rolled my eyes, took her outstretched hand, placed my other hand on her waist and began a slow waltz around the room.

She was continuing her explanation, "Did you know that when I attended Hogwarts, there was no Halloween party, and the Christmas party was a very different affair—no dancing, just a banquet, Christmas songs, the school choir. It was fun, but I think almost all of the students would have preferred a dance as well."

I smirked. "You mean all the female students."

She smirked too. "Of course."

She went on. "So, I never danced all the years that I was at Hogwarts."

I wondered who had been the Headmaster in that era, so I asked, "When was that?"

She barked a laugh. "Don't you know it's rude to ask a lady her age?"

I chuckled. "Yeh, I guess so. I was just wondering what Headmaster didn't like dances?"

She smiled. "Oh, I was in the Dumbledore era, smarty pants. I might have graduated just a couple of years ago."

I smiled, too. "You know, I'm pretty sure that I'd have remembered you if you'd been a student during the last ten years or so."

"Well, thank you, I guess. I'm not sure whether to take that as a compliment or not."

I smiled more broadly. "It's probably a little of both."

"I thought so."

There was a break in the conversation, and I realized that the band had switched to a different song. I was beginning to think of breaking off the dance when Pam seemed to realize that. She said, "You know, I've got an awful lot of missed dances to make up for."

"Really?"

The dance rhythm had definitely turned slower, and I found her closer. My hand was now more at her back than her side.

She was now more whispering in my ear than saying to my face, "Yes, I never got a dance with the groom at a certain recent wedding. I figure he owes me at least one dance plus another one or two as accumulated interest."

I chuckled. "I think I need to talk with your CPA. He may be cheating you."

"Ohhhh, do you think that I'm entitled to more?"

I opened my mouth to answer, but I didn't have a ready reply. She didn't hesitate but said, "Doesn't silence betoken consent?"

All that I could think to say was, "Not always." I suddenly realized that my cheek was feeling the warmth of hers. I knew that it was time for a change in the status quo. I said, "I'm feeling a little dry. How about finding something to drink?"

I felt her hair brush my cheek as she pulled back a little so that I could see her face, "Yes, a drink. That sounds good. I hear that you have a small but strategically stocked cabinet of potables."

I laughed inside. At last I had a good answer. I took her hand and strode off for the refreshment table. "Technically, I'm a chaperon at this event, and I have to maintain absolute sobriety."

I could hear the pout in her voice as she said, "Oh, pooh."

The tone of voice, not the words, struck a chord somewhere in my memory, but I couldn't quite bring to mind what it was. We reached the table, and I asked, "What's your poison? We have pumpkin juice, non-alcoholic punch, butter beers, iced tea, and something else that I don't recognize. It's probably fine, but I'm not taking a chance on it."

I turned to her and waited. She considered a minute and said, "Oh, I'll have punch. Now, why didn't I bring a flask of something good in my purse?"

I laughed. "I'm glad you didn't. I'd have to bust you for bringing alcohol to a school event. Very bad for the M. O. M.'s reputation."

I got her punch and had a butter beer. We walked over to an empty bench and sat. She asked me a question that surprised me, "Are you happy here?"

"What in the world do you mean? Are you about to offer me a job?"

"No. I just meant that over the last ten years or so that you've been here, Hogwarts has seemed to be the center for all sorts of excitement. But this year seems to be shaping up as a blah year."

I stared at her wondering if this were going anywhere. "Frankly, I think it's a nice change. Are you trying to stir up trouble?"

"No. no." She said it in a sort of whine. "It's just that in past years, there's always some spice in the air. You know. It just felt like anything might happen. A lot of the time it wasn't good but that uncertainty was exhilarating. Like when Sirius Black was haunting the castle. Don't you think?"

I wondered what was going on. This was definitely not the sort of conversation that you expected from the Chair of the Board of the school. I said so, "Come on, I thought the Board liked boring years. I thought that was what you guys wanted."

She just shook her head as though trying to shed a pesky fly. "Oh, never mind. Let's get back on the floor and dance." She put her empty cup down and took my hand, dragging me back to the dance floor.

I hesitantly said, "Ooo. Kayyy."

The band was still playing slow. She put an arm around my waist and one resting on my shoulder, and we shoved off. After a minute her head was resting on her hand on my shoulder. We didn't say anything.

After a while the band called a break between sets. We walked over to the refreshment table. When we'd collected a plate of mints, nuts, and a piece of cake, we found an abandoned spot along one of the tables. We sat.

"You know, I've been thinking about your boring idea."

She ogled at me. "I had a boring idea?"

"No. No. I mean your idea that school is boring and maybe not as effective without some . . . well, danger. I hate to admit it, but you might be right."

"You're damn right, I'm right. What can we do about it?"

Stranger and stranger. Should a Board member be using that sort of language. I reflected, but decided that as politican she might. "Introduce some fake danger. You know, the second year that I was at Hogwarts,

Dumbledore announced at the opening banquet that everyone should stay off the third floor if they didn't want to die."

She sniggered. "And you'd announce that about the fourth floor even though there's no problem with the fourth?"

"It's worth a try."

She simply said a forceful, "NO."

She thought a minute. "You know, Hagrid always had a way of finding dangerous animals to teach about in Magical Creatures. Maybe we could get him to go back to some of the old lesson plans."

I laughed. "Hagrid's had a lifetime's worth of trouble because of those old lesson plans. I think we can spare him more." I hesitated a minute and said, "You mean like bringing in a dragon."

She looked off to the left and nodded her head. "It wouldn't be the first time." She laughed and repeated her forceful, "NO."

"Well, we could always bring back old Valdy."

She rolled her eyes as she placed a hand on my wrist. "Now, that's just plain stupid." We both laughed.

By this time, the band had started up again. She took my hand and dragged me out on the floor. The first dance was a moderate tempo. If it were any faster, I'd have sat down right away. Somehow she convinced me to dip her a time or two.

Then the tempo turned really slow. Someone dialed the lights in the Great Hall down. I suddenly found both my arms around her, and her chin was resting on a shoulder. Her cheek was against my cheek, and I could feel her warm, moist breath on my ear. She said something. It was so soft that even with her mouth at my ear, I couldn't tell what it was that she said. Then I felt something wet on my cheek. To this day, I don't know if it were a breath of a kiss or a tear.

The next thing I knew, she pulled away from me and with her head turned said, "I've got a . . . a . . . board meeting tomorrow. I've got to go." She ran off across the dance floor toward the fireplace. There was something strange about her gait. I couldn't quite make out what in the dim room. I took a step toward her, and I almost tripped on something. I looked down and saw one of her flats. It had somehow worked off. I picked it up and ran after her. It was hopeless. She had reached the fireplace before I'd fairly begun. She reached into the pot of floo powder and was gone in a green flare. I stopped running.

The next day, the slipper was sitting on my desk in my office.

Minerva had gotten back to the Head's apartment even later than I had. She yawned as she came to bed. "What a boring night. The board had to see everything. They came back to the Great Hall, had some refreshments, and I think a couple danced a bit. I hope that your Halloween curse is broken." The last was said with some tentativeness.

I shrugged, "Yes, I guess so. Neither Brahms nor his wife showed up— unless they were really well-disguised. The Chair of the Board hung around for a good while. I made sure she had something to drink and eat. I danced some with her."

"She didn't talk about budget did she? She usually brings that up at every board meeting she attends."

I scratched my head, "No, but she did talk about education."

Minerva rolled her eyes. "She didn't bore you with some crazy theory, did she?"

I drawled out, "Well, sort of."

"What was it?"

"Well, she thought that Magical education would suffer without some sort of real threat around."

Minerva turned to me and said, "Did she suggest one? She didn't suggest something like bringing a new Riddle along?"

I laughed. "No. No. She said that was a really stupid idea."

"Good."

Minerva stretched out and turned toward me. "I thought that she wasn't going to be able to attend tonight. It must have been a last minute decision."

"Yeh, she arrived after you and the rest of the Board left on your tour. But she left in a hurry before you got back."

Minerva was definitely thinking of something else. Her thigh had mysteriously become uncovered. Her last words were, "Probably another party she had to attend." Then she giggled.

I sat at my desk, finishing some grading. I really didn't want to tackle returning the slipper, so I temporized, somehow hoping it would magically disappear on its own. Actually, that almost did happen.

The door opened. I looked up and my mouth opened to say something.

However, Aurora beat me to it. "Halloween's gone. I just came to point out how I was a good girl last night."

I nodded. "You mean gloat. Yeh. I guess I can't fault you. Bravo."

She tsked, "Tsk, tsk, tsk. Don't be nasty. This is not gloating."

She walked over to my desk and noticed the slipper. "A transparent slipper. Cute. I think it's probably too small for you, though. What happened to its mate?"

I frowned. "Well, I know whose it is. Did you know that the Minister of Magic showed up last night? She somehow lost this slipper. The trouble is that I want to get it back to her, but . . ."

Aurora nodded wisely. "But. But, you've not mentioned it to Minerva. But you can't send it to her magically on your own. But you want to avoid embarrassment.

"Just to show you how good a girl I can be, I'd be happy to send it off by owl."

"That would be swell. Oh, yes. I'd like to send a little note along. Just a minute." I reached into my drawer and pulled out a piece of parchment. I tore a small square off and wrote on it with a ball-point.

When I finished, I started to read it aloud. Aurora interrupted me. "You don't have to do that. I'll respect your privacy. I promise that only the recipient will read it."

I shook my head. "That's OK. It's better if someone else knows:

"Dear Pam, You left this slipper behind. I tried to catch you before you left but didn't succeed. Thanks for hanging for a while. It was a great evening. Wendt."

She laughed. "Just what a girl wants to hear. 'Thanks for hanging.' But, at least, you did say it was a great evening."

She picked up the slipper and the note and walked off airily. She stopped at the door, and turning, said, "I think my work here is finished . . . for now."

That was the last that I heard about that incident. I occasionally thought about sending a note to the Minister—just to see if she really had been at Hogwarts that night. Every time I was tempted, I was faced with the question of what I would do if I found out that she hadn't been. As time passed and nothing developed, I decided that there wasn't any reason to know the truth.

Christmas at Home

The final day of end of term exams had come and gone. The Christmas party had arrived. Minerva had finished her end of term speech. It was simple. It was straight-forward. It was short. I loved it.

She had said, "Happy Christmas to all. Change if you will for the party. Come back. Enjoy. Don't forget to leave your books behind when you leave for holiday."

I complemented her on the speech. I decided to stay in the Great Hall as the band set up. I had already donned my party robes, and I was going to enjoy the entire party. The process was much like Halloween had been. The house elves set up refreshments. The band set up and warmed up. Why they bothered warming up I have never understood. I couldn't tell any difference between the practice and the performance.

Minerva returned in her party robes that I had not seen her wear before. They were green with red diagonal stripes. They were drawn tight around her waist like a muggle dress. I let her know in no uncertain terms how much I liked them.

She said, "This design is supposed to make dancing much easier than traditional robe design. I intend to test that thoroughly tonight."

I replied, "Then why wait? The band will play its required heavy metal song, and then I hope will relapse into gentle strains."

My prediction was correct. They did. We danced most of the first set. At one point we stopped for something to drink. As we approached the table, Minerva commented, "I have a special treat for you."

I didn't express any of the doubts I had about her "special treats." We reached the table, and I found cans of American soft drinks. I looked them over and commented, "Very good. Coca Cola—always welcome. Seven-Up—once my favorite. Diet Sprite—well, there's always going to be the occasional disappointment."

At that Minerva stared at me, "The distributor assured me these were the most popular American sodas."

"Oh, you did fine." I nuzzled her as I said that. I selected a Coke and popped the top.

Minerva marveled, "Oh, so that's how you do that. I wondered. It seemed like there wasn't an obvious way to open it up." Meanwhile, I was looking for a glass and some ice.

Minerva noticed and asked, "You seem to be looking for something."

"Yes, soda is traditionally served over ice in a glass." By this time, I'd located a nested stack of glasses and some ice. I demonstrated. "First, take a sip straight out of the can."

She did and shrugged. "I don't know what the big fuss is about."

I then filled a glass with ice and poured the rest of the Coke over it. When the fizz subsided, I handed it to her and said, "Now try this."

She took a sip and a smile crossed her face. "I see what you mean."

She changed topic. "It's a little hard to believe that Aurora has missed two parties without doing something with or to you."

I commented, "A pleasant surprise." I scanned the room and spotted her. "There she is over there dancing with Brahms. She seems to be enjoying herself."

Minerva sniffed. "Well, she should. Let's go back to the dance floor."

The rest of the evening went uneventfully except for one incident. Brahms dragged Aurora over to us and said, "Let's swap partners for a dance or two."

We did. When Aurora and I waltzed out of earshot, she said, "Notice. I didn't even put Nicky up to it."

I replied, "I'm proud of you. Two whole parties in the same year and no crazy schemes."

She smiled a wan smile. "Oh, yes. It's hard to give up old habits. How is married life treating you?"

"Very well. There's no more sneaking around when we're at school. We still have to be careful about PDA's during the terms, but there's so much opportunity in private that it doesn't seem too bad. How about you?"

"We never had your problem. It was always OK for us to date and have PDA's—again not during regular terms in public. I don't know how you two stood it."

I sighed. "Well, when it's the only game in town, you are thankful for what you have."

She sighed, too. "You know that it wasn't the only game in town."

"For me it was."

28

She leant in closer and said, "Let's just dance for a while." We did. After a while she said, "You know, the Christmas and Easter holidays always seemed special to me. Being here without teaching duties, with the castle almost empty just felt like I was in another Universe completely divorced from the one that we always live in. It seemed like a place where all the normal rules disappeared—where anything might happen."

I said, "The first couple of years, I would have agreed with you. Especially Christmas holiday always seemed like you were in another world."

She didn't say anything but nodded her head. After a while she asked softly, "You wouldn't consider staying over the holiday, would you?" She quickly added, "You and Minerva?"

I grimaced while my head was turned from her. "Oh, we are meeting the relatives for the first time since we were married. "

I could feel her nod her head. "Yes, we plan that for Easter. Nicky has talked me into going skiing for the first time. We're going to the Alps. I dread it. Flying down the hills, dodging trees, trying to keep from falling over—how could you actually like that?"

I chuckled. It wasn't kind, but I couldn't help it.

She exclaimed, "What?"

"Oh, it's just the idea of someone who flies brooms twice as fast as skis and goes hundreds of feet up in the air being afraid of skiing."

She shuddered involuntarily. "You are so insensitive!"

"Sorry. It was beyond my control."

We danced in silence for a while longer. Then she sighed and said so softly that I had to replay it in my mind a couple of times to be sure I'd got it right. "Oh, I wish this didn't have to end."

I wasn't going to press for it to end, but shortly the band took control of that out of our hands. They reached the end of their second set.

We had drifted far from Minerva and the Boy Genius. They headed back toward us. I turned to Aurora and said, "I kind of wish it didn't have to end just yet myself."

I had my back turned from the other pair. Aurora quickly hugged me and planted the fastest kiss on my lips that I'd ever felt. She stepped back and said, "Have a wonderful holiday if I don't see you again before you leave."

I nodded and said, "I wish exactly the same for you." She smiled at that.

□

The next day, we were in the Great Hall having breakfast with the students and teachers who had stayed on for the Christmas party—at least those who had decided to get up in time for breakfast rather than just in time for the Hogwarts Express. As I'd expected, everyone had overdone it, and only a few sleepy students had shown up along with an almost equal number of sleepy staff.

Minerva and I had packed the day before, so we were ready to leave for the holiday as soon as the Hogwarts Express left. In the past, Minerva (and I) had been responsible for making sure that all students in her "house" were on the train or on their way home in some other way. Since she no longer had a "house", her duties just consisted of staying until the "house" heads reported in that everyone was on their way home and was someone else's responsibility.

We had spent a leisurely time getting down to breakfast. We'd brought our luggage, such as it was, down to the Great Hall, and we intended to leave by floo from the Great Hall as soon as the report was in.

I'd just gotten well into my sunny-side up eggs and bagels when an owl flew into the Great Hall. It circled the hall once and headed for the dais. I thought to myself, "Oh, no!" as it flew low over me and dropped down to land next to my plate.

Minerva chuckled, "Well, you seem to have a friend for breakfast."

The owl held out a claw that had a letter attached to it. Minerva "oohed" as she looked at it. She said, "That's one of those new-fangled letters that have a tear-strip for a signature. This must be important."

I grumbled. "This is worse than a cell phone. With a cell phone, you can just not answer a call. These pesky birds will just stay with you until you take the letter or, like this one, even sign for it."

"What does it say?" she asked as she looked over my shoulder.

I opened it and discovered that it was from Gringotts. Minerva read it out loud. Fortunately, nobody was close enough to hear. She said,

> "Dear Mr. Wendt,
>
> We have enclosed a draft agenda for the next Board meeting of Gringotts, Inc. to happen Jan. 15. Please review it, particularly the abstract of your presentation for accuracy.
>
> If you have any changes, please provide them prior to Dec. 31 so they may be included in the final agenda.

30

Best Regards, etc. etc.

There was a page of parchment behind the cover letter. Minerva put her hand on my shoulder and said, "Well, what does the agenda say."

I turned around and grimaced. "You know perfectly well that I can't tell you. That is confidential Gringotts info, and I can't reveal it to anyone without prior permission."

She sat down next to me and stared into my eyes. "Oh, you know it's easier to ask forgiveness than permission." Then she winked her right eye.

"No can do. Now, you either go back to the Head's seat so that I can read this and see how much I hate it, or I'll just wait until we're at Maggie's before I do that." She got up a little grumpily and started to turn.

I added, "Oh, one more thing. Could you give me a lift to Diagon Alley tomorrow?"

"Oh, I suppose." She backed away, hoping I'd change my mind. I didn't.

Instead, I switched my attention to the first page of the attachment. It was a hand-written agenda. The usual items were listed. There was always a report on profit and loss for the quarter and a report on projections. Sometimes there was followup on issues from previous meetings. Then there was my item.

> An Analysis of Trends in the Velocity of Money, including a projection of the future Velocity of M3 and Higher Monetary Measures.

> Abstract: The Velocity of the various measures of money was depressed to essentially zero by the alien invasion. It has been rising but primarily as M1 velocity. The velocity of M2 has been increasing slowly. Questions answered include, how quickly will M2 and M3 velocity approach pre-invasion values?

I took an introductory course in Economics as a college student, and I had a pretty basic knowledge of the idea of Velocity of Money, but why would they think that I was qualified to speak on that?

Then I turned the page and found a rather nice line chart. It was a graph of the velocity of the various money supplies over the last 24 months, including the current month that wasn't complete. It surely looked like someone had access to a computer and knew how to use Excel. I wondered if that room that Gringotts kept with a printer also had a laptop or two.

The chart itself was pretty dramatic. It showed that prior to the alien invasion, the velocity of money had been pretty steady for all money types. After that, the velocity quickly dropped to close to zero for all money types. Then, after the invasion had been repulsed, the velocity of M1 had recovered pretty well over the last several months, though still not to its pre-invasion level. The other measures had very slowly recovered. Since all those other measures of money measured what Grigotts dealt in, I could see why they were concerned.

About that point, I heard a cleared throat. I looked up and saw Minerva standing in front of me. She asked, "Were you thinking of staying at Hogwarts for the holiday, because if you were . . . "

I looked around the hall and saw that it was empty except for us. I said, "I suppose the Express has left the station."

She nodded, "What about us? Are we leaving the station?"

I was still dazed, so I just said, "Sure."

□□

When we walked into Maggie's cottage I was happy to see that the only person present was Maggie. I had no idea how many relatives would show up to greet the newlyweds, but any more than Maggie would not have been welcome to me.

Maggie was still not completely at peace with the idea of having a muggle for a brother-in-law, but she was not bad about it. She helped us settle into the guest room.

We had a light lunch with her at which we discussed the holiday. She had it pretty well plotted out. We would spend every evening with one or another of the cousins, nieces, and nephews. At least the first couple of days would be spent shopping for gifts.

I had to admire the fact that Minerva had a well-developed system for tracking the friends and relatives who needed gifts. She had them all grouped by family. Each had tendencies for gifts that they liked. She had just incorporated my family into this system.

All this was laid out at lunch. Minerva had her long parchment on the table. We discussed them. You might think that I was overwhelmed by this. I was not. I had a few alternate tasks laid out myself.

For one thing, the holidays were the only time that we had much time to see films. I insisted that we had to build in time for that pastime of mine. Minerva was clearly disturbed that her carefully plotted time-table was to be displaced. I held my ground.

"You really can't expect to monopolize all the opportunities for fun in this holiday. This time of year, the motion picture industry releases many of its best, or at least, most entertaining movies. They are only in the theatres for a couple of months at most. This is the only time that we have to see them."

Minerva was not without resources for her view. She said, "Oh, but aren't there these. . . uh . . . what do you call them DUIs or whatever. They let you see movies any time."

I smiled, which should have been a clue to her that she'd lost the argument. I quietly pointed out, "Oh, but you know that DVD's can only be played on machines that require electricity. No electricity at Hogwarts. So this really is the only chance to see these movies."

She wasn't ready to give up. "But, the BG is installed in the Shrieking Shak. There's plenty of ekeltricity there, AND he has DWI players."

I frowned and tried to communicate by expression how unfair she was being to Brahms. "That is his office. He has staff there around the clock. It would be a real imposition to use his machines."

I almost laughed at her quandary. She wouldn't dream of imposing on someone. She pursed her lips, deep in thought. She was no doubt trying to come up with a counter-proposal.

During this Maggie was just sitting back, apparently enjoying the show. She probably was thinking that she warned her sis about getting involved with a muggle.

I went on with my argument. "Anyway, even if we had a way of playing DVD's that still is not the same as seeing movies in a theatre. It's all the difference between seeing a band perform live and listening to a gramophone recording. It's not just the big screen, but the crowd reaction is valuable too. Movies are even worse that way because bands do have concerts after they release music. Movies almost never come back to theatres once the original run is over. It's really use it or lose it."

Minerva hung her head. "I suppose you're right. It's wrong of me to want to do everything that I'm used to doing at Christmas time."

She went on. "OK. What movies do you want to see and when can we do that?"

I shrugged. I don't know. I've not looked at a muggle newspaper in a few days. You have to check the movie listings and then decide what and where to see them."

I could see that Minerva was at the limits of her patience, so I quickly added, "When we go into London tomorrow to shop, I'll pick up a newspaper or two, and we can decide."

She just said in a flat tone, "OK. We can do that tomorrow when we go shopping in Diagon Alley."

We took a long walk in the neighborhood in the afternoon. In the evening, we went to one of the niece's for dinner. I'd not met the family before. They had been briefed about my being a muggle and were pretty much polite and pleasant. They had kids. I spent a lot of time with them. One, a girl, was a second year at Hogwarts, and the other was a ten year old boy. They'd both spent a lot of time with muggle kids, and we actually got along pretty well.

I asked them if they had a board game that they liked. That brought an enthusiastic reply. They liked a game they called "Trip to Gringotts." It turned out to be a clone of Monopoly. The little girl apparently liked being the "Goblin", better known among muggles as the "Banker". She took great joy in laying the game out and counting out fake galleon coins to everyone. Apparently the family played it enough that everyone in the family had their favorite moving piece. That left the broomstick and the minature Hogwarts Express train for Minerva and me to fight over.

Minerva smiled a mischievous smile and said, "I know what Mr. Wendt likes. He'll take the Express. So, I'll be broomstick."

The game was actually a good way to have conversation among the adults and keep the kids entertained. There were plenty of gaps in the play when adults could talk, and it wasn't a tragedy if there were blank spaces.

The niece asked innocently why I liked the Express piece. Minerva chortled, "You must ask Wendt."

The niece turned to me. I said, "Well, it's simple. I like traveling by train, especially the Express."

Minerva could hardly hold back her laughter. The niece apparently didn't notice. She said, "Oh, you know, I always liked the Express. In a way it was my favorite thing about Hogwarts. I always looked forward to those day long train rides." She hesitated and added, "Even now, I'm sad occasionally that I don't have a reason to ride the Express."

As the evening progressed an idea occurred to me. I asked Minerva, "You know, the Express just turns around the next day and returns to track 9 ¾ at Kings' Cross, right?"

Minerva looked at me suspiciously, "I don't know. I suppose so."

"Well, then, Mrs. Rupert ... and her husband could ride up to Hogwarts with the students, stay at the Three Broomsticks, say, and return the next day? Right?"

Minerva hemmed. "Maybe. I can't remember it ever having been done."

I persisted. "But there isn't any rule against it, is there?"

She didn't say anything. Mrs. Rupert was silent too as we disassembled the game. Not surprisingly, the grand-niece had won. She was the most intense about the game, and of course, the adults weren't pushing any advantages they had during the game.

Then I had a thought. "Minerva, I understand that it's probably better for a parent—at least of a 1st or 2nd year—not to go along on the train, but couldn't a parent ride in the teacher's car. No one would have to interact with them. There's always room in that car."

Minerva grimaced. "Oh, maybe."

We finished and said goodbye to the Rupert family. We disapparated from their porch. We arrived down the street from Maggie's house. Minerva took my arm and said, "Why in the world did you add that last suggestion. Having parents on the train would just be a damn nuisance."

I stared at her and said, "Look, the issue hasn't come up in hundreds of years, has it?"

She grumbled. "I suppose not."

"Then is it likely that droves of parents will line up to ride the Express?"

She shook her head back and forth like a boxer bobbing and weaving, "Oh, I suppose not. Still."

I was disgusted with her. "Use your head. She's not going to ask to do that."

Minerva focused a gimlet eye on me. "And why not, now that you've raised the possibility."

It was my turn to shake my head. "She doesn't really miss the Express that much. She is just having nostalgia for her youth. She sees the end coming for her kids being in school. Just the idea of it being possible to turn back the clock for a day or two will more than satisfy her."

Minerva wasn't sold, but she said, "Maybe. We'll see."

□
□□

The next day, bright and early, we got up and disapparated to the street next to the Cauldron. We entered and were seated for breakfast. Tom was delighted that we were giving him custom, and we hadn't even used his floo.

We proceeded to Diagon Alley. We entered Gringotts. Minerva needed some gold for her Christmas purchases, and I was there to try to talk myself off the agenda of the Board Meeting.

We entered and approached the concierge's desk. Before we arrived, he ran around the desk and extended his hand to me. "Mr. Wendt. It's so good to see you!" Then he seemed to notice Minerva. He added, "And Mrs. Wendt, of course. What can we possibly do for you?"

Minerva stared at the two of us and said, "I'll just go to our vault and get a little gold out, shall I?"

I nodded.

I turned to the goblin and asked. "Is there any possibility that I can get on Glazblatt's calendar sometime today?"

The goblin expressed surprise, "Sometime? I'll take you in to see him right now myself."

Minerva was still standing nearby. She said, "Well, Wendt, I think that you and your drinking buddies will be occupied for some time." Whenever I met with anyone without her whether it was the likes of Filch or business partners, she referred to them as my drinking buddies. She went on, "I'll be at the Cauldron for lunch if you can tear yourself free from them."

I nodded. The goblin took me by the arm and pulled me away, "Quickly. I don't want to waste any of your valuable time!"

So, we went into the interior of the bank. I knew the route pretty well. We reached Glazblatt's outer office. The secretary recognized me and said, "Please sit Mr. Wendt. I don't think Glazblatt is meeting with anyone important, I'll see if I can get you in right away.

With that, she opened the inner door, stuck her head in, and said something in Gobbledygook. There was a lengthy conversation after which she turned to me and said, "Mr. Glazblatt will be pleased to see you now." With that she opened the door wide and invited me in.

Only Glazblatt was in the office. I supposed that his guest must have left by the other door into the office. Glazblatt stood, walked around the table, and extended his hand, saying, "Welcome. Welcome. What can I do for you?" He motioned to his human-sized plush red leather chair.

I sat and said, "I'll not waste your time. I'm flattered that you would invite me to speak at the Board meeting, but I really don't feel qualified to address the topic."

He shook his head sadly. "Oh, if we had anyone in the bank who was competent to speak on it, I'd be happy to have them do so. This topic is much more a muggle topic than a wizarding or even Goblin topic. I won't admit anyone to Board meetings even as a guest speaker unless I have some familiarity with him. It's either you or no one."

I shook my head. "How in the world am I going to develop any amount of expertise in the couple of weeks that I have available?"

Glazblatt smiled. "You've been in lots of tighter deadlines. You always manage one way or another."

I sat a while considering. I closed my eyes, and I'm afraid that my mouth may have opened. Glazblatt became alarmed. "Mr. Wendt. Are you all right?"

I opened my eyes and said, "Yes. Yes. I'll offer you a deal."

What passed for a smile among goblins appeared on his face, and he said, "Yes, yes. What is it?"

"Here's my offer. There's no negotiating. Take it or leave it. If you don't take it, I won't even show up at the Board meeting."

He frowned and said, "How much choice do I have?"

I nodded. "OK. Here it is. I take the next two weeks to do research and develop ideas. At the end of that time, I tell you if I'll speak or not. You accept my decision without question. Furthermore, if I need any resources to complete my research, you provide them."

He nodded slowly as he considered and then extended his hand, "Done."

I took his hand and said, "And done."

I got up and left the office by the door that I'd entered. The concierge goblin had left. The secretary offered to guide me back to the front of the bank.

I replied, "That won't be necessary. I know my way."

She nodded her agreement, and I turned to leave. She said, "Oh, wait. Are you sure that you don't need another appointment?"

I shook my head and left. During my reverie I'd come up with a plan. I would start with the current issues of economics journals—the *Economist*, the *Wall Street Journal*, even *The Times of London*. Then I would hit the libraries to read recent issues. Surely someone had written about this.

When I hit the street, it was too early for lunch, so I decided to go to Flourish and Blotts to start my research. I entered and went directly to the periodical section. They had magical newspapers from England and most of Europe. They also usually had some muggle newspapers. I worked my way through the stacks of newspapers. The only thing I found was the *Times*.

I paid for the paper and went to the little lounge area that they had to begin reading the Business section. I quickly scanned the headlines. There was nothing that obviously spoke to my issue. I then began reading the first paragraph of any article that seemed like it could apply to my problem. There wasn't anything.

By that time, I thought that it was close enough to noon that I could go to the Cauldron and get a table. I'd order something to drink and wait for Minerva to arrive while I read the other sections.

Tom greeted me with obvious pleasure. "You'll be joining us for lunch, will you?"

I agreed, told him that Minerva would be joining me a little later, and I'd just take a hot tea until she did. He suggested a small table. I took it and buried my nose in the opinion section.

I hadn't finished that section when Minerva arrived, and we had lunch. She was disappointed that I hadn't tracked her down after getting out of Gringotts.

I then reached a tricky spot in the conversation. "Minerva, I've got to do some research for the Board meeting. I'm going to have to go looking for a library where I can . . ."

I didn't get to finish. She expressed her unhappiness that I wouldn't join her for afternoon shopping. "This is our very first Christmas as husband and wife. You can't be bothered on the very first day of Christmas shopping to help me!"

My mouth opened and closed without anything exiting it. Finally, I said, "Look, you have a point. I'll help you shop this afternoon, but tomorrow morning, I've got to do this research."

She was obviously unhappy but must have decided that half a loaf was better than none and agreed. We spent the afternoon in three different stores, finding amazing bargains that would overwhelm our relatives and friends. Meanwhile, I collected an ever growing collection of bags from the stores that we visited. Finally, Minerva bought an Omni-Size magic bag that we could put them all in. Then, it was not that difficult to carry our bargains. The only problem was that every time we added a new bag we had to re-organize the bags in the Omni-Size to accommodate a new one.

That evening we went to a cousin's home to visit. He and his wife gave me the once-over and declared, "muggle."

I agreed, and after that the evening wasn't that bad. The cousin and his wife both cooked, and their meal was actually quite good. It wasn't quite up to Hogwarts standard, but I enjoyed it thoroughly. He turned out to have a sneaking interest in most things muggle.

Minerva and I were both peppered with questions about muggle inventions—like cell phones, Microwave Popcorn, and music records.

It turned out that he was a classical music fan. We talked about the London Symphony orchestra versus the Cleveland Symphony and the Chicago Symphony. After dinner, he took me to his den. He showed me his gramophone and his collection of classical vinyl. He had some amazing recordings in his collection. I thought I was going to weep at the quality and breadth of his collection. He picked up an album that had Rachmaninoff performing his own *Second Piano Concerto*. He was about to put it on the gramophone.

I said, "Oh, don't. You have to save that for really special occasions."

He chuckled, "This is a special occasion."

I gave up. As the first chords sounded, we took seats. He asked me, "I have heard of these things called compact disks. What is all the fuss about?"

I definitely was going to cry then. I composed myself and said, "Look. Your gramophone is amazing. If you only had access to electricity, you could have a compact disc player. You could listen to this music with fidelity that you wouldn't believe. You could play them hundreds of times without scratches or pops or hiss."

I quickly added, "Now, there are people who argue that vinyl is easily better than CD. I don't get their argument. I just think you should have the opportunity for a direct comparison."

He nodded and said, "We've thought about having electricity. It just didn't seem like it was something we needed. If you really think that we could have this wonderful music with electricity, then maybe."

I nodded quickly. "You can get a sample of it right now. I have a cell phone with a little music on it. The quality isn't great but you can get an idea. That is, if the level of magic here is low enough to let it play."

I took out my cell phone and brought up the music player. I didn't have Rachmaninoff's *Second*, but I did have his *Third*. I turned it on. It actually worked! We sat there listening to the tinny, tiny speaker playing Rachmaninoff. He actually did weep for joy.

I said, "I think that electricity could work here—at least in this room."

"That does it, I'm getting a CD player!"

The *Economist* Throws a Party

The next day, Minerva agreed to drop me off at a library near Maggie's house. She was still not happy about my spending the morning at the library, but we would meet for lunch and shopping afterward.

The library was rather nice. It didn't have the widest selection of journals, but it did have The *Economist* and the *Wall Street Journal*. I decided to start with the *Journal* and then do the *Economist* and then go back a day at a time. The *Journal* was pretty much a glorified version of the business pages of the *Times*. But in the very first *Economist* that I picked up, I hit pay dirt on page three.

On page three there was a half-page advert for a conference on January 5 about the role of money in the post-alien economy. The ad listed speakers, topics, break-out sessions, and contact information. It was going to happen at Cambridge. There would be speakers from universities and major banks. I found a xerox copier and copied the advert. I went back to my table with it. I scrawled on the back of the copy, "Get me in here!"

I folded it up and put it in my purse and returned to the journals. I read until Minerva arrived for lunch. There was nothing else that came close to matching my first find.

We went to a muggle cafe. Minerva's opening statement was, "I suppose you'll want to come back tomorrow and every day until the holiday is over."

I smiled beneficently. "No. No. My work here is done. However, I will need help sending an owl to Gringott's tomorrow."

She regarded me suspiciously, but she knew me well enough to know when I was telling the unvarnished truth. It was a pleasant lunch.

The rest of the days up until Christmas went as she had planned—well, except for one afternoon when we saw of *Master and Commander*.

□

Christmas Eve was a special occasion. We went to Cousin Beryl's home, which turned out to be almost a castle. All of the relatives that we'd seen plus more showed up. People had come in from all over Europe and even one couple from the States.

Beryl walked around from group to group of closely related people. Minerva and I came along in her train. She would introduce us to each as Mr. and Mrs. Wendt. Of course, nearly everyone knew and recognized Minerva. The ones that we'd visited knew and recognized me. To everyone, though, I was introduced as a Professor at Hogwarts School of Witchcraft and Wizardry.

Of course, she didn't add, unless pressed, of what it was that I was a professor. Most people didn't really care. Most were perfectly OK with my being a muggle.

One very proper matron asked, "And what did you do during the war?"

I asked her which war she meant. It turned out that she meant, of course, the war against Riddle. I was tempted to reply with a quote from Pink Floyd, "I traded a bit part in the war for a lead role in a cage." That was technically pretty close to the truth. I'd spent the first part in the war in a detention cell of the SAS. Of course, later, one of the things I did was help run refugees to the States. I didn't mention that.

What I did say was, "I was a consultant for the British muggle government. I advised them on policies for resisting Riddle."

She didn't know quite how to take that. Minerva gave me such a kick to the shin when I'd answered that it was lucky that the matron was speechless for the moment.

Minerva started to give her a more accurate account of what I'd been up to. I turned sharply around to face her and gave her a look that matched the shin kick for intensity. She just grumbled and said, "Wendt underestimates his efforts."

She sniffed and said, "No doubt you'd say that."

I could see Minerva's dander rising. I took her firmly by the hand and said, "Let's see if we can find Aunt Beryl." We walked away and shortly did find Aunt Beryl. She was standing at a refreshment table.

Fortunately, she was alone for the moment. I asked her, "I suppose it's too much to hope that you will join us for our usual New Year's Eve party?"

She chuckled. "After this," she extended her arm and pointed around to the crowd of people in the ballroom, "I can't think of anything I'd rather do. Yes, expect me at your sister's at sunset."

41

There was a string quartet that played through most of the evening. There was no dancing. I was greatly appreciative of that. Minerva and I had had enough socializing before midnight. We left shortly after the stroke of midnight.

□□

On Christmas day, we ate, opened presents, ate some more, and played parlor games. There were just the three of us until the mid-afternoon when Professor Slughorn arrived.

Of course, Minerva was concerned that something had happened at Hogwarts. I had a different idea. I asked him, 'Would you stay for left-overs for dinner? I'm sure it's lonely at Hogwarts."

A wan smile creased his face,."Well, yes. This was more a social call than an emergency."

I didn't have the nerve to ask what had happened to all his influential contacts from school.

I suggested the game of "yes and no". No one had heard of it under that name. When I explained it, everyone sighed in relief, "Of course, Twenty Questions."

I was at a distinct disadvantage. Everyone picked obscure Magical things or Fantastic Animals. I did know a few of the more common ones such as Phoenixes, but they had things like Mandragoras and bow-truckles and so on.

I had my revenge though. On my turn the questions went something like this:

"Is it an animal?"

"No."

"Is it vegetable?"

"No."

"All right. Is it something that is larger than a bread box?"

"Barely, yes."

"Is it smaller than a table?"

"Yes."

"Is it a book?"

"No."

"Is it a tool?"

"No."

"Is it useful around the house?"

"Not really."

"Is it used on a farm?"

"No."

42

"Is it used by a Healer or a what is that you muggles call your Healers?"

"Doctors. And no."

"Is it used for fun?"

"Yes. By the way, you've used half your questions."

The going got slower then since they didn't want to waste their questions. Minerva asked, "Is it something that only muggles use?"

"Yes."

"Is it something that ordinary muggles would use?"

"Yes."

"Is it something having to do with entertainment?"

"Yes."

"Is it radio?"

"No."

Minerva seemed to have a glimmer. "Oh, I know. Is it, uh . . . is it what you call telly?"

"No."

They began to be really careful then. Minerva asked, "Is it a DWI?"

I couldn't help laughing. "No. And I think you mean, DVD."

Maggie had an inspiration. "What about that other thing that looks a lot like the DWI, you know . . uh . . CDR."

"I have to give you points for ingenuity. But, no."

Slughorn asked, "Is it a gramophone?"

Maggie said, "That's good, but we use them too."

"Maggie's right, no."

Minerva said, "I have three ideas. I'm pretty sure one of them is right, but we have only two questions left. Does anyone else want to guess something?" Nobody did. She went on, "Is it a VCR tape?"

"Sorry, no."

With only one question left, she pondered hard and then asked, "Is it a computer?"

I drew my "no" out. "Sorry, no."

Minerva then stamped a foot and said, "It's got to be a movie, then."

I admitted that she was right.

43

Gringotts Comes Through

Boxing Day was blessedly boring. Nothing at all happened. The next day, an owl showed up outside the kitchen window. It pecked on the glass once and was promptly let in. It walked up to me and dropped its cargo onto my plate of bacon and eggs.

"Why do they always do that to me?"

Minerva glanced at it and observed that it was from Gringotts. Everyone got up, walked around the kitchen table poised to look over my shoulder.

I said, "Sorry, this looks like official business. I have signed a non-disclosure agreement with the goblins and can't let you see it."

Minerva and her sister reluctantly returned to their places, and I slit the rather thick envelope open. Inside there were several items along with a cover letter. The cover letter said:

"Dear Professor Wendt,

> Please find enclosed a ticket with your confirmation number to the *Economist* Conference on the Future of Money, a ticket to the lunch, a fact sheet containing frequently asked questions about the Conference, a brochure describing the keynote event and breakout sessions.

> "If you have any questions about the Conference, please direct them to the contact people listed in the FAQ sheet. Other questions you are invited cordially

to direct to me. It will be my great
pleasure to assist you in any way that you
might conceivably desire.

Javeen, private assistant to Glazblatt.

I smiled. It seemed to me that this conference was public knowledge, and I could share that I was going to it. So, I kept the cover letter but laid the other items on the table and said, "It's not confidential that I'm attending this conference. Look to your heart's content."

They did.

Minerva's immediate reaction was, "This is a business conference, isn't it?"

I nodded.

"Then you'll need something better to wear than that ratty old suit that predates Stanford."

I stared at her. "Why in the world?"

She sniffed. "Well, in the first place, it doesn't fit you that well. Second, you'll be representing Gringotts, won't you?"

I answered cautiously, "Yes."

"Well, you want them to think that Gringotts is a business-like organization, don't you?"

I growled, "Since when were you concerned about the reputation of Gringotts?"

"Since my man was representing them. We're going right now to a good muggle men's store and buy you a suit befitting your position on the Board of Directors of Gringotts."

I knew when I had lost, so I just nodded agreement.

For a witch, she knew an awful lot about muggle men's clothing. We got out the most recent *Times* that we had, and she searched through the adverts for a good store to find me a suit.

She picked three names out of the adverts, and I found myself outside a well-known store by 10 AM. I wished that we could just find something at this first store and be done with it.

Apparently, it wasn't all that strange for wives to accompany their husbands on these sorts of expeditions. We entered the store and found a salesman immediately approaching us. He introduced himself and offered his services.

I decided that I needed to take charge. I said that it was simple. I just wanted to buy a suit appropriate for business meetings. It turned out that it mattered a little whom the meetings would be with.

I probably made a mistake in admitting that I'd be meeting with banking representatives from around the world.

He nodded and led us to the high-end part of the store. He asked what color I was looking for. I, at least, had a good idea of that. I declared, "I want dark grey." Minerva nodded agreement.

He nodded sagely and asked, "Single or Double."

Fortunately, Minerva was there to ask the stupid questions. She asked, "Single or Double what?"

The salesman made it easy anyway. "Why madame, single or double breasted." He then took two suit coats off of racks and displayed them. He had a double-breasted in his right hand and the single-breasted in his left.

Minerva oohed over the double-breasted and nodded her head encouragingly. "Double, I think." Then she saw my face and said, "Noooo, I suppose we really want single-breasted."

I nodded encouragingly. Then we looked at infinitesimal differences in colors among dark greys. I selected one at random.

The salesman said, "Of course, custom-tailoring is complementary, so let's go see our tailor."

I saw a problem. "I really need it by New Year's Eve."

Minerva stared at me. I calmly answered, "I know the meeting isn't until the next week, but we really have no time for a second adjustment if it's not ready this year."

The salesman solicitously said, "I'm afraid that we can only meet that schedule for an additional fee."

I shrugged. It was going to be expensive at this store anyway. Why should I bother about even more expense. "OK. Let's go talk to the tailor."

I had to wait for two more gentlemen to be fitted. It was well after noon before we got out of the shop, but I counted myself lucky that we could get out without visiting a second or even third shop.

□

New Year's Eve was a busy day. I received a call just after noon about the suit. The alterations were ready.

Minerva transported me there, and it took us a good hour and a half to wait in line to pick up our suit. I had begun thinking of it as our suit. I had to try it on. There was a small issue with the pants length of one leg. The tailor insisted on correcting it on the spot. It would only take a jiffy, don't you know.

Well, it was a long jiffy.

Then we had to do some last minute shopping for food and little party favors. We did that at Diagon Alley. For party favors we decided to take a chance on Weasley Wizard Weezes. It turned out to be a good choice. They had some perfectly good things like "poppers", paper origami dragons that actually flew around for up to a half hour, and noise-makers of various sorts. They had fire-crackers. I was rather reluctant to take a chance on them, but Minerva insisted that we must have at least one. So, we bought a fairly large one shaped like a red dragon.

Minerva helped Maggie work on food prep. I insisted I'd do all the cleanup if they just did the food. They finally forced me to make a green salad. That was something that I felt competent to do.

Besides the four of us (Beryl, Maggie, and the Wendts), there was one other guest. We had invited Professor Slughorn. He was very thankful for having both Christmas and New Year's Eve handled.

The meal was memorable in the best possible way. Nothing memorable happened. Afterwards, Professor Slughorn would, commenting on the evening, say something like, "We had a bang-up time. There were party games, treats, and . . uh . . yes, I guess we had dinner too."

We had finished the meal and were settling down to some conversation over coffee and tea when there was a knock on the door. Minerva got up and said, "I suppose I should mention that I've invited a mystery guest this evening."

Everyone looked at me as she went to the door. I just shrugged. No one had the slightest who it was—least of all me.

We heard the door open and then close. The hall closet door opened and closed. I could tell because it was a bit sticky. Then Minerva led Pam Myers into the living room. Everyone was perfectly surprised. I stood as did Slughorn. I extended my hand, which she took briefly and released.

Minerva was speaking. "As most of you know, there is traditionally a Back Alley Bridge tournament held in this house on New Year's Eve. Since we have five guests, I decided that it would only be fun if we invited a sixth, the perfect number for Back Alley Bridge. Also, it's appropriate because everyone is familiar with the game in this household. It would only be fair to match Professor Slughorn with another novice. I couldn't think of anyone better than the Minister of Magic."

Actually, I could think of a number of better people, but I wasn't going to say so out loud. I was pretty sure that there wasn't a Legilimens in the group, so it was safe to say that to myself.

No one seemed particularly surprised. Even Slughorn seemed charmed. He took Pam's hand and touched his lips to it. It was a work of a minute to go to the dining room and clear the table. Cards were brought out.

Minerva explained the rules and divided us up into teams. There was a little dispute as to who would be my partner. Both Beryl and Minerva had that position in mind. I decided the question by choosing Aunt Beryl. That delighted her greatly. Maggie and Minerva weren't sad to be partners. Myers and Slughorn seemed to be strangely happy to be partners. I wondered if there were some back story there, but I sure wasn't going to take a chance at ruining the evening by asking about it.

Back Alley Bridge, like contract bridge, has a strong element of chance. The game frequently has wild swings of score as the hands progress. At one point, Pam and Horace were well behind, but by the end of the first set of games, it was quite close. A whim of luck put Maggie and Minerva in the lead by a few points at the end. Pam and Horace came in second by a single point with Beryl and I leading from the rear.

The next set was different. This time skill played a larger role. Beryl and I won by a fairly large margin. That delighted Beryl. Pam and Horace were taking it amazingly well. They were delightedly chatting away about life at Hogwarts when Minerva noted, "We missed midnight."

At that point it was already 12:45. Maggie brought out a bottle of champagne. We toasted the New Year. Pam and Horace had entwined arms as they drank their toast. It nearly came a cropper when they almost spilled each others' drinks, but we all got a good-natured chuckle out of it.

Beryl, as she often did, stayed the night. Minerva and I gave up our room to her and took the attic garret. There was some argument over who would take what room. During that argument, Pam and Horace snuck off. I did not miss the brief exchange between them, though.

Horace said, "Allow me to see you home safely, please."

Pam had said, "How gallant! Yes, you may. You may pop your head in for a quick nightcap as well."

□□

The rest of the holiday finished quietly with both Minerva and my doing some lesson planning. On the final day, we went to the Cauldron to take the floo to Hogwarts.

We ordered a quick drink from Tom as usual. Then we entered the floo. Minerva took up some floo powder and said, "Headmistress's Office, Hogwarts. Columbus, Ohio." Then she threw down the floo powder and we landed unceremoniously in the floo of the Headmistress's Office.

I asked, "What in the world has Columbus, Ohio got to do with anything?"

She looked over and said, "Well, it was that Auror's idea. I just got around to implementing it."

48

I searched my memory trying to think when an Auror had suggested Columbus Ohio as a part of the incantation to get to her office.

She supplied the reason. "Surely you remember when that Auror suggested that I put a password on my floo entrance so that no one could break in."

Then it came to me. "Oh, sure. That was a long time ago. You're only getting around to it now?"

She shrugged. Then another thought occurred to me. "So, Columbus, Ohio is your password?"

She nodded.

"That's not a very good idea."

"And why not. It's easy to remember."

I rolled my eyes, "Yes, easy to remember but also easy to guess. You need to make it a harder-to-guess password."

"Well all right, Mr. Technical, what would you suggest?"

I thought a minute. "Well, it should have numbers in it and maybe special characters."

She screwed up her eye in concentration and asked, "What kind of special characters?"

"Oh, you know, like the pound sign."

"Oh, you mean like: February 7, 1947"

I said, "I guess so. Just so long as that date isn't a special date to you."

"I just made it up."

"And you can remember it easily?"

"Maybe." She thought a minute. "I want to be able to use my own floo in my own office. I think maybe I'll stick to something really easy to remember."

A Day at Cambridge

The day began with an argument over breakfast. Minerva was saying, "How can you prefer a 'continental breakfast' at Cambridge to a Real Breakfast Made by Real Hogwarts House Elves!"

The way she said it, everything was capitalized. My answer was easy, "Look, the goblins of Gringotts paid for the whole trip, including the breakfast buffet at Cambridge. It would be ungrateful to turn it down."

She rolled her eyes but gave in. "OK. Where is it that you're going?"

"The Bodleian Library, Blackwell Hall. I need to get there quickly, if I want to have any time to actually eat any of the breakfast."

She was still not happy, but she dusted my new suit off for the fifth time and declared that I was presentable—just. She took my hand, and we walked into the floo in her office. She threw down the powder and we were on our way.

Why she bothered with all the brushing off of my suit before we left was beyond me. I was now covered with soot. A quick *scurgio* spell got me pretty well cleaned off. I just tossed a few galleons onto the bar of the Cauldron and said, "Got to fly, Tom, sorry."

We walked outside and disapparated onto the Cambridge Campus outside Blackwell Hall. Minerva dusted me off again and said, "Go get 'em tiger!"

I frowned and walked up to the main door. At least the conference was well marked. Inside, there was a welcome table manned by several young ladies. Each had a range of the alphabet on a tent label in front of her. I walked up to the Q—Z table.

The young lady asked me for my name. I gave it. She rifled through a pile of name tags. After a bit, she said, "Oh, yes. Wendt with a 'D'."

I said, "Right, with an 'R'."

She laughed. Then as she stared at the name tag, she asked, "It says here that you are with Gringotts bank?"

I smiled. "Guilty."

She showed even more consternation and asked, "It also says that you're a member of the Board of Directors."

"Guilty again."

She said, "Oh, pardon me. My name's Quinn. I'm sorry to be nosy, but it's pretty unusual for members of a bank's Board to show up at one of these."

I shrugged.

She said, "Hmmmm. Also, I've not heard of Gringotts. Where is it headquartered?

"Well, actually, it's here in England, but it's a pretty small bank. We have branches in a number of countries, but not many in any one country— even here."

She looked more puzzled than ever. "What is your cap?"

I was puzzled for a moment. Then I realized what she was asking just before she supplied it. "Oh, our captalization. I'm sorry. I signed a non-disclosure. I can't even tell you that."

She nodded. "A man of mystery, eh?"

I sighed. "Afraid so."

Then she seemed to have a thought, "Hey! Are you attending the luncheon here?"

I nodded.

"Let's sit at the same table. You have piqued my curiosity."

I shrugged, "OK. I guess I shouldn't have much trouble spotting you."

"Why not?"

I shrugged again. "You appearance is distinctive."

"I'm not sure how I should take that."

"Nor am I. I've got to get in if I'm going to have some of your wonderful continental breakfast."

She frowned and said *soto voce*, "No need to hurry." She quickly added, "I almost forgot. There's a change in speakers for the keynote panel. It's all here on this sheet. Everyone's supposed to get one."

She was right.

□

After kicking myself for not having breakfast at Hogwarts, I skipped all the networking going on in the halls and headed directly to the meeting room.

There I found that I could get a seat in the third row. Once I was settled

51

in, I looked at the corrected agenda, and my mouth dropped. The speaker who'd had to drop out at the last moment was replaced by a familiar name —Dr. Richard Feynman! What in the world was going on?

I waited in much anticipation.

At 9 AM, the director of the conference came out on the stage where there were four chairs and a podium in place. He went to the podium, tested the microphone, and announced, "Welcome to the first annual *Economist* Conference on the Future of Money.

"This Conference was called because of the near extermination of money caused by the invasion of the Earth by the aliens who called themselves 'Souls'. Nearly six months after the end of their domination of the Earth, the world's economies are run on a mixture of cash, also known as M1, various forms of credit, and the alien system that is a variation on the Marxist paradigm.

"In this first conference, we want to give the banks, governments, and industries guidance as to the likely future of the use of money in our developing economic system.

"To start the conference we have a key-note panel of experts. There are three. Each will present a different perspective. Each will speak for not longer than twenty minutes. We will then take a break and resume at 10:30 AM. There will be a panel discussion, which we hope will be limited to forty-five minutes, followed by an open question and answer session. As soon as that ends, we will adjourn for lunch."

"Our first speaker is Dr. Leslie Chambers of University College London. He will present the traditionalist view that the use of money will eventually resume its original function in the world economic system.

"Our second speaker is Dr. Mansur Kuthrapali of the University of Calcuta who will present the position that the future of money is quite limited and that even the current level of use will decay to the vanishing point.

"Finally, we had a cancellation. Dr. Robert Cummings of the University of California, Los Angeles has had an emergency appendectomy and will be replaced by Dr. Richard Feynman of California Technical Institute of Pasadena, California. He will present the position that the long term state of the economy will be a mixed system including both extensive use of money and a near Marxist subsystem. Frankly, I can't wait to hear what he has to say.

"So, without further ado, I'll call the participants out one at a time. They will speak and then be seated for our panel discussion segment. Please welcome Dr. Leslie Chambers, University Collge London."

There was a general round of applause for Chambers. He came out and presented his position. It would be fair to characterize it as claiming that the alien invasion represented a perturbation to the economic system. Now that their influence was gone, the system would return to a state of equilibrium that would be very close to the original state.

As I listened, it struck me more and more that this was not analysis. It was analysis by analogy. He was taking physics ideas and trying to apply them to much more complicated systems. He might be right, but it would be more by accident than by research.

He finished and had polite applause and, really, more than polite. Then the host introduced Kuthrapali. Kuthrapali was interesting. He didn't try to convince by arguing why the money-less society was coming. He simply outlined all the advantages of the money-less society.

The main advantage was that it solved the problem that had first been recognized by Marx but had always been put off. Modern methods of production had finally caught up with Marx's vision. Very few people were required to produce the basic requirements of life.

He pointed out that those basic requirements included now a number of things that a decade ago would not have seemed so basic. They included simple cell phones, clothing, food, even computers were on the verge of becoming nearly free. He portrayed two different worlds—one where eveyone had access to the basics of life and a few luxuries simply because they were alive. The other was one where the majority of people—maybe the vast majority—lived in abject poverty or were almost slaves. They would not have access to even the simple basics that he had just described. He painted a gruesome picture of a world that wasn't that far away.

He argued that accepting the gift that the aliens had given us of an economic system where everyone did reasonably well, and few did very well was by far the more acceptable one for everyone—including the very well off.

At the end of his talk there was scattered applause. I thought that I had to applaud, although I was afraid that his picture of a disastrous future was the most likely event.

Then, the host introduced Feynman. He gave a brief review of Feynman's accomplishments and finished by proclaiming Feynman to be a jack of all trades AND a master of most, including burglary, painting, information technology, and most significantly—physics. He had worked in collaboration with economists and those in other fields. He was the person suggested by Dr. Cummings to replace himself.

Feynman took the podium and thanked the host for his kind description. He began with a story:

"I feel like one of the pickpockets who frequented hangings a century or so ago. They were like magicians who direct your attention elsewhere while picking your pocket. We've just seen the world economic system hung. While you are still gazing with amazement, I will pick your intellectual pockets.

"Anyone who comes to a podium like this. . ." With that he walked away from the podium and began pacing back and forth, directing his gaze now here, now there about the audience as he spoke. ". . . Anyone, standing here claiming that they can predict the economic future, is a fraud. Maybe he is defrauding himself more than anyone else. Economics is not a science yet. Maybe it will never be.

"I want to make one primary suggestion. I happen to agree that Dr. Kuthrapali is right about one thing. The basic commodities of life are nearly free. They should be completely free.

"If something is not a commodity, then it should be considered a luxury.

"Then money can be used for its legitimate purpose—a way of directing research and development toward projects that really are preferred by people. So, luxuries should be developed as dictated by the dollars and pounds and yen of people."

He continued developing this theme, and by the end of the talk, I was convinced that his idea of money co-existing with the alien scheme was worth investigating further.

When he finished the discussion, he was met with what I would call bewildered applause. There were clearly people in the audience who supported him strongly. There were also a lot of people who were just polite.

The host declared a twenty minute break. I decided to retain my good seat near the front and just wait. I also, made notes on the talks that I could develop into a presentation for the goblins.

When the twenty minutes were up, the host called the crowd to order. All three speakers returned to the stage and sat. The host sat on stage right. He asked the first question, which was enough of a start for the panelists to continue the discussion until the host called a stop.

The first question was, "What proof do you have that the world economy is returning to the equilibrium that you described, Dr. Chambers?"

Chambers called for a slide to be projected on the screen behind the panel. It was a graph that was not that different from the one that the goblins had sent me. Chambers even had fitted the curves of the velocity of the various money supplies and projected a date when they would be close to the equilibrium point.

Feynman asked if there were a chart with error bars and if there were uncertainties available for the fits.

Chambers answered that there were but that he'd not wanted to obscure the data with them.

Feynman just stared at him and finally commented, "That is where the data is."

Kuthrapali asked Feynman how the money-less commodity economy could co-exist with the moneyed economy. "For example, even commodities require raw materials. Will they be obtained freely?"

Feynman's answer was that companies that produced raw materials will sell them both for the production of commodities and the production of luxuries. There would be plenty of profit for the raw material producers even if they gave them away to the commodity producers.

That statement sparked a lengthy debate about just how that could work. Would people actually work for companies that produced only commodities for free?

Feynman replied, "Of course. They do right now. Haven't you heard of Linux and free software." Apparently no one on the dais had.

Finally, the host had to call an end to the discussion and opened the panel for questions from the floor. There were a couple of people with microphones circulating in the crowd so that people with questions could be heard easily.

A couple of people asked very technical questions of Chambers and Kuthrapali. Then the questions seemed to dissipate. So I stood up.

Everyone who asked a question was to give their name and organizational affiliation. I was recognized and when I had the microphone said, 'James Wendt, Board of Directors, Gringotts Bank.

"Professor Feynman, my question is for you. You make a sharp distinction between commodities and luxuries. Just where does health care fall?"

Feynman squinted out, apparently to get a better view of me. Then he asked, "You aren't the same Wendt who recruited me to speak at a commencement address, are you?"

I was not entirely surprised that he remembered me. I simply said, "Yes, that's right."

He asked if I'd quit Hogwarts. I answered that I hadn't. Then he smiled and said, "You didn't happen to bring that Dursley along with you? I'd like to say hello to him."

All I could do was say, "No, sir. I'm afraid I didn't."

He said that was too bad and then answered my question. He said, "Well, that's a difficult question. We have to get our categories straight.

Parts of health care are commodities. For example, vaccines, basic health exams, good nutrition are commodities. On the other hand, kidney transplants, exotic chemotherapy for cancer, and so on are not. The dividing line between the two would not be easy to chart, but I think it's possible and should be done, don't you?"

I could only say, "Yes, I think you're right."

I returned the mike and sat down. There were a number of questions afterward. The host then called a halt to the questions and dismissed us for lunch.

I reached the hall that had been set up for lunch. I didn't have to search for the young lady who'd helped me when I arrived. She ran over and said, "Come this way, Dr. Wendt. I've got a table held for us. Her name tag said her name was Quinn."

We arrived at the table and found there were already six people there—five guys and another woman. Quinn and I sat. She introduced me around. Apparently they all worked for Barclays who were co-sponsors of the event.

One of the guys asked, "Do you really know Professor Feynman?" There were nods around the table.

I shrugged. "Yes, I do. And by the way, Quinn introduced me as Dr. Wendt. I don't have a Ph'd—just a master's degree from Stanford."

As we were speaking, waiters brought salads. Quinn apologized and asked rapidly, "How did you get to know Feynman, and what about this Hogwarts school? Are you also on their board?"

I couldn't help laughing. "I know about Hogwarts because I'm an instructor there. Just to forestall questions, let me say that I'm a lowly instructor there of English Literature. It's a small residential finishing school in the far north of Scotland—hard to get to and hard to get into."

One of the guys said, "That doesn't explain how you got to know Feynman."

I nodded sagely. "No, it doesn't. I suppose that it wouldn't hurt to tell you that story."

□□

I was a graduate student at Stanford, studying English Literature. One day, there was a notice on a bulletin board. It said that Dr. Richard Feynman was going to be visiting SLAC. For those of you who've not heard of it, SLAC is a sort of acronym for the Stanford Linear Accelerator. It's a physics research facility operated by Stanford.

I'd heard of Feynman and thought that it would be fun to hear him speak, so on that Thursday morning, I skipped a class on the origins of the English novel and drove out to SLAC. Feynman is a lot funnier than he was today.

He started his talk in the crowded auditorium where he was speaking, "OK. I always like to get a feel for my crowd before I start. So, please, everyone stand up."

We did, a bit surprised.

He said, "OK. Stretch. I don't want anyone falling asleep on my watch."

We did. Then he said, "OK. Everyone on the staff here at SLAC, please sit." A good number of people sat—probably close to half. His comment was, "Anything to get out of work, eh?"

Then he said, "Now, would all of you who are physics graduate students, please sit."

After they'd sat, there were probably about one quarter left standing. He then said, "Now, would anyone who's an undergraduate physics student, please sit."

That left a scattering—maybe about one in ten or fewer. "OK, anyone from the press, please sit."

After that, there were maybe a dozen or so standing. "That many?" I was the one closest to the stage. He said, "You," apparently meaning me, "What's your profession?"

I looked around to make sure that he was talking to me. He left no doubt, "Yes, you in the fourth row."

I said, "I'm a Stanford graduate student."

"What field? Chemistry? Math? Biology?"

I answered, "English Literature."

He laughed, "Why in the world are you here?"

All I could think to say was the truth, "It's complicated."

"Well, then, why don't you join me for lunch? I'd like to know just how complicated it could be."

Feynman's talk was about String Theory. He gave a brief history of the development of String Theory and then dove into details. I'm afraid that I don't remember any of them. Anyway, when he'd finished talking there was time for questions. No one seemed to have any or maybe it was that no one wanted to embarrass themselves with a stupid question. I wasn't afraid because, frankly, I'd already embarrassed myself.

I stood. Feynman recognized me by saying, "You again. I hope you have a really good question."

That almost did me in, but I asked my question anyway, "Well, sir, as I see it, String Theory really isn't disconfirmable. Why do people spend so much time on it?"

Feynman said, "That is a good question. Does anyone out there have an answer?"

No one dared to stand up, but somebody shouted out, "It's a beautiful theory."

Feynman nodded, "Yes, it is a beautiful theory." He walked across the stage and turned back to start a walk back across the stage. Before he'd gotten very far, he looked up and turned toward the audience. "The red-head in the first row is pretty, but I wouldn't take it on her say-so that String Theory was true.

"The answer is correct. You see, physicists are enamored of beauty. They will run away from their good wife, the scientific method, to have a fling with beauty. But much of the time, beauty lets them down in the end.

"An example of that is the Perfect Cosmological Principle. In its simplicity it's even more beautiful than String Theory. It also appears to be false. The Cosmic Background radiation has proved her false.

"Ah well, that's always the story with beauty."

That seemed to be the end of questions. No one else wanted to take a chance with Feynman. As people began to wander off, Feynman addressed me again, "You there. Yes, you. I wasn't kidding. I'm going to have pizza and beer with a couple of my graduate students. Would you come along?"

I was delighted, of course. Apparently, there was one pizzeria that he frequented when he was at SLAC. He gave me an address ,and I agreed to go there and join them.

It turned out to be almost a hole-in-the-wall. There were a few tables and a long counter where people sat and ate. One of his graduate students had grabbed an empty table. The rest of us ordered slices of pizza. I wasn't much of a beer-drinker, but I ordered a Pabst Blue Ribbon and joined them.

The first thing that I noticed was that the red-head in the front row was one of his graduate students. Her name turned out to be Marilyn. I couldn't help asking her, "You let him get away with that kind of crack about you?"

She smiled, "Oh, he knows that he'll pay for it later."

Feynman took over the conversation. "OK, Mr. . . who are you anyway?"

"Wendt. James Wendt."

"OK, Mr. Wendt, how is it that an English Literature major knows so much about Physics, hummm?"

"Well, it's a long story."

"We've got all of lunch."

When I started college at The Ohio State University, I thought that I would be a dual major—physics and pre-med. That didn't survive too long when I realized all the non-physics classes that I'd have to take. So, I changed to pure physics.

That seemed to go pretty well, but I had to take some humanities. I decided that I'd take an English Literature class on the modern novel. I liked to read and thought it would be a pretty easy class that would look good on my transcript.

It turned out to be a harder class than I'd counted on. I wasn't doing great in it, and I began to wonder if dropping it wasn't the better part of valor.

However, something strange happened. One day, I stayed after class to ask a question. I wasn't one of the instructor's better students, but she was kind to me.

As a matter of fact, she wasn't just kind. We got into a lengthy discussion about one of the authors that we were reading. The novel was *Light in August*. It turned out to be a really fascinating discussion. During the course of the discussion, I began to notice that the instructor was actually rather pretty. She was black, had long lustrous hair that she usually wore in a large sort of bun at the back of her head, and her eyes seemed to shine when she talked about the book. She had family that lived close to where Faulkner grew up.

I began to take a lot more interest in the class. I worked hard. I thought hard about the books that we read. I spent real time re-reading and thinking about the essays that I wrote for the class.

I began discussing things with her after every class. The amazing thing was that she didn't come to discourage me—ever. There weren't many other students with questions after class, but I found that I just wanted everyone else to ask their questions so that we could have an undisturbed talk. The class, which I had every day, was the highlight of the day.

Toward the end of the quarter, one of the other students approached me after class. He wasn't doing very well in class. Somehow he realized that I was doing rather well in class. I hadn't thought about it much. My essays had more red on them than they ever had before, but there were also good grades. The red was mostly suggestions about different approaches to the topic of the essay. One essay had a whole page of red comments and suggestions paper-clipped to the back of it.

Anyway, he had this idea that he thought was great. Why didn't a few of us in the class invite Ms. Brock to dinner—just a thank you for being a good teacher and all that. Then, maybe, a little of the good feelings would slide off into final grades.

I ordinarily would have made the fun of that suggestion that it so richly deserved, but it fed into my interest in inviting her out for something after the quarter was over. The other guy was excited that I had a similar idea.

In the end, it never came to anything. On the day of the final exam in the class, I decided that I could ask her out. I didn't know how I'd make it clear that I wasn't just brown-nosing, but I figured that there must be a way.

Anyway, the final exam came. I wrote a great exam. I was sure of it. Even though I finished it ten minutes early, I held on to it, pretending to check it over and over. I even made a couple of minor corrections that I quickly rescinded. Finally, the last of the other students handed in their papers, and I brought my blue book up. She smiled at me and took it.

I thought it was then or never. I opened my mouth to ask her out for dinner or maybe just coffee. What actually came out was a choked off, miserable thank you for a wonderful class. I made the stupid comment that I thought it would change my life. The moment those words were out of my mouth I regretted them. But they were on the air, like the hand-writing on the wall, never to be called back.

We just stood looking at each other for a minute or ten. Then she said that she had to get on her way, and it was over.

The funny thing was that her class did change my life. I took another literature course the next quarter. It didn't have Ms. Brock as an instructor, but that course proved to me that I really did love literature, and it wasn't just the effect of Ms. Brock. The quarter after that, I changed my major to English Literature.

The red-head asked, "How was she?"

I shook my head, still bemused by recollection of Ms. Brock. I said, "Sorry. You asked?"

She repeated, "I asked, 'How was she?'"

I was still a bit befuddled. "You mean how was she as a teacher or a writer or . . ."

Feynman laughed, "Marilyn meant how was she in bed? Right?"

"Sure, after all that you must have hooked up some time. Certainly not until a while after your grade was safely in the book." She leaned closer, "Was she worth all the angst?"

"I'll tell you how she was. She was perfect. She was smart. She had a sense of humor. She was beautiful—oh, so very, very beautiful.

"One time her slip was showing—literally. That pure white lacy slip that she was wearing was just visible below the edge of her skirt. Through the pure white lace, you could just see the pure black creamy skin. It nearly drove me crazy that day."

I laughed. "I'll tell you something ironic." I hesitated to think about how to put it.

Marilyn interrupted me. "You mean to tell me that after all that, you never got together?"

I nodded.

"You are such a putz! Of course, she was into you. Why else the good grades and long, I'm sure, heart-felt comments on the papers and the talks."

I had to admit that I was—a putz. Every now and then I do wonder how being with her would have been.

Feynman summed it up admirably. "You got into English Literature for a skirt."

I shrugged a "yes."

⊞⊟

I said, "So, that's how I knew Feynman. He's got a really good memory. About a dozen years later when I was looking for a commencement speaker, one of the people that I got in contact with was Feynman. I knew it was a long shot. He remembered me and agreed to come.

"In all the years that I've been at Hogwarts, there's never been a better speaker."

Quinn asked, "Well, what about this Dursley? What's the story with him?"

"To be honest, I haven't the slightest idea. He's on the staff at Hogwarts. I guess the two must have met after the commencement. Maybe they became drinking buddies; I don't know."

The pizzas had arrived, and we concentrated on them for a while. After lunch, Quinn pulled me aside. She had another question. "How is it that an instructor at a finishing school—even a great finishing school gets to be on the Board of Directors of an international bank—even a small international bank?"

I shrugged. "I'm sort of a token member of the board. You know, boards seem to want a diverse membership."

She pushed further. "What kind of token?"

I thought about it a minute and was forced to answer, "I'm afraid that I

61

can't say."

She stared at me and asked, "Confidentiality?"

I nodded.

She reached into her purse and pulled out a business card. "Here, if you ever need professional help . . . or . . . personal, get in touch."

I glanced at the card and put it into my brief case. It was almost time for the breakout sessions, and I'd not really decided which to attend.

I quickly turned back to her, "Quinn?"

She turned quickly as well, "Yes? What can I do?"

"I'd like to get a copy of the slides from this morning, including the ones not shown."

She deflated, "Oh, did you provide an email address?"

I had provided one. I rarely ever used it. It was from the time when I'd tried to run away from England.

"Well, we'll email all the slides from the presentations, including the breakout sessions to everyone."

"Thanks."

The breakout sessions were not nearly as interesting as the keynote panel. After the conference, I went to a wizarding bar. Well, really, I went to the street where the wizarding bar was. I stood around for almost half an hour waiting for Minerva to show up.

She finally did. "Well, Wendt, let's go home. I've saved something good for you. We can go down to the kitchens and get something to eat, too." We went into the bar, bought a drink, and then we took the floo to Hogwarts.

The Board is Bored

We were standing in the Waiting Room outside the Conference Room that the Board used when they met. We'd just come through the floo using the special ticket that every board member received that gave admittance to the special floo.

Javeen, the personal assistant to Glazblatt was in the Waiting Room, checking ID's and conducting people into the Conference Room. She looked Minerva up and down. "You've been here before, haven't you?"

Minerva sniffed. "Yes, I have."

Javeen said, "You can wait here if you have to, but the meetings sometimes take a very, very long time."

Minerva sat on a sofa and said, "That's all right. I have lesson plans to work on—lots and lots of lesson plans."

Javeen said, "No, really, if you're concerned about him getting somewhere," then she turned to me and put a hand on my forearm, "I'd be very, very happy to take him wherever in the world he'd like to go."

Minerva sniffed, "That's my role. Now, trot off to your meeting, and you'll find me waiting for you whenever it's done."

Javeen pulled on my arm to lead me to the door of the Conference Room, opened it ever so slowly, and led me in. She announced, "Mr. James Wendt of Hogwarts." With that she squeezed my arm and ever so slowly closed the door behind me.

The Conference Room table was not full yet. I quickly found the tent name plate with my name and took my seat.

Glazblatt was sitting at the head of the table. He glanced nervously up at the clock. It was still five minutes until meeting time, but he was evidently in a hurry. I placed my briefcase on the table, opened it and brought out the pages that I was going to use as my main exhibit.

The last couple of attendees arrived. Glazblatt started the meeting. There was the report on profit and loss, expenses and income.

Income had been somewhat less than normal. It was attributed to some people downsizing their vaults and a few closing their vaults completely. No one seemed particularly concerned with the trend.

Then my turn came.

I handed out my exhibit. It was different from the attachment that Glazblatt sent me with the draft agenda. It had error bars, and trend lines for the velocity of the various money supplies. I'd provided my own money supply definitions. I separated M1 from M2 and called it M2prime. I separated M2 from M3 and called it M3prime.

I explained. "I'm supposed to report on the future of money. M1 is not of interest to us. M2prime and M3prime measure the velocity of money where you earn your profit. The more turns that these money supplies make, the more profit you make. You get a percentage of each of these.

"The projections are based on work by Dr. Chambers of The University College London. Notice the size of the error bars. They show that there's a lot of uncertainty at this point. They also show that your business will improve with time. The forecast covers four quarters into the future.

"I have to tell you that there is a minority report that suggests that the velocity of money will eventually decline and may go completely to zero. I don't think that will happen, but you should make plans in case that happens."

Everyone around the table looked dismayed. I couldn't imagine what they thought I might have to say that was particularly good. Economics, after all, is the dismal science or maybe it's pseudo-science as Feynman would say.

Eventually, one person did speak. He asked the obvious question. There was no obvious answer. "What do you think you can do to prepare for the end of money?"

"I don't have any good ideas. There is just one thing that one of the speakers at a symposium on this topic suggested."

Suddenly all eyes were focused on me. "He suggested that the future role of money may be guiding research and development of what he called luxury items.

"You must understand that what he thinks of as luxury items may not be the same as what you think."

Gorblatt muttered, "Don't make us beg. What are luxury items."

I thought for a moment as I tried to formulate my answer. "Well, you already have a good start. There are very few truly destitute wizards. Why is that?"

There was utter silence for several minutes. Then a small voice at the other end of the table squeaked, "With magic, any wizard can supply most of the basic necessities of life." He burrowed back in his seat fearing that the obvious answer must be wrong for some reason.

"Oh, you're right. Anything that a wizard can't fairly easily supply for himself is a luxury item.

That same voice was emboldened. He said, "Then that means that things like Healer's services and elf-made wine. . . and. . . and vaults are luxury items."

I looked around and saw some smiles breaking out. Goblatt was even smiling. He asked, "Then, we just go on with business as usual?"

I shook my head. "No. You need to invest in the invention of new luxuries. Eventually magic will turn all luxuries into basics."

That had the board stumped. I amplified, "There are muggle investment firms that specialize in this already. They invest in risky new businesses that depend on new inventions or unusual business models.

"Every now and then they make it big. Most of the time, they fail and your money is lost."

Everyone around the table looked from one to another. Then the lone voice at the other end of the table raised a reluctant hand. "May I submit a motion?"

Gorblatt nodded.

The goblin said, "I move that a working group be formed to investigate . . . uh . . . these unusual opportunities."

I supplied, "Sometimes among muggles they call those opportunities 'Black Swans'. Oh, by the way, I second the motion."

Glazblatt said, "Whatever they are, there is a second. Is there discussion?"

There were a few comments. The bold were in favor of the idea. The timid wanted to stick to tried and true methods of old. I finally moved the previous question.

There were no objections. The motion passed six to three. There was the usual final business of all these meetings: the suggestion and approval of the next meeting date and the discussion of new business topics for the next meeting, etc.

The meeting was adjourned. I gathered my left-over exhibit papers. Some people took the exhibits. Someone suggested going out together for lunch. I wasn't interested even though Glazblat wanted me to join him. I steadfastly maintained that I had to get back to school to prepare for the next classes.

Glazblatt asked, "Why do you stay with that school? You're independently wealthy now. You could easily live on your residual income by itself." He added, "In some luxury."

I could only smile and say, "I can't think of anything more exciting to do."

Glazblatt shrugged and gave that funny burst of exhaled breath that seemed to pass for a laugh. "Well, best of luck with that."

We left the room. Javeen came over and said, "SHE insisted on staying. But I'd be overjoyed to take you ANYwhere."

I walked over to Minerva who got up and kissed me rapidly. She took my hand firmly in hers, and we walked to the floo. She picked up some floo powder, and we were in her office after a couple of paces.

She only then asked, "How was that meeting?"

"I can't tell you any details but nothing bad happened."

She thought about that comment for a minute as she sat on the sofa in her office. She patted the spot next to her.

I didn't need more encouragement. She commented before we got down to business, "You said it at the beginning of the school year."

"What did I say?"

"This year is shaping up to be ho-hum."

I ran my hand under her robe and replied, "Perhaps not totally ho-hum."

June At Hogwarts

Someday I will write an account of the tumultuous events that led to a meeting with the Head of the FBI that most recent June. Until then I can only say that we were in the United States on a sensitive assignment. At the end of that assignment we were in that infamous building that the FBI inhabits, the J. Edgar Hoover Building. We packed our meager belongings from our office in its basement. Besides the last couple of days when we'd been writing our reports for the FBI, we'd been scattered all over the globe tracking down sources, interrogating witnesses, and sometimes risking our lives.

Now, we were sitting behind desks in a windowless basement office. Sally and I were the only two who had a lot of experience with keyboards, so we were doing the typing. Minerva would walk around, dictating as she walked. So did Phil.

Mr. & Mrs. Brahms had already left for Hogwarts. They argued that they had done very little outside of the Shrieking Shack, so why couldn't they write their report there?

They left almost immediately, but returned for the "Lessons Learned" meeting. Then they returned to England the same day.

As we finished our reports on the last day before the LL meeting, I asked Phil what his plans were.

He seemed a bit flustered, especially when Sally turned her attention to him and asked, "Yeh, Phil. What are you planning to do?"

He looked around at us apparently hoping that one of us had the answer. His gaze settled between Minerva and me. It went back and forth as though looking for a sympathetic audience. "Well, I got an owl post from the Secretary of Magic. . ."

Here Minerva rolled her eyes. Almost in perfect unison both she and

Sally held out hands.

Phil frowned, took out his wand, and a wave of it produced a small scroll. He handed it to me, saying, "Why don't you read it, Wendt?"

I wasn't sure just how anxious I was to have the dubious honor, but I unrolled it and began reading, "Mr. Pearson , . . ."

Phil grimaced, and I proceeded, "Mr. Pearson, I, as the Head of the Magical Government in the United States, have the right and the duty to . . ."

Here Minerva echoed, "The Right AND Duty."

I went on. "To review the actions of American Magical subjects who assist other Magical governments, especially Auror Offices. I request and require that you . . ."

Sally interrupted again, "Isn't he ever going to get around to it?"

I kept reading. "I request and require that you draft a report for my eyes only. "

Sally laughed. "Well, that let's you out Phil."

I drove on. "In order to do this, I've received permission from the British Minister of Magic to re-assign you to the British Auror Office as a liaison until you completely fulfill your assignment."

Minerva said, "I suppose that you need to get to work on fulfilling this . . . assignment."

Sally didn't look all that happy, but Phil pointed out the silver lining. He sat down next to Sally and gazed into her eyes. "You realize, of course, that means that I have to find someplace to stay in England while I'm on special assignment."

Sally's eyes widened, and she nodded slowly. "You know, I might just have an idea about where you could stay."

Minerva kicked me in the shin for no apparent reason and said, "Allow me to offer Hogwarts as a place that you could stay, right, Wendt?"

Then I got it. "Oh, of course. You would be more than welcome to use my back office bedroom while you're visiting. Let me assure you that it is very comfortable, and the bed is also very comfortable and able to accommodate more than one . . ."

At that point, another swift kick to the shin ended my eloquence on the features of the bed.

Phil accepted my invitation. Sally thanked me profusely. Minerva just smiled.

There was an immediate return to work. Of course, there were slight adjustments in location. Phil dictated and looked over Sally's shoulder as he spoke. Minerva also looked over my shoulder, but she nuzzled my ear and whispered, "Doesn't that laptop you're using move—like to a different room."

I replied, "I suppose. Did you have a room in mind?"

"Noooo. Just not this one."

I nodded resignedly, stood, and led her out of the room.

As soon as we'd left our office Minerva asked where we were going.

"The only place I know of where we don't have to break in—the cafeteria."

□

The next day, we had our meeting with the Special Ops Director. Then we had an argument about how to get home. Minerva wanted to take a port key. I wanted to use the same way we arrived—by airplane.

In a way, the happy couple determined our route home. They wanted to fly first class. Minerva insisted that we had to give them the privacy they deserved. We could only do that by going home by port key.

I groused but gave in. However, I insisted that we travel by train to the New York port key Authority Office.

We took the Metro to the train station. I bought tickets. We boarded and got settled in. As we waited for the train to leave the station, Minerva gave me a strange stare.

"OK. What is it?"

She put her hand on my thigh and said, "You aren't planning to stop at Princeton Junction, are you?"

I couldn't help laughing. "You know, the idea hadn't entered my mind, but now that you mention it, it would be fun, wouldn't it?"

Minerva growled, "Not on my life, you don't."

"Oh, come on. It wouldn't be that bad. There aren't any Deatheaters left. I'd just get off and buy a newspaper and get right back on."

She groused but agreed, provided that we both got off and bought the paper. We did. I found a Princeton newspaper in the newsstand in the small station. We re-boarded the train none the worse for wear, and I stuck out my tongue at Minerva.

We arrived in New York and looked up the port key Authority immediately. It was below Grand Central Station, of course. We had had enough experience of this that we had no trouble filling out the parchmentwork to get a port key.

The only question that provided us with any trouble was "Did you visit the United States for business or pleasure?"

We replied that it was business. The functionary who reviewed the application stopped on that question, He asked, "What was that business?

Your application says that you are both teachers."

Minerva was about to make a "it's none of your business" statement when I took the opportunity to kick her in the shins. I answered, "Well, sir, we are teachers, but every teacher has to have a side line these days. I'm a consultant."

The functionary asked, "Just what sort of consultant?"

I had to smile. "National Security."

He stared at me and then asked, "You'll have to be more specific."

Minerva gave me an "I told you so" look and let me go on.

I said, "Well, you no doubt remember when Tom Riddle was a national security threat in England?"

He nodded cautiously.

"Well, the British government hired me to advise them on dealing with Riddle."

He stared at me even more suspiciously. "And your advice was?"

I had to think that one over. Eventually, I came up with the real answer, "Don't try to kill him."

The functionary laughed, "Right smart. And good advice." Then he stamped our form and said, "Come back here tomorrow morning, and your port key will be ready—one way, to depart at your pleasure, for the Ministry of Magic."

As we ascended to the muggle level by escalator, Minerva asked, "Was that your advice, really?"

"Sure. Of course, we did a lot of other things as you know, but the advice amounted to that."

We reached the muggle level. When we did, Minerva suggested that she knew a good hotel in New York from the last time that we'd been there. It was the Churchill.

I had no objection, so we disapparated there. I checked us in. We proceeded to our room. While I was unpacking, there was a tapping at the window. I glanced over to see an owl perched on the window sill.

I opened the window and watched the owl hop in. He seemed to have no inclination to give me his letter, so I shrugged and shouted for Minerva. "Special Delivery for you."

Minerva came out, accepted the parchment, unrolled it, and read to herself. She hummed and whistled as she read. After she was finished, she handed it to me. I started to unroll it but she gave me the gist.

"A student from long ago heard that we were in the country and wanted me to drop by and visit for the evening. Do you mind if I go?"

"Of course, not. Is it formal or can I go casual?"

She bit her lip, "Well, really, this is an old, old friend, I'd actually

70

kind of like to go on my own."

I shrugged, "No Problemo. I'll just go down to the lobby, buy a copy of the *Times* and work the crossword."

She shook her head. "What is it with you and your newspapers?"

I said, "I like to keep up on the news, and there's nothing like a newspaper of record for doing that."

Minerva quickly changed into nicer robes. I quickly changed into more casual jeans, and we parted—her by disapparation and me by the elevator.

I found the coffee shop, bought a copy of the *Times,* and took it into a booth in the bar. A waitress stared at me, but took my order for hot tea, and I set about reading the front page.

□□

I'd almost finished the front section when I heard a voice ask, "Do you mind if I have the front section when you're finished?"

I was just finishing an article. I said, "Not at all. Give me two minutes, and I'll be done."

I finished the section, folded it, looked up, and gaped at the woman standing in front of me.

She was about five foot seven, had long brown hair, was wearing some sort of ship's officer's uniform—civilian. I gaped because I was sure that I ought to recognize her but didn't.

She took hold of the front section and had gently started pulling it away from me. "I thought you were going to let me have this section?"

I came back to myself and said, "Oh, yes. Yes. I'm sorry for staring. It's just that you . . ."

She was staring now too. "Uh huh. Me too. I think that I ought to recognize you." Then she gasped. "You're James. . ."

I had recognized her as well. "Jennifer!"

She nodded. I immediately invited her to sit. She did.

I signaled the waitress. "What would you like?"

Her face colored a bit, and she said, "What you're having. It's hot tea isn't it?"

I nodded. We sat there for minutes on end gazing at each other. Neither of us said anything. Eventually, she asked, "So?"

I knew what she meant. I said, "If we start, we'll be here all night."

She nodded. "You're right. I know a little more about you than you do about me, but always you had this trick of being able to figure things out about me that I thought were deep dark secrets. Do the trick."

71

I shook my head. "It never did me much good."

She still was determined. "Do the trick."

I gave in. "OK. You know what you always hated the most about that trick?"

She smiled. "Yeh. You could have claimed it was magic, plain and simple, but you never let it just be. It couldn't be magic. No, you had to explain everything."

"Yeh. You're right. I understood loads about you but practically nothing about me." I took a deep breath and said, "Here goes.

"First, you're wearing a ship's uniform."

She shook her head. "You never change, do you?"

"No."

I went on, "It's obviously no uniform of any navy that I know—which isn't many—US, British, French.

"So, you're not in any service.

"You aren't in the Merchant Marine. Nobody wears uniforms like that —fancy—in the Marine.

"So, you've got to work for a cruise line.

"You were in finance when we . . . " I stopped because I couldn't bring myself to say, ". . . were together."

She put her hand on my wrist. Her mouth formed a hard line, and then she said, "Could I have something hard?"

I nodded and signaled for the waitress. She came. I said, "The lady would like a . . ."

She looked up at the waitress and said, "Jameson whiskey."

I was surprised but agreed, "Same—on some rocks, please." The waitress smiled. I guessed Jennifer was more used to hard drinks than hard conversation.

"Anyway, my guess is that you—with your background in finance— are something more like an accountant. . . "

She said just one word, 'Purser."

I nodded. "OK. This is the beginning of the summer season, so you're on a re-positioning cruise to someplace in northern Europe."

She was silent. Whether it was because the waitress had just returned with our drinks or because she wanted to hear more, I didn't know. The waitress had presented the bill, and I'd written my room number on it. She said to me but looked at Jennifer, "All right, room 818 do you want to run a tab?"

I nodded.

The waitress turned, walked away, and turned back just before she reached the bar.

I took a sip and went on, "It's ironic. A couple of years ago I booked a passage on a re-positioning cruise. . . "

She smiled. "But you never got to take it."

I took her left hand and and raised it to the light. "Right. Anyway, to get back to you. I don't see a ring or even the shadow of a ring. If you were ever married, it was a long time ago.

"So, your job with the cruise line is more than a job—it's a career. There's nobody serious."

I stopped for another sip and for thought. Could I come up with any more magic? After I'd swished my drink around in my mouth a time or two I said, "You clearly left your job with the investment bank sometime after . . ." Again, I couldn't bring myself to name the end of our relationship. I temporized with another sip. Then it hit me. She had said that she knew that I had never taken that cruise ship. I went on. "You have been an officer on the cruise ship for several years. You must have been an employee for several years before that. I doubt that you would have gone directly to a cruise ship from the bank. That means at least a year or two before you left the bank. That takes us back to Inverness, doesn't it?"

She stared at me as she took a sip. "You are just as infuriating as you ever were. Did you ever try to find me?" Her gaze turned inward, and she said, "Of course not. You would have found me if you'd tried. So you didn't try."

I could only admit it, "No. I didn't."

We stared at each other for a time. I finished my last gulp of drink as did she. The waitress noticed and came for our glasses, "The same?"

We looked at each other. I said, "Yes."

As we waited, she said, "You never used to drink."

"No. I picked up the habit shortly after . . ."

She nodded. "Me, too."

Then she surprised me. "Maybe I have picked up your other bad habit. I will do the trick with you."

□
□□

"I was pretty sure that we split because you had another fancy lady."

She stopped dead, having named the elephant. She took a sip and went on, "You never tried to get in touch again. That sealed it for me. I see that you are married." She dangled her empty ring finger. "But it's recent. I think within the last year or so. Your ring has a fancy serrated edge. It looks bright and new. It wouldn't if it were much more than a year old."

She lowered her eyes as she swirled the liquid in the glass, and then

73

she looked up at me again. "Did your first fancy lady split with you?"

I was preparing to answer, but she beat me to it. "No. If you had split with her, I think that you'd have returned to me. You didn't.

"That must mean that there was some reason that you couldn't get married for years. Was she already married to someone? And you waited faithfully for her to be freed?"

She took a sip and went on. "No. I don't think so. If that were it, I think you'd still be with me. You'd have dropped me like a hot potato when she became 'available,' but you'd still have been with me.

"So what was it? She was available but wouldn't marry you. She kept you dangling on a hook. You had your little trysts from time to time, but she wouldn't marry. That's it, isn't it."

Again, she didn't give me a chance to answer but plunged on, "There was something or someone else." She took a quick pull on her drink, threw her head back and laughed. "It wasn't a triangle, was it? She had her fancy man, and you had her as your fancy lady. That would be too rich!"

She shook her head. "No. It wasn't a triangle. Something happened. She was ready to marry finally. Was it the invasion of the 'Souls'? Did she finally realize how precarious life is? That you have to seize what you can when you can?"

We both sat and waited. She then was finished. "Tell me about it. What happened? How did she decide to marry you?"

I had been swirling my drink, listening to the clink of ice against ice and ice against glass. I took a stiff drink, let it settle, and then started.

"You had it mostly right. I did have a fancy lady. It wasn't a triangle, and it wasn't pride on her part. She was afraid for me."

Jennifer stared at me. "How is that possible? You're the gentlest man I've ever known. What was she afraid of?"

This definitely required a good shot to get started on. I took that shot, swirled what was left in the glass, and thought a minute.

"OK. The only people who know what I'm about to tell you besides relatives and people directly involved is. . ." I tried to think if anyone else knew. Nope. No one else. So, I said that, "You are about to be the only one. Will you swear not to tell anyone else?"

She took a shot as well. Then she ran her right hand index finger across her left breast in an "X" and said, 'Cross my heart and hope to die."

The irony of that unexpected oath struck me hard. Maybe it was partly the Jameson laughing, but it didn't seem that funny to me. I was laughing so hard that I was hardly making a sound other than an occasional moan.

Jennifer just stared at me in bewilderment. "What's so funny?"

I got control of myself and leaned forward toward her. "If you only knew just how literally some people take that sort of oath, you'd not joke about it."

She was apparently offended that I would think that she wasn't serious. "I meant every word." She said it in the exaggerated way that people who have been drinking do when they have had just enough to loosen their inhibitions but still have a fair idea of what they are saying.

I nodded. "Well, that's maybe a good place to start—with that oath.

"There are people who actually can enforce that oath. If you swear that oath to them, your life is on the line."

She seemed to sober a bit and looked at me from an angle. "You mean gangsters or Cosa Nostra or whatever?"

"No. No. I mean something entirely different." I stopped and looked into my glass—perhaps for inspiration. Just then our faithful waitress arrived and asked helpfully, "Another?"

Jennifer nodded, and then she asked me, "And you were saying?"

"Well, let me try to explain this with an analogy. " I paused to put my argument together. "OK. Suppose that you went into your doctor for an annual checkup. She always has a mammogram made. She calls you back into her office for a review of testing. When you arrive, she says, 'I have an important result for you. Your mammogram came back with some very troubling spots. I want you to make an appointment with an oncologist who I think is good.'

"Now, you hem and haw and say something like, 'Sounds important. I'll get around to it pretty soon.'

"You doc says, 'I'm serious. You need to do that right away. Will you swear to me that you'll do that when you get home.'

"You say, 'Sure, cross my heart and hope to die.'

"She says, 'I guarantee you that you will die, if you break that promise.'"

Jennifer said, "I kind of get that, but surely that's a special case. . . Isn't it?"

I shook my head.

Just then we both noticed that the waitress had been standing there listening with rapt attention. She delivered the drinks and said to Jennifer, 'Girl, you go see that oncologist tomorrow morning first thing, you hear?"

Jennifer just gaped at her.

The waitress didn't give her a chance to answer. She turned to go. Jennifer said, "Wait."

The waitress turned back. Jennifer said, "Put this drink and the rest on my tab."

The waitress pulled out the tab and drew a line across it and then handed the tab and her pen to Jennifer, who wrote her room number on it. The waitress looked at it and said, looking at me, "Room 644. Hmmm Hmmmm. I think somebody is going to have a good time tonight."

We both took a sip of our refreshed drinks, and Jennifer said, "You were saying?"

"I was saying that wanting to know more about swearing that you hope to die is like standing on the banks of the Rubicon."

She answered almost immediately, "You mean the river in Italy that it was forbidden for a Roman army to cross. So that once I cross that frontier, there's no going back."

I nodded and said, "Right."

She thought about it a minute and asked, "Can you tell me why it's my Rubicon without my actually crossing it?"

I puzzled out my answer in the fresh glass that was sitting in front of me. "OK. Yes.

"Let's go back to your poor doctor. She wants you to see an oncologist. You do. In your first interview after tests, you discover that the oncologist doesn't believe you need chemotherapy or surgery. So what do you do?"

Jennifer now stared into her glass. Finally, she said, "OK. I guess I wouldn't keep that oncologist, and . . ."

I nodded. "And?"

"And I suppose that maybe I don't trust my doc so much. Why would she think that I needed an oncologist?"

"Right. Now, suppose that instead of going to your doc's recommended oncologist, you found your own oncologist who agreed with your doc?"

She puzzled that for a long while. "I suppose that I'd just assume my doc was just fine, and I'd keep going to see her."

"Right. The question is 'Would you want to have that additional information?'"

She took a deep breath and then a deep sip of her drink. "Yes, I guess I'll never have another chance to learn whatever it is that I'm sitting on the banks of the Rubicon staring at." She stopped again and then said, "Yes. I'm sticking my toes in the Rubicon and wading out into the stream. What do you have?"

"OK. The way the 'Cross My Heart and Hope to Die' oath works is MAGIC."

She just stared at me uncomprehendingly. Then she asked, "I guess I missed it. What did you say?"

I said, "The Unbreakable Oath. Yes, that's what they call it. That Oath works by Magic."

She took in the enormity of that claim. Even a little tipsy and not paying complete attention, she got it. Her mouth opened and then closed. Her next reaction was to exclaim, "You're serious, aren't you?"

I nodded. "Yes, There's a whole lot more that we could talk about if you want to, but that's it. There is real magic. I've seen it, felt it, been blasted around the world by it."

She shook her head, whether in disbelief or despair, I couldn't tell. Then she said, "So your 'fancy lady' is . . . was . . . a witch?"

"Yes."

She just sat and stared for a while. Then she said, "And her problem with you was 'Guess Who's Coming to Dinner'?"

I agreed but added, "It wasn't that simple. As a matter of fact that wasn't the biggest problem. As a non-Magical, I was in serious danger from the Wizards and Witches who hate muggles."

She smiled. "That's what they call normal people, right?"

"Yeh."

She went on, "So, somehow you're out of danger now?"

"Yeh. The muggle-haters were organized by a guy whose name was Riddle—Tom Riddle. He started a right war against the people who disagreed with him. He lost it and his life in the war."

"So, the war went on from the time I met you until last year?"

"Not exactly. It ended over two years ago, but Minerva—that's my fancy lady—is stubborn. It took that long to change her mind."

I asked her, "So what happened to you? Was I close?"

She shook her head, "You were disgustingly close. I sometimes wondered how it would be to be with you. Would you drive me crazy always anticipating what I would do and say?"

I assumed it was a rhetorical question, but she snapped her fingers in front of my face, "I was serious. What did you think? What would it be like being with you?"

I stared at her a minute, and when she looked like she was going to snap her fingers again, I said, "Give me a break. I need a couple of minutes to think about it. You're only asking me what the rest of my life would be like!"

What I was thinking about was what might have happened if we had met for the first time now. She was so very tentative when we were together before. She never or rarely said what she really wanted. This young woman (and she was still young!) knew what she wanted and said so. I probably was as tentative as she was.

Then, I had my answer, "We would have driven each other crazy just like we did then, but you are a different person now. I'm a different person too. You wouldn't let me drive you crazy. You'd be on top of it."

She nodded. "Yesh. I can see that," Her faint smile that had brightened her face from the second drink on, grew noticeably brighter. She said, "Well, I pined for you for a year in Inverness. Then I decided that you were a lost cause. I moved back to London and got a job in a Starbucks."

"Never."

"Yes. It was just temp—for about a month while I looked for a job. I found one pretty quickly. The Merchant Marine were looking to hire more women. I got into a training program to be a ship's purser. I passed with top marks."

I nodded. "I don't doubt it for a second."

She laughed. "Damn straight. I got a job with the Maersk line. I seemed to be always on ships that rounded the Horn of Africa.

"On my fifth voyage we were attacked by pirates. They didn't know what they were doing, and we repelled them. That was it for me. I'd had a year in. I thought that was enough to let me apply to a cruise line.

"I started looking for a position on a cruise line. I had to start at the bottom. My stint in Starbucks was good enough to get me a spot working a coffee bar on a ship."

I smiled as I said, "Probably your looks didn't hurt either."

She snorted and went on, "After a year or so, a Junior Purser position opened up on a different cruise ship. I got it."

She stopped for breath and a sip of Jameson. Then she went on, "I never forgot you. As a matter of fact, I never had a serious date from the time that we split.

"Oh, I had a bunch of first dates, but the single staff of the cruise ships that I was on began calling me the ice maiden." She stopped again and laughed.

"Do you know that for a while, before the ice maiden phase, the female staff began to think that I was gay. I got invited out more than once by women who thought I was too cute for the guys."

I couldn't resist asking "I always wondered how lesbians know other lesbians when they see them."

She drawled, "Ooooo, they don't. They just guess and sometimes get lucky. They never got lucky with me."

"And you never met anyone who . . . well . . . meant more to you?"

She shook her head but then said, "At least until a couple of years ago when you were on my cruise ship."

I stared at her. "I was never on the cruise."

She laughed at that. "Well, you are technically right, but on this one cruise, your name was on the cabin door and there were clothes in the closet. That incident almost got me fired."

Then the light began to dawn 'Yes, that was the summer that I was fired from Hogwarts."

She looked the question. I answered, "Hogwarts was the school where I taught. There was a change of Headmaster. My fancy lady fired me."

She laughed. "She had a strict code of ethics if she fired you because you were dating. Or were you doing more?"

"None of your business. That was at the height of the war. She fired me to save my life. I bought passage to the Caribbean on a re-positioning cruise."

"I was on that cruise. But you didn't go. MI5 or somebody tried to make it look like you were on the ship. You had me fooled. That's pretty good, fooling a ship's purser about that."

I took a sip and said, "Right. I wish I could claim to have had something to do with it. I was rotting in jail at the time."

She looked at me with something like wonder. "You are just about the last person that I would expect to be in prison. I guess you beat me. I didn't even make it to the brig." She hesitated and added, "Though I did come pretty close that once."

We both had a good laugh at that. Somehow, Jennifer's hand had landed on my forearm. We both were surprised. By common consent we withdrew.

I asked her, "What would have landed you in the brig?"

"Oh, I was determined to find out if the James Wendt on the passenger manifest was the same James Wendt that I knew and . . . loved. . ." She seemed surprised to have let that slip. "Anyway I got the passengers in the neighboring cabin to help me break into your cabin. Those Dursleys were a crazy bunch."

My jaw dropped. Meanwhile, our waitress had brought another round to our table unbidden. She said "It's on the house." She winked at Jennifer.

Jennifer shook her head as though to clear the cobwebs. "Do I look gay? I'd swear that waitress winked at me."

I shook my head. I returned to the Dursleys, "You don't mean Vernon, Petunia, and Dudley?"

Jennifer nodded, "As a matter of fact, yes."

The bun in which she had had her hair pulled up had been loosening all night, and that last nod had undone it. Her hair tumbled down over her shoulders and back.

I had to ask, "It's a crazy world, don't you think?"

She nodded and her hair worked around her left shoulder onto her left breast. She said, "It is crazy. You know that you owe me, don't you?"

I searched my memory. What could I owe her. Nothing obvious occurred to me. So, I shook my head "no."

She said, "Sure you do!" Her voice had gotten pretty loud by now. She wasn't being unpleasant, just assertive.

I said, "I don't get it. What do I owe you. I'll be happy to repay you with interest."

She nodded slowly "Yes, with interest."

"So?"

"Don't shyou remember the time shyou helped me move into my apartment?"

Then it came back to me. She was moving from London to Inverness. She had this new roommate. I'd embarrassed Jennifer by not sleeping with her. My mouth formed a big "O" as I realized what she was talking about.

To my surprise, Jennifer leaned across the small table where we were seated. The big "O" that my mouth formed was the perfect target for her lips. It was not a long kiss, but she had clearly enjoyed it.

Just then, our friendly waitress showed up and said, "OK, you two. You've had your limit. I'm declaring your curfew. Get to bed."

Jennifer was up first and took my hand, dragging it weakly, "Come on. You heard the lady."

The lady was still there and helped propel me along behind Jennifer. She added to Jennifer, "Now, honey, don't you forget to get to that oncologist."

Jennifer just laughed. We reached the elevator. She punched the up button and we waited an eternity for it to show up. We were the only ones in it. She said, "Lesh's see. I know the floor. Sure I do." I didn't see what floor she punched.

The door opened and we stumbled out. She still had my hand. She guided me down the hall. We reached a door. She slid an electronic key into the lock that miraculously opened. I hadn't been sure that we were at either of our doors.

We entered, and she closed the door by leaning against it. "Welsh, here we are. Are shyou ready to pay up?"

That woke me up. I looked around and somehow knew that this was not my room.

Jennifer's hand crept up my forearm. She suddenly seemed a whole lot more sober. She said with a great deal of determination, "You owe me."

Later, when I thought about it, I supposed that I really did owe her. That one incident had possibly turned the whole course of our relationship.

If I'd slept with her that night so very long ago, she might have seen that I was just another guy. She might have accepted our breakup as just another signpost on her life that pointed somewhere else than at me. I wondered if what I'd done this last night might have unmade that incident.

What I said was, "You're right. I owe you." In my drunken state, I didn't doubt that I could give her a great night. "I'll give you a night nobody could forget!"

Her left hand came up to my right shoulder, and her hair spilled over my arm. "I'll be jussh fine with a good night."

It's funny what will excite your sexual appetites. That hair draped over my arm was it for me. I found that I was fully ready to give her a grand night. I tried and failed to lift her up and onto the bed. It was OK. She pulled me down onto her. I was afraid that my eagerness would undo me. The alcohol probably prevented that. Instead, I gave my full concentration to her. We ended an hour of decent foreplay and sex in each other's arms by my spooning her.

She asked a question that I was not able to answer then and probably will never be able to answer. "What would you have done if this were a dozen or so years ago."

I thought about that as I held her in my arms. I eventually said, "You and I didn't exist a dozen years ago. If we had, it would have been a different universe. I don't know."

We held each other and napped for a while. I woke and tried to dress without waking Jennifer. She woke."You're going back to her."

I nodded as I looked down at her long soft body encased in her long soft hair. "Yes. You deserve the good. Go and find it."

I fumbled back to my room hoping that I'd not find Minerva there waiting for me.

Miraculously, she wasn't. The message light on my phone was flashing. I retrieved the message. Minerva and her old girl friend had decided that she should stay the night. Minerva would be back at 7 AM, so I'd better get some sleep.

I glanced at my wrist. It was 2:30 AM. I could still get some sleep.

I showered quickly and fell asleep on the bed as soon as my legs hit the sheets.

The next morning, I was awakened by a sharp blow to an exposed leg. "Whaaa?" I argued.

Minerva was toweling her long grey hair dry. She asked, "Are you ever

81

going to get up? You were dead asleep when I got back a couple of hours ago.

I said, "Sure, carouse all night and get home just in time to attack me."

She sat on the bed next to me, "Ohhh! My poor little baby. Let Mother make it all better with a kiss."

Her hair draped over my face as we kissed. When we broke, she said, "I see that you've been doing a little carousing yourself. I smell Johnny Walker or the like."

All I could say was, "Right you are."

I took the second shower of the young morning and prepared myself for the onslaught of disapparation. "Minerva, I'll go down and check out. Just leave our keys up here in the room."

I grabbed my duffel bag and headed for the elevator. I went directly to the front desk and checked out. As I was finishing, someone else got in line behind me.

I turned to go and saw Jennifer. She looked the perfect ship's Purser in her gleaming white uniform that was pressed until you could cut your knee on the crease. Her hair was drawn up in a tight bun at the nape of her neck. It was just barely discernibly brown.

She handed her key over to the clerk and said over her shoulder, "Just check me out. I don't need a receipt."

We gazed at each other for a few interminable seconds. I said, "I so wish things could have come out differently long ago."

She smiled a smile that was unbecoming of a bright young officer. "You never told me the rest of your story. I'd like to hear it someday. I have a feeling that if you'd been with me, the world would be a good bit worse off, wouldn't it?"

I smiled too. "It would be a different universe. Who could say?"

I then turned to the clerk and finished checking out as well. When I turned away from the front desk, I saw Minerva coming from the elevator toward me, and Jennifer was just leaving through the revolving door to the street.

Minerva asked if we were ready to go. I nodded and took her hand. We walked toward a hall that led to meeting rooms. As we departed from view of the front desk, we disapparated to Grand Central Station. We found the little pub that had a floo connection in the back of the Common Room. I bought a bottle of Coke, and we took the floo to the port key Authority.

Our port key was waiting for us. We picked it up and left the office. Minerva was ready to use it right away, but I had put it in my purse.

Minerva was suspicious. She asked, "When do you plan on using that port key?"

82

I smiled. "I have a little surprise for you. Take us to LaGuardia."

She was even more suspicious. "What is a lagarden?"

I decided that I had to come clean. "It's LaGuardia. It's an airport. We're going on a little sight-seeing trip."

She shrugged. "Well we could use a holiday after that last adventure." She disapparated us there. We went through security and found our gate. At the gate as we were waiting for our flight, she asked a question. "Who was that woman in uniform you were talking to at the hotel?"

"Oh, she was checking out, too. She'd had a rough night. Some guy had kept her awake half the night."

Minerva nodded. "Yes, probably having a party in his room. How did you sleep?"

"Not great. It wasn't a guy partying. I just couldn't seem to get settled. You know how it is when you try to sleep in an unfamiliar bed."

She laughed, "Have we been doing anything beside that lately?"

She wanted to know where we were going. She had glanced at her ticket, but didn't recognize the abbreviation for our destination airport.

I said, "It's a town in Tennessee—Chattanooga."

"And I suppose Tennessee is somewhere in the States?"

"Sure."

"What's in Chattanooga for us?"

"Oh, let's just wait and see."

She did. The flight was barely an hour long. When we arrived, I gave her an address of where I wanted to disapparate. It was on the Tennessee Riverfront.

When Minerva realized that she grabbed my arm and stopped me in my tracks as we approached a dock. "We're not going on a boat by any chance are we?"

I shrugged. She slumped. "And you talk about Wizard ways of travel. A boat? Really!"

"Yes, a really boat. You'll enjoy it. Just wait and see."

I dragged her up the gang plank to the deck. An officer intercepted us and asked for our ticketing documents. I had them, of course. He examined them and directed us to our cabin that was on the second floor. He was surprised at our lack of luggage. Of course, I had my trusty duffel bag that had traveled around the world with me recently. It was small and modest, but it served me well. Minerva, of course, had her large handbag that held more than my duffel bag did.

I had spent some real money to get us a very comfortable cabin. It had a small veranda and real antique furniture that was perhaps not ante-bellum, but at least was from the 19th century. As I pointed out these features, I remarked on river travel in the 19th century. "Riverboats were powered by steam engines that drove the big paddle-wheels such as the ones that propel this boat. The steam engines were fairly dangerous. Every now and then one would explode and sink the riverboat, set it on fire, and send shrapnel flying everywhere for hundreds of yards around the boat."

Minerva gaped at me and said, "You see. These boats are death-traps. We're not really going to sail on this one, are we?"

"Oh, that was in the 19th century. Steam powered passenger boats have been illegal for far more than a hundred years. I believe that I read that there is one steam-powered riverboat left. It's a ¼ scale replica of a Mississippi riverboat. I think it's located in Texas somewhere. This boat is perfectly safe."

I took her in my arms and said, "You're as safe as houses in this boat. As a matter of fact, you're safer than in my arms."

She chuckled, "I'd probably be safer than in your arms in that Texas steam-powered boat."

I gave her a generous kiss and said, "Anyway, even if something bad did happen, you're never more than a mile from shore. You could disapparate there with me, and we'd be just fine."

With that she took a good look around the cabin and delivered her verdict, "Well, it is pretty posh. I suppose it might not be that bad."

I shook my head in disbelief. "Not that bad. This is a floating palace."

She asked, "This is a nice cabin, but what can we do on this cruise?"

I exclaimed, "What can you do? Come over here." I led her out on the veranda. "Look across the river. The scenery is spectacular. You can sit on the veranda and admire the view as you placidly sail down the stream. The cuisine may not quite be up to Hogwarts standards, but it will be very good. We'll stop at several ports along the way. You can sample the night-life in these spots. I think we'll stop at one planta. . ."

She interrupted me. "Stop with the tourist brochure already. OK. It may be interesting. I'm willing to give it a shot."

So, the cruise started mid-afternoon in Chattanooga. We watched the shoreline drift by. She found that we were traveling too slowly to keep her attention riveted on the passing scenery. She took up a book and alternated reading and viewing.

I was fascinated that first afternoon and could hardly pull my eyes from the scenery.

Dinnertime came. We went down to the dining hall. It was not the Great Hall, but it had a fine view of the river. The food was excellent. Even Minerva had a hard time choosing between paying attention to her meal and the scenery that was passing by us.

Toward the end of the meal, the ship's purser gave a talk about the history of the river and the land around it. The Civil War featured prominently in the talk. Minerva commented on the point. "It seems like every place we go in your country the Civil War looms. When we were in Washington, just across the river was the Arlington Cemetery full of memories of that war. Your greatest president was alive during the war. His memorial may not be the largest, but it is the most beautiful. This entire cruise goes through land where battles were fought seemingly continuously through the war."

She hesitated in thought, "You know, I think I saw a Civil War Memorial in New York City in Central Park."

I laughed at that. "You mean when Archie Goodwin was squiring you around while I was being tortured in various hospitals."

She punched me in the shoulder, and I declared it was time to head for our cabin.

Minerva asked me if I didn't want to stay for the movie they were going to show.

I replied. "Not this one. It's the first Lord of the Rings movie. I want to see it when I'm in a proper theater."

She shrugged.

I lead her up to our cabin.

When we reached our cabin, the sun was pretty close to the horizon. I invited her out to the veranda. There was a chaise lounge chair there as well as a normal chair. I suggested that we share the lounge chair and watch the sun set. It was rather nice with a fair amount of color.

She was sort of in my lap, rather like being spooned by me. We both enjoyed it a good bit. As the last light dimmed, the stars came out nicely. We napped and finally decided that it was time for proper sleep.

The next day, I spent some time studying the cruise brochure. I noticed something that I thought might be fun to do that night. I checked on it in the Business Room that had a computer and a slow Internet connection.

At lunch, I announced to Minerva that I had a little outing planned for the evening after dinner. Her eyes perked up, and she asked what. I said, "It will be a little surprise."

It became a guessing game. She guessed that we were going to Nashville for some "country music" whatever that was. Then she guessed that I'd found another couple that knew Back Alley Bridge. I denied both.

Through the afternoon she kept guessing. I'd found another Magical couple? No. We were going to have a poker tournament? No. I added, "That's not a bad idea and appropriate for a river cruise. Back when riverboats were a big deal one of the common pastimes was playing poker. Professional gamblers were present on every boat and made a decent living playing against amateurs."

By dinner, our appetites were up. She was anxious to find out what I had in mind. After dinner I led her up to our room. She was disappointed, "We're going to have sex. Big deal."

I laughed. "I think it's a big deal, but no, we're not having sex." That seemed to disappoint her.

"We are going to disapparate. Take us to Jackson, Tennessee."

She shrugged but held out her hand. I took it, and we disappeared. We re-appeared in downtown Jackson. Minerva looked around and said, "So?"

"Now disapparate us to the baseball field."

We arrived in the parking lot behind an empty bus. I led Minerva around it and on to the ticket office. We bought two of the last seats behind home plate.

I said, "I hope you saved some room for a hot dog and soda."

Minerva nodded. "Besides a boring sport we get mediocre cuisine."

I shook my head and said, "Don't judge either before you've experienced them."

I bought us a couple of hot dogs and Cokes, and we found our seats. Minerva asked, "OK. What's so great about baseball?"

All I said was, "Watch and see."

Minerva waited and eventually asked, "Aren't you going to explain the game to me? How can I enjoy it if I don't understand it?"

I thought about the last time that I'd tried explaining baseball to wizards. It was on a submarine. I'd used salt and pepper shakers and cutlery. It was not so good. I said, "I think you'll enjoy it more if you figure out the rules for yourself."

She stared at me with no result. Then she shrugged.

She took a bite of her hot dog and made a face. It was looking like a long game. I said, "Why don't you go back and get a little mustard for that dog?"

She made another face but did get up and go back to the condiment stand. By the time she got back, the game had started, and the first batter had grounded out to the shortstop. Minerva asked, "Something happened while I was gone."

I said, "Yeh. The first batter grounded out to the shortstop."

She just asked, "What?"

I said, "Just watch the game and enjoy."

She gave me a sour look but took a bite of her dog. Her expression wasn't that bad.

The first inning ended with a man getting a walk to take first base. The next man struck out for the last out.

Minerva wanted an explanation. I said, "You tell me what you think happened."

She said, "Well, there seem to be two teams. One gets to throw balls at the other. If someone hits a ball, they can run to that bag over there. But if the other team gets the ball to the bag first, the player who hit the ball is done." She paused and asked, "How am I doing?"

"Not bad. But the teams have changed places. You'd better keep watching."

She turned back to the field and watched the bottom half of the first. She finished the hot dog and commented, "That dog wasn't bad. Can I have another?"

I shrugged and said, "Sure. Just remember to use muggle money when you buy it."

She stared at me, "When I buy it? Aren't you going to get it for me?"

"You got the mustard just fine. Try stepping up to buying something."

She was a little exasperated. She pointed out, "I missed some of the game when I went for the mustard."

I nodded. "Right. That's why I'm not going."

She stared at me. "Well, I'm not missing any of the game either."

I nodded. "Suit yourself."

She stubbornly stayed in her seat until the bottom of the third inning. "Oh, won't you please go get me a hot dog?"

I smiled as I turned to her. "Sure. I'd be happy to."

In the top of the fifth inning, the away team scored a run. Minerva jumped up and screamed, "Huzzah!"

She asked, "What was it that just happened?"

"Tell me."

She smiled. "Well, the man who hit the ball first ended up touching all the bags and got back where he started. But what does it mean?"

"That's the object of the game. The team that does that more wins."

Her eyes lit up with pleasure. "Ooooo. Why couldn't you tell me that at the beginning?"

"It wouldn't have been as much fun for either you or me."

The game was tied going into the ninth inning. Minerva asked me how long the games go. "Well, usually each team gets nine tries to score. This would ordinarily be the last turn, but if it ends up a tied score, they keep going."

She said, "I'm going for the first team that batted. Who are you rooting for?"

I laughed. "The umpires."

She stared at me. I cleared it up for her, "Oh, you would call them referees." She pondered that while we watched the game. The visitors got someone to third with two out. The next man up hit a dribbler down the first base line. The pitcher ran up and got it. He threw the man out at first.

Minerva stood and clapped hard. "Then she realized that the runner on third hadn't scored." She turned to me and said, "Why wasn't that a run for my team?"

I said, "The runner was forced out at first."

She immediately replied, "But the man on third reached the last bag before that happened!" in an aggrieved tone.

I shrugged. "Sorry, force outs always beat runners to home plate."

She stared at me and then said, "That's not fair!"

I shrugged again. "That's the game."

"Oh, Pooh. Maybe we can keep the other team from scoring."

The other team scored three runs on a home run in the bottom of the ninth.

Minerva took it philosophically. "Well, everyone seems happy."

"The home team always bats last."

We walked slowly out of the stadium. Minerva turned to me, "Can we come again tomorrow night?"

I said, "Maybe. We'll have to see if they have a game here tomorrow."

She sighed. "Maybe baseball isn't such a bad game after all."

I agreed. "Maybe."

We disapparated back to our cabin and got a good night's sleep in—sans sex.

The next day we arrived at the Ohio River. We docked in the Ohio, and a small ship's boat took people who wanted to have dinner on shore or go to the Performing Arts Center of Paducah. I gave Minerva her choice—baseball or Paducah. She gritted her teeth and chose Paducah.

We ate at the Italian Grill on Broadway and saw a play at the Four Rivers Center. The Italian was decent but nothing more. The play was a play about the settling of Kentucky. It was informative and entertaining—sort of.

When we got back to our cabin, Minerva regretted her choice. But she was a good sport about it.

The next day we went down the Ohio. Minerva was restless all day but wouldn't reveal why. At dinner, she admitted her guilty secret. "Can we go to see baseball tonight?"

I admitted that we could try. We returned to our cabin at a run. I don't know what other passengers thought we were up to. I didn't care. We disapparated to the Jackson ballpark. It was as dead as a doornail. Minerva swore. You don't see that very often.

I let her venting end and mildly mentioned, "You know, Jackson is not the only place with baseball."

She stared at me. "You could have mentioned."

"I just did."

"We're burning moonlight. Where are we going?"

I thought a moment. "Try the Great American Ballpark."

She asked, "Where is it?"

I shook my head. "There's only one."

We clasp hands and ended up in a parking garage.

Minerva looked around and said, "This doesn't seem like much of a ballpark. How did I miss?"

"I don't think you did. I think it's over our heads."

The expression on her face showed that she clearly didn't believe me. I said, "Just walk. I'll show you." We walked up a couple of flights of stairs and arrived."

She asked, "You mean to say that there was ground over our heads?"

"Technically, no. This is a BIG ballpark. They don't use much soil, but they do have natural grass."

She stared again. "Is having natural grass unusual?"

I said, "Not all ballparks do."

We bought tickets, hot dogs, soda, as before. Minerva immediately noticed several things. "This place is expensive. Jackson was much cheaper."

I just said, "This is the BIGS."

Then she was disappointed at how far away from the field our seats were. I opened my mouth to comment on the BIGS. She anticipated me and asked, "What are the BIGS anyway?"

"The top level of the sport. They have the best players. The biggest ballparks . . ."

Minerva finished, "The highest prices."

I nodded.

She enjoyed the game but commented when it was over, and we were back in our cabin in bed. "I wish there had been a game at Jackson."

"Me too."

The next day we were fast approaching the Mississippi. Minerva asked if there would be rapids at the confluence of the two rivers.

"No, the Mississippi may be the Father of Rivers. If so, the Ohio is the Mother of Rivers. When the two meet, it is not the tempestuous embrace of young lovers but the peaceful blending of love."

Sitting on our veranda, we had a peaceful blending.

The next day we'd passed onto the Mississippi. Minerva was looking forward to Memphis, as was I. The cruise would stop there two nights and one full day so that we could tour the city.

We decided to see the Aquarium and find a venue to listen to the blues. However, when I suggested going to see Graceland, Minerva was clueless.

"What is Graceland?"

I said, "It was the home of the King."

Minerva, of course, didn't know what "King" I was talking about. I quickly supplied details. "The King is Elvis Presley. He probably did more to invent and popularize Rock & Roll music than any other musician. I think that anyone interested in music should visit his home and museum."

Minerva reluctantly agreed to the tour. The Aquarium was on the waterfront, though a nice hike from where our boat docked. Minerva is always up for a good walk, so we walked there. We then took a cab to Graceland. Minerva preferred the Aquarium to Graceland but didn't really complain.

The highlight of the stay for the both of us was the dinner and show that the tour company had arranged that night at one of the nightclubs of Memphis. I'm glad that they arranged it. I wouldn't have known which were safe neighborhoods and which were not.

The meal was better than on the boat. The music, the Blues, was very much to my tastes. Minerva seemed to enjoy it too. She declared it was good music to talk over. None-the-less I thought she really enjoyed it.

That evening—for the first time on the cruise—we made love. That isn't so unusual. Traveling really takes it out of you—even on a leisurely boat tour. Someday—I vowed—I'd get her to take a repositioning cruise. Then I think there really would be love-making.

The next day was to be the next to last. Really, it would be the last full day. We stopped at a plantation on the west side of the Mississippi. It was called the Lakeport Plantation. The tour line had arranged a special late tour at 4 PM including a meal typical of pre-bellum southern cuisine. Minerva found it interesting but not as good as what we had in Memphis.

That night was our last night on the boat. There was a vote taken among the passengers. Would we stay docked overnight and then proceed the next day after sunrise to Vicksburg or proceed overnight and arrive in time for breakfast on the boat. If we waited for the morning, we could have lunch on the boat as we came into Vicksburg.

The vote was fairly overwhelming. At least 75% of the passengers wanted to stay docked until the morning to maximize the time for viewing the river in daylight.

The captain, whom we'd hardly seen during the cruise, announced the results but made an important announcement. "Ladies and Gentlemen, most people prefer to cruise during daylight on the Mississippi. However, we understand that doing that and arriving in the early afternoon may be a hardship for some. If there is anyone like that on board, please see the purser immediately. I don't promise that we'll change our plans for you, but depending on circumstances, we might."

Then the purser announced a little surprise. The riverboats, especially those on the Mississippi, had been known for gambling. She then announced, "You've been such a good group that we're going to set up a little casino here in the dining room. It will take us about a half hour. That will give you a chance to freshen up, and if you have evening attire, you can change into it. Then you can come down and try your luck.

"I have to warn you that you will not be gambling for money. The laws of the states we're going through forbid that. But we will have real chips, a craps table, a couple of poker tables, and a roulette wheel. And perhaps, a couple of tables for 21 depending on your interests."

Minerva and I went up to our room and changed into our evening best, which was the same as our evening worst. We came down to the transformed dining room. The staff had changed into appropriate costumes for a 19th century riverboat.

Everyone started with the same stake—ten thousand dollars worth of chips. It was announced that at midnight, the three with the most chips would win prizes. The top person would get free passage on this cruise anytime during the next year. Second prize was a pair of tickets to a concert the next night in Vicksburg by the Dixie Chicks. Neither Minerva nor I had heard of them, but we agreed if one of us won, we'd go to the concert. The third prize was a pair of tickets to any regular season Cincinnati Reds game. Minerva wasn't as excited about that.

Minerva wanted to play all the games—none of which she'd played before. However, she added, "I want your advice on what is the best game to play to win one of the prizes."

I smiled. "Well, it depends on a number of things."

She frowned. "Do you have to do that?"

"Do what?"

"You know—explain everything."

I frowned, "Strange you're not the only one to tell me that recently."

Minerva just said, "Well, duh."

I said, "OK. I'll explain as little as I can, but I have to at least tell you how to bet if you're going to really try to win something."

Minerva nodded, "I guess that's fair. OK. Go ahead."

"O.K." I exaggerated the letters. "You've got to remember that you're betting against the house as well as the other players in most of these games. The house always has a built-in advantage, so your best strategy if you're playing against the house is to take the plays that will minimize your loses. That would be playing craps. Now, I'm not saying that you wouldn't make money. I'm just saying that the smart strategy is to play to lose slowly."

Minerva said, "I don't like the sound of craps."

"You don't even know what it is."

"I don't care. What's the next best game."

I thought a minute. "Well, if you know the game fairly well, it's poker —a card game. You're not playing against the house. The house will provide a dealer, but they only take a percentage of the winnings—not anything if you don't win."

"Oh, great!"

"Look. I like competition as much as the next guy."

She interrupted me. "You like it more than the next guy."

"OK. OK. Still, I think the best strategy for you, since you don't really know any of the games, is to go around and play all of them for ten or fifteen minutes. Then pick the one that you like the best and stick with it. If you end up liking craps, I'll give you a little advice on how to lose slowly. Besides, if you don't win, at least you'll have a good time."

She agreed to that. We made a tour of the tables. I played a couple of times so that she could see the technique. Then I let her loose on the games.

They did have twenty-one setup on one table. After we'd made the grand tour Minerva declared that she liked twenty-one best. "What are you going to play?"

"I think I'll play a little poker—just enough to get discouraged. Then, I'll come here and join you at twenty-one."

As the night wore on, we discovered that it was a lot like Vegas. They provided you free drinks—alcoholic if you liked. I ordered Dewars whiskey on the rocks. I intended to nurse it through the entire night. It took me longer than I expected to get discouraged with poker. I'd nearly finished the whiskey when I left for the twenty-one table. When I got there, I ordered another and stuck to my determination that it would be my last of the night.

Minerva was doing pretty well at twenty-one. I couldn't tell from her stack of chips whether she was up or down. I'd lost a little more than a thousand by playing conservatively.

Minerva was so intent on the game that she hardly nodded at me when I arrived. As it approached midnight, I'd actually only lost another thousand. While I'd been at the table, Minerva had been winning, but I had no idea where she stood.

At the very end, most of the players had given up or gone broke. There was only one other player at our table. He didn't have much left.

Midnight struck, and most of those left. They didn't even turn in their chips to be counted. There were a total of nine of us who did.

Minerva ended up positive on the night. She had something north of twelve thousand. I was less negative than I expected, but I still had a little less than eight thousand.

The grand winner had over twenty thousand in chips. Minerva came in second with some other woman coming in a close third with something like eleven-five. I counted myself lucky to end in the upper division at fifth place.

We fell into bed and were asleep before our heads hit the pillows.

When we awoke the next day, we discovered that we weren't in Vicksburg. I'm glad that we had decided to stay moored.

After breakfast, we walked the decks to get a good view of both sides of the river. Minerva held my waist from behind and whispered in my ear, "I'm glad we did this. I almost wish it would never end."

I smiled happily. "Well, courtesy of the cruise line it won't end until tomorrow."

She was surprised but then realized what I was talking about. "You mean the concert tonight."

"Sure."

We checked into a hotel after leaving the ship and went to the concert. At a break at the end of a set, I commented to Minerva, "Well, now you've heard all the main music forms that were invented in the States—Rock,

Blues, Country and Western."

That night we made love again.

The next morning, Minerva was anxious to get back to Hogwarts. She insisted on using the port key from our room.

I had another idea. "Why don't we go to New York, stay the night, and leave from there?"

She asked, "Why?"

"Well, I was wrong last night. I forgot about Jazz. New York is the best place to go for jazz. We go to a jazz club, stay the night, and then use the port key."

Her brow wrinkled in concentration. "No. What reason would we have to come back to the States if we've heard all your home-invented music forms, hmmm."

I smiled and admitted that she had me.

The Announcement

We arrived outside the Port Key Office in the Ministry of Magic. We went in, reported our return, and received a surprise.

There was a letter waiting for us. The receptionist was pretty mysterious about it. She just said that an American had left it here for Minerva and me.

There's this thing between Minerva and me when we receive mail addressed to the both of us. Neither of us wants to open it. I ended up opening it.

I said, "Big deal. Sally wants to meet us for breakfast, lunch, or dinner —whichever is appropriate for when we arrive. Phil is to be the messenger. We're to go up to the Auror Office. If he's there, he takes over. If not, we send him an owl and he communicates. Easy-peasy."

It was 2:30 PM BST. We went up to the Auror Office and looked up Phil. He was camped in a cubicle near the back of the big room. When he saw me enter the cube, he jumped up and said, "Great to see you. Was it a good trip?"

Minerva nodded with a big smile on her face. "Well, you saw the message. How about dinner?"

We said in unison, "Fine."

"How about five. I get off here then, but if you'd like to go earlier, it wouldn't be a problem."

Minerva said, "I'd like to spend some time in Madame Malkin's. And I'm sure that Wendt would like to spend some time in Flourish & Blotts."

I nodded. "Yeh. At least, I'd better."

Minerva kicked my shin.

Phil was oblivious and said, "I'll go get Sally, and we can meet at the Cauldron at five."

We took the floo to the Cauldron. Tom greeted us as usual. I said, "Tom, we'll be back with re-enforcements for dinner. Never fear."

Minerva and I went on through to Diagon Alley. She took my arm and said, "Let's go to Madame Malkins."

I said, "But I want to go to Flourish & Blotts, remember?"

She growled but didn't otherwise object. I knew that she wanted me to look at some new robes for the next academic year. I would surprise her by heading over to Malkins around 4 PM or so.

I bought a copy of *The Prophet* just in case I was wrong about Minerva's intentions for me. I'd not yet convinced Blotts to stock the *London Times* regularly. *The Prophet* was a poor substitute but any port in a storm.

I arrived at Malkins and found that Minerva indeed was in the men's section checking out the latest style in robes. We had our usual negotiations about how many suits of robes I would buy. We reached our usual compromise of two. I chose conservative styles and was fitted. Luckily, we escaped before 5 PM.

We had to hike over to the Cauldron pretty darn quickly. We arrived just as Phil and Sally walked out of the floo. Sally came over to me and hugged me. That was not unusual. What was unusual was that she seemed really happy. Phil got us a tabl---e, and we all sat.

Tom came over and named our usual drinks. I was agreeing as Sally interrupted me. "This is kind of a special occasion. Tom, do you have any champagne?"

He smiled. "I think I can find a bottle."

I thought, "I'm sure he can—for a price."

Phil said, "First things first. I am paying tonight, including the champagne, and there will be no argument."

I said, "So who's arguing?"

Phil and Sally looked at each other and went through a sort of wordless communication which ended by Sally saying, "I have the most wonderful news."

Minerva stared at her, and I could tell that she wanted to say something but was holding back. Then Sally and Phil said, almost in unison, "We're getting married." They both laughed as they said it.

Minerva said enthusiastically, "I knew it. I just knew it!"

I said, "I can't tell you how happy I am for you both. Sally, we've been through a lot together. You deserve this happiness as much as anyone I've ever known. Congratulations!"

Minerva insisted on knowing all details. By this time, Tom had arrived with a bottle of champagne and glasses. I noticed that he had five glasses. I said, "I think Tom should be the next person to know the news."

Phil agreed. "Tom, please pour five glasses."

I said, "Let's raise our glasses to the health and happiness of the future Mr. and Mrs. Pearson."

We clinked glasses, and Tom emptied his in a single swallow. We then ordered dinner.

Sally began talking immediately about their plans. "I'm glad you and Wendt are here. I've some ideas, and I wanted to check out what you two think of them."

She then started spitting out ideas rapid fire. "Of course, we want the wedding to be at Hogwarts. I've talked with my parents. They think that will be fine. Most of my friends would just come for the wedding itself. We could bring them up on the Express and they could stay overnight at Hogwarts. I've been thinking of who would be bridesmaids. I've a few ideas.

"There's so many other things: invitations, wedding cake, grooms cake, party favors, and on and on."

Minerva seemed as excited as she was. She offered the services of the house elves for the rehearsal dinner and the reception. All would be the school's wedding gift to the couple.

I looked over at Phil and said, "Not that much for us to do?"

He said, "You've not heard talk for hours on end about the wedding."

When Sally and Minerva stopped for breath, I asked, "How many muggles are you going to invite?"

That brought the discussion to a halt. Sally thought and eventually said, "I'd not really thought about details of who would come. . . We've been talking about one hundred guests in total—half from my side.

"But, many of them would be magical—probably half anyway. Then there would be my family. All of them know about magic—maybe a dozen or so. Everyone here at Hogwarts, of course. That would be maybe three dozen. But I think that I could steal some of Phil's fifty who all have to come from the States. That would maybe leave about two dozen. I'd probably invite eight or ten from the SAS unit. They all know about magic. Then there would be half a dozen or so from my college days. That would leave. . . oh . . . maybe ten or so school chums. They're the only ones who don't know about magic already. Probably half of them would blow it off. So maybe half a dozen tops who don't already know about magic."

I said, "But those few will be surprised for sure at King's Cross when they board the train."

Phil had a suggestion. "Some of my friends could meet yours at King's Cross, explain the situation, and help them through the barrier."

I had another idea. "Does the train go on an ordinary track when it leaves King's Cross?"

Minerva pondered that a moment. "Yes, I'm pretty sure it does."

"And," I went on, "It goes through ordinary train stations, right."

Minerva frowned. "You know very well that it does."

I went on, "Could we arrange for it to stop at one of those—say one close to London to pick up passengers?"

She nodded. Sally became enthusiastic again, "The train is pretty much an ordinary train. The muggle guests board at. . . say. . . Oxford and ride up to the Hogsmeade Station. They walk up to the castle. All this time, Phil's friends are doing little magic spells to show them what magic's about. They are amazed and happy for me. It's wonderful."

I thought about it looking for holes. Right away, Minerva named one or two. She said, "There are the ghosts."

I said, "Well, we could ask them to sort of lie low."

Sally was not entirely happy with that. She said, "I'd hate to disappoint poor Sir Nicholas."

I frowned. "Well, I guess there's going to have to be a crash course on magic and ghosts, and I suppose that we can't keep that bloody poltergeist away."

Minerva's smile turned grim. "I can deal with him."

I smiled. "Well, it can't be any worse than when I came to Hogwarts at first."

Minerva's reply was, "Don't be pessimistic."

After talking it through until the dinner was finished, we had decided that there weren't any insuperable problems with the wedding at Hogwarts.

Both Minerva, and I were dead tired. We took the floo directly to our apartment. I don't know where Phil and Sally went, and I don't care.

The Bridesmaid's Dilemma

The trouble for me began with a meeting of the bride-to-be, Minerva, and me. I thought that it would be an easy meeting where the most difficult task that I would get assigned might be deciding how much to contribute to the cost of the wedding.

Sally's father had died in the first Iraq war. Her mother's pension along with her earnings had allowed them to live fairly comfortably and even finance half of Sally's Uni education. She had paid off her half by now, but neither of the ladies were exactly well-to-do. I was completely happy with the idea of financing the majority or even the vast majority of Sally's wedding.

I thought the hardest part of the meeting would be working out a budget for the wedding and deciding how much of the expense that I would leave unfunded so that her Mum could retain pride without being beggared by the expense.

We met in the Head's Office. We'd all spent a lot of time in it over the past couple of years, and were very comfortable there.

Sally was always very organized, so she had an agenda with estimated times for each item. She handed out copies of the agenda. I glanced down the list. The first item was, as I'd expected, "Estimated wedding costs and requested contributions." That had half an hour dedicated to it.

The next item was simply, "Father of the Bride". That had only five minutes allocated.

The next item was "Bridesmaids, flower girl, and miscellaneous". It had forty minutes allocated to it. That one seemed like a yawner to me. Or at least, it was one that I expected to yawn through even if the ladies sweated bullets over it.

The meeting got off to a good start. Sally had a handout that listed the major expense items of the wedding and her estimate of costs. She opened by saying, "Minerva, there are a lot of items on here that I don't have a good way of estimating. I was a MOH once for a muggle friend. I was involved with most of the planning, and I know what a number of the items cost for her wedding.

"However, there are items here that I don't know how to estimate. Let's start with the rehearsal dinner. I'd like to have it in the Teacher's Lounge. That's large enough to accommodate everyone in the wedding party. Is that all right with you?"

Minerva smiled a stiff smile that told me that we'd already hit a snag right off the git-go. I couldn't image what it would be. Surely, Minerva wouldn't deny that simple and reasonable request? Would she?

Minerva started in slowly as she would in helping a slow but beloved student with a difficult transfiguration. "Dear, I want you to have the perfect wedding. If you want to use the Teacher's Lounge for your rehearsal dinner, I'm perfectly happy for you to use it."

Then she blinked her eyes. That was a sign that there was a "but" coming. "But, you've put down here an estimate of two hundred fifty galleons for rental."

Sally's bright smile that she'd started the meeting with sagged a bit, "Not enough. What would you like to charge."

Minerva shook her head sadly as though a favorite pet had just died, "Sally, Sally, Sally. How can you not know that we will not charge you a thin knut for rental of the Teacher's Lounge, or for that matter, for rental of the Great Hall."

Sally's eyes widened to the size of pie plates, but then her temper got engaged. "I can't allow it!" I almost expected her to pound the Head's desk, but she didn't. "You would charge any other member of staff for the rental of meeting rooms or the Great Hall for goodness sake!"

By the end of the speech her eyes were flashing, and a quick glance showed that the Head was equally determined. I was tempted to let them go to it, but heaven only knew when we'd be done with the meeting if I just stood back and let this go on. I decided to intervene. It was a risky decision, but it was a decision rooted in self-defense.

I raised my voice and said, "Ladies, allow me to make a suggestion."

The both of them discovered that they had a new target for their ire— me. Minerva said, "I'm the Head of this institution, and I'll decide whom I charge and whom not."

Sally opened her mouth to say something, but I interrupted again. "Whoa, whoa, whoa. Just let me get a word in, and I think you'll both be pleased."

Minerva cocked her head. She'd heard me come up with some inventive ideas in my time. She seemed to be willing to let me speak. However, Sally was not so disposed, "Look boss. I know that I work for you, but you've got to let me do this my way."

She was looking directly at me, so I guessed that she must be referring to me as "boss" even though Minerva was her boss. I broke in and said, "Am I ever going to break you of that awful habit of calling me 'boss?'"

She was pretty mad, but she managed to give a half-way polite reply, "No, boss."

I plunged on ahead. "Look, there's a compromise that I think you will both like.

"First, Minerva, I've heard you say more than once that the scholarship fund for needy students needs replenishing, and you hate to go to the Minister of Magic to ask for more money."

Minerva nodded warily. I went on, "Why don't you come up with reasonable charges for rent, and Sally will contribute that to the scholarship fund?"

Sally seemed to want to object, although I can't imagine what she'd object to. I didn't give her a chance to come up with something. I hurried on. "Now, Sally, you know that the majority of the costs of this wedding are going to be paid by . . . uh . . . a wealthy benefactor."

She jumped in, "You mean by you."

I nodded and smiled and went on, "So, why don't the two of you get together and come up with a round sum. Then, we'll talk about how much gets funded by you and your Mum and how much by me."

The both of them were wary. Minerva asked Sally, "Do you see anything wrong with it?"

Sally shook her head and said, "No. Just so long as you don't low-ball the fees."

Minerva shook her head and asked, "Low-ball?"

Sally answered, "Yeh. Haven't you ever heard your husband use that word. It's from that silly game they play in the States."

Minerva turned to me. "What does that mean?"

I shook my head. I wondered how much she'd picked up of any knowledge of baseball on our tour of the States. "It means just what it sounds like. Don't make a low estimate."

We then turned to coming up with reasonable fees for the use of the castle, grounds, and so forth.

Relieved that we'd passed that danger point, I wondered what could possibly go wrong with the next agenda item. Of course, there was the possibility that I might be nominated, but there were so many objections to me as stand-in father of the bride that I didn't even consider it. After all, I was, if anything, slightly younger than Sally. On top of that was the fact that I'd fight nomination tooth and nail.

I needn't have worried. Sally named her candidate. "I'd like you to get in touch with Colonel Parker. We went through a lot together, and let's face it, he's closer to my Dad's age." She stopped, took a deep breath, and said, "to the age my Dad would have been than you are."

That would be easy. Well, pretty easy. I supposed that he'd be willing.

The last agenda item seemed like something that I'd have no interest in, and I could either stay and be bored or leave and get something useful done. So, I stood.

Minerva and Sally said in unison, "Where are you going?"

I looked from one to the other and shrugged, "Well, to be honest, I've really not got any interest in bridesmaid's dresses or THE color of the wedding or who will be disappointed at not having their daughter be flower girl. I couldn't help you if I stayed, I'd just get bored."

Minerva seemed to be relenting, but Sally didn't. She said "You've got a very important role to play."

I scoffed, "With the bridesmaids?"

She replied, "With one in particular—the Maid of Honor."

"Is there some wedding tradition I don't know about?"

Sally shook her head, "No. The girl I want to be MOH is a muggle. We have been friends since private school. I already contacted her, and she's agreed. Somebody has to give her the scoop on magic, wizards, Hogwarts, and so on." She gave an airy wave with her left hand as she said, "so on". Then she added, "You're it."

"Why me? She's not my friend. You're the natural for this. You've known her since private school. You're BFF's or whatever. She would believe you a lot more than she would me."

Sally came as close as she ever did to whining as she said, "Ooo, Wendt, just do it. You've got tons of experience at introducing people to the idea of magic. You did me and all those SAS officers and the people on the submarine. This would be a cinch for you."

I was not giving in that easily. "Oh, come on. Why can't she be introduced to the wonderful world of wizardry on the Express at the same time everyone else is?"

Minerva just clucked her tongue, and Sally said, "That would defeat the whole purpose of having an MOH."

"How so?"

"Well, the purpose of an MOH is to help the bride-to-be plan. She shares all the fun little secrets of the bride-to-be. She knows the bride-to-be and knows the little touches that make the wedding just so, so perfect."

I kept my stern look. But Sally continued, "Surely even you can see that the MOH has to be present with bride-to-be long before the wedding. Some of it could be away from magic places, but some of it definitely has to be here and even a few other magic venues."

I was reluctantly coming around but Minerva added the coup de grace. "You Americans have a saying, 'If Mum ain't happy, ain't nobody happy.'"

I surrendered. "All right. All right. Just where and when does this extravaganza of painful and embarrassing revelation happen. Or do I have to plan it myself?"

Sally answered, "Oh, that's not a problem. It will be a fun occasion. Haley Poetzl, Minerva, you, and I are going to a bridal shop to shop for the bridal gown next Saturday."

I muttered, "Great. I suppose you have a cover story for why I'm there."

Minerva smirked,."Of course. I'm Sally's boss and old friend. I'm there because I want to make sure the wedding is wonderful. And you're my devoted husband who is concerned with all my closest concerns."

I had to admit that they had me foxed.

□

The day of choosing the bridal gown arrived. I realized that I had no honorable alternative to going and taking my bitter medicine. I spent a good bit of the night tossing and turning. At times, I was barely asleep, and at others, I was awake practicing the speech that I would have to give to the Maid of Honor. It was hard to tell which was which.

When the alarm rang, I'd actually gotten an hour or two of sleep and hazily stumbled out of bed. Minerva was already in the bathroom. She'd showered and was toweling off as I knocked on the door. She invited me in.

She was bright and cheery. Why shouldn't she be? She didn't have to do anything in the least unpleasant. As a matter of fact, all women seem to take a great delight in helping other women get married.

On the other hand, I had no delight in giving this MOH a crash course on muggle-Wizard relations.

We had what would have been a wonderful breakfast in the Great Hall. It was Saturday and there were hardly any students present. The delights were totally lost on me. All too soon, the three of us, Minerva, Sally, and I were stepping into the Great Hall floo.

We arrived in the Cauldron's floo. I was so depressed that I just waved

103

a hand at the woman who was running the bar this morning and walked to the bar. I put down several galleons and said, "Both you and Tom should have a drink."

She smiled and wished us a good day. I could only reply a sullen, "Right."

We left the Cauldron. Once on the street, Minerva took our hands again, and we suddenly found ourselves in an alley. Immediately outside the alley was a bridal shop. Sally joyously led us in. We'd arranged to meet at the Cauldron for dinner after I'd finished my odious task.

The interior was tastefully decorated in pastel colors. Thank God none of them were pink. The proprietor led us to a room where I found that a young woman was seated. She immediately rose when we entered the room.

She strode to us and looked to be ready to introduce herself when Sally beat her to it. Sally looked at me and said, "And this is James Wendt and his wife, my boss."

Haley extended a hand and said, "Pleased to meet you." She apparently had long hair. It was tied up in a bun on top of her head in a fashion that Minerva had never worn. It was an intense black that was deeper than any that I'd ever seen. She was wearing a pair of wide-rim black glasses that challenged her hair for the deepest black that I'd ever seen. Her face was broader than average but somehow it seemed to suit her perfectly. She wore an ankle length white skirt and a dark blue blouse.

Sally then said, "This is Haley Poetzl, boss."

I grimaced. Things were starting off every bit as badly as I feared. I just mumbled, "Don't call me boss."

Sally didn't loose any of her bright banter. She turned to Haley and said, "Don't pay attention to him. He isn't really my boss. He just used to be."

Haley's smile didn't lessen. She said, "I'm pleased to meet you both. Sally has said quite a lot of good things about you, Mr. Wendt."

All I could think of to say was, "She's much kinder than I deserve."

A bright smile lit her face as she said, "I doubt that very much."

All I could do was shrug.

Our hostess from the establishment invited us to sit on some armchairs that were arranged in a semicircle. The opposite side of the semicircle was a semicircle of mirrors. She suggested that the ladies accompany her to view her selection of dresses.

She turned to me and said, "You, Mr. Wendt, would probably be more comfortable here. We'll select a few likely dresses and return here so that Ms. Harker can try them on."

With that, they left the room, which was beginning to seem more and more like a tomb to me. There was a coffee table with a variety of magazines laid tastefully out. They had titles like "Today's Bride", "Modern Honeymoons", and "House and Garden". I guess the last was for the benefit of mothers of the bride and so on. God! Why hadn't I brought a copy of *Scientific American*. And, why didn't they have a copy of the *Times?*!

I whiled away the endless wait trying to search for something of interest in "Homes and Gardens."

After an eternity, the ladies returned. There was an additional lady with them. Sally introduced her as her mother, Mina Harker. She was shorter than Sally by an inch or two. Her hair was blond shot with platinum. It was just long enough to draw up behind her head in a nondescript hairdo for which I have no name.

She wore a short skirt of tan and a pastel green top. She extended her hand, which grasped mine firmly. She turned to her daughter and asked, "How is it that we've never met?"

Sally was caught speechless for once. "I don't know."

The hostess had several dresses in her arms. She invited us all to sit while she arrayed the dresses on hangers around the room.

Mina turned to Haley and said, "I'm so glad that Sal chose you as her Maid of Honor. You have always been my favorite of her friends."

Haley turned a little red. It might have been more noticeable if her fairly dark skin hadn't masked it. What she said was, "I'm very honored Mrs. Harker. It's my first time as Maid of Honor."

Mina nodded and said, "And you should have been married too, but it seems that people don't always get what they deserve."

Haley's face turned noticeably redder, and I began looking for a hole that I might crawl into. There being none, I simply tried to see if I could develop that Zen skill of disappearing. Sally didn't seem much more comfortable than I, but she had nothing to say.

After the second eternity that day, Sally suggested that Haley try one of the dresses on so that she, Sally, could see what it looked like on another woman. She took it into the dressing room with her. After she'd left, Mina said, "Poor Haley. Do you know why she hasn't gotten an offer?"

Sally said, "Now, Mum, you know perfectly well that modern women have other concerns than getting married."

That conversation continued a bit comparing the virtues of married life with a job and pure devotion to one's occupation. The only comfort that I had in all of this was that, as bad as it was, what was coming would be even worse.

Haley returned. She stepped in front of us but far enough back that we could see the back of the dress in the mirrors. I won't even attempt to describe any of the dresses or this one's effect on Haley's appearance except for a couple of things.

First, the hostess suggested that Haley take her glasses off. When she did, the general agreement was that the effect was positive. Everyone (and in the bridal shop when I say everyone, I'm excluding myself) agreed that she should wear contacts to all wedding events.

Second, I suggested that Haley let her hair down. It would certainly be worn down at the wedding. Of course, Haley wouldn't be wearing the dress, but I was curious.

At this point, something occurred to me that impelled me to make a comment. I said, "Excuse me. If you can tolerate an amateur's comment, I'd like to suggest something."

Everyone shrugged, so I proceeded. "Haley, would you put your glasses back on, please?"

Everyone stared at me in disbelief—including Haley. However, I stood my ground. "It's easy and I'd appreciate your indulgence."

Again everyone shrugged. Haley put her glasses on and shook her hair to restore the long jet black hair to its original form. It fell smoothly over both shoulders, back, and breasts to her waist and beyond.

She just stood there. So, I said, "Please turn around slowly and while you're doing it, have a look in the mirror."

She did so. When she finished her rotation, she had a real smile on her face. She said, "I like it. I don't understand it, but I think I like how I look, wearing my glasses."

Mina was opposed. She turned to Sally and said quite candidly, "Sal, dear, Haley is far too striking wearing those glasses. She will draw all attention to herself."

Sally said, "You know, I think I agree." Then she turned to Haley and said, "You are really striking in that dress with your hair down and wearing those glasses. I really hate to have to ruin your effect, but would you mind wearing contacts for the wedding?"

Haley looked from one of us to another. Finally, she settled on me, "What do you think, Mr. Wendt? Am I too . . . oh . . . pretty in these glasses?"

I looked at her face carefully and expressed my opinion, "You are indeed stunning. I think it's the combination of your long black hair accompanied by your bold black glasses. You might not have the ideal classic appearance, but every eye will be focused on you. I can't believe that you don't realize the effect you have."

She seemed perplexed. Then she had an idea, "Do you mind if I wear my glasses for the rehearsal? That would not be disruptive."

That compromise seemed to satisfy everyone. Again, I wasn't satisfied, and I didn't care whether or not Sally had all the attention during the wedding. It might seem unkind but I thought that the Maid of Honor ought to have some glory too.

Sally tried that dress on and two more dresses. There was not general agreement about a preference for any of the dresses so far.

We went through the rest of the dresses, and they picked one. Everyone wanted my opinion on the dresses but I plead utter ignorance of fashion—especially where it applied to weddings.

When the painful experience finally ended, Sally announced that she, Minerva, and her Mum had some business (unnamed), and that Haley and I should go have some lunch where she was sure that we'd find topics to discuss.

I nodded sullenly, sneered internally, and asked Haley where she would like to go for lunch.

She thought a moment and said, "Let's just go to my hotel. It's got a decent restaurant, and it will be convenient for me."

I agreed. When we arrived, it was already after 1 PM, so we didn't have much trouble getting the table that I wanted—one for two in a corner removed from most other diners. All the better for doing the explanation that I was going to have to do.

She ordered a cup of tea.

I said, "If you don't mind, I'm going to have something harder."

"Isn't this a little early?"

I smiled a wan smile and assured her that it was a special occasion. She agreed and decided to change her order to a glass of red wine. Even before the drinks arrived, her spirits brightened. I would not have thought that possible, but I guess it's not every day that you get to be an MOH.

We concentrated on the menu and ordered before we got down to the real business of the lunch. She kicked it off, "Mr. Wendt." She hesitated, "May I call you Jim?"

Her bright attitude caused me to sink deeper into a funk. "Oh, sure. Why not. I guess we'll all be much more acquainted before the wedding's over."

She smiled and said, "Exactly! Sally says that you are the best person to explain to me about some aspects of her fiancé that I should know before the wedding."

I nodded. The time of maximum dynamic stress had arrived. This would be it.

But, it wasn't. She went on. "Well, I think you should know something about me before you tell me about Phil. Don't you think."

Anything that would put the moment of reckoning off was good for me, so I nodded judiciously.

□□

How could that smile keep getting wider? It did as she began, "Sally and I met in college. We were roommates. We rented a flat together. I met her by pure luck. There was a service at the school that matched people with apartments that the school had vetted.

"Ours was a partnership made in heaven. She was a third year student who knew all the ropes, and I was a freshman when we met. I was fresh off the farm—literally. My Mum had a small house at the edge of town that had been a farmhouse.

"Sally was sophisticated and smart and beautiful—everything that I wasn't." She hesitated and said, "And maybe still am not."

I interrupted. "Just as a point of information, be fair to yourself. Have you forgotten that you have to wear contact lenses because the mother of the bride is worried that you will steal everyone's eyes away from her daughter?

"And really, as an impartial observer, I agree. You are quite stunning."

She still had left her hair down and was wearing her glasses.

"Don't forget that Sally chose you for Maid of Honor. She's pretty darn smart herself, and she wouldn't choose someone for so much responsibility for her wedding if she didn't trust her abilities completely."

I hesitated a minute as I thought, and then another idea occurred to me. "You have not seen her in tough situations. She is relentless and unforgiving. She insists on good performance from everyone."

Haley who had been looking down had lifted her eyes and chuckled, "Even from her 'boss?'"

I just said, "I won't comment on that."

"Well, you seem convinced."

I smiled. "Even if you aren't?"

Something of her old joy came back. "I guess if you think so, I shouldn't argue."

"Believe me. That is an argument that you'd lose."

She went on. "Sally always seemed to have dates, and she knew all the professors. She advised me on whose classes to take, and whose to avoid like the black death.

"Her wardrobe was not large but she had lots of good outfits. Dad

108

spent a lot of money on mine, but I was never happy with them."

Her smile regained its original brilliance—maybe due to the change of topic that she was about to bring up. "Now, you've got to talk. What is the story about Phil?"

It had to happen eventually. I was about to start when the waiter returned with our dishes. Haley said, "Saved by the bell . . . peppers." I had ordered stuffed peppers.

I asked for a refill of my Dewars. Haley still had plenty of wine. We ate for a while and, as our appetites disappeared, so did my reasons for putting off talking.

I leaned back and said, "This is rather a long story. I hope you're prepared to spend the afternoon working through it. I'd hate to have to take a break in the middle."

She had pushed her plate back and put her elbows on the table so that she could rest her chin on her hands. "Sally said it might be long, so I'm prepared for a siege."

I nodded. No more reasons to procrastinate. "OK. We have to go back a number of years.

"You may have guessed that I'm not from around here."

She chuckled. "No! You mean you're not from Islington?"

"Laugh you may, but if you haven't guessed that I'm from the States, you're going to the bottom of the class."

Her smile grew further. "So, you're a Yank from New York City?"

It was my turn to chuckle. "No, I grew up in the state of Ohio, which you may never have heard of. I went to college there and graduated with a degree in English Literature. Then I went to graduate school at Stanford. I think you may have heard of it."

She nodded by rocking her hands supporting her head back and forth —a strange mannerism, especially as she kept her attention locked on me.

She asked, "Strange background for someone who works for the SAS, isn't it?"

"You might think so, but I have two extenuating circumstances. One is that I got fired from my teaching job. The second is that I was more drafted into working for intelligence than volunteering. Also, I have only ever worked for them as a contractor—not as a permanent employee."

Her eyes, which I had just noticed were a jet black, had gotten ever wider. I didn't imagine they could do that.

That was a trail that I didn't want to go down, so I just said, "That's another story. Maybe some black night Sally will talk me into telling you about it. I wouldn't trust her to tell it straight."

Her eyes clouded somewhat. She asked, "Why a black night? Is it a bad story?"

I considered before saying, "I don't know what kind of story it is. James Joyce said that some stories are night stories. He meant that they are ambiguous stories—clouded by darkness."

She looked down at her long ignored glass of wine. "Maybe I need something stronger than this for that story."

I chuckled. "It wouldn't hurt.

"But to get back to the story at hand, I have to go well back earlier from that story that we were just talking about."

She nodded that strange nod of hers and agreed. "OK. Another time. But the bond between bride and MOH is strong. Sally will make you tell that story some time."

"Yeh," I thought, "She just might."

What I said was, "I was fresh out of college. As a student of English Literature, I thought that I ought to spend some time in the land of the mother tongue. I came over here intending to work for a year or two, learning the land of Shakespeare, Donne, and Jane Austen. What actually happened was that I couldn't get a job other than at Starbucks until I was almost flat broke.

"I was desperate, and I found a job that called for desperation." I expected a comment or question at this point, but Haley just continued to gaze at me from her hands that cradled her cheeks.

I went on. "I saw a job posting in the *Times* and answered it. They were looking for an English Literature teacher for a small public school. It was residential and in an obscure corner of Scotland. The advert didn't say all of that, but I soon discovered that after I answered the advert.

"I was living in a rooming house with some students who were hardly younger than I was. One day, there was a tap on the window that persisted. I discovered an owl on the window ledge. It seemed determined to get in.

"When I did let it in, I discovered that it had a small note tied to one of its claws. I removed it and read the note."

Here Haley sat bolt upright and asked, "What in the world was it?"

"It was a response to my answering the advert. It proposed an appointment to discuss my response further."

She grasped my arm and said, "That's really spooky. I wouldn't have gone for anything."

"Maybe I shouldn't have, but I was desperate. It was either go to the meeting or go back to Ohio."

She made a face and said, "Ugh!"

I nodded. "I didn't think I had much choice."

I stopped to gather courage and think about my next step. Haley

110

squeezed my arm harder and demanded, "Well! What happened?"

"I went to the meeting. It was in Hyde Park at the old boat dock."

She stared and squeezed again. "Yes?"

"There was an old man there. He had a boat. We got in it, and he paddled us out on the pond. He interviewed me for the job. He was the Headmaster."

She released her breath. "Well, all that build up for a boat ride on a pond?"

I shook my head. "You had to be there to understand. I was convinced by the time that the interview had ended that this school was . . . well . . ."

She supplied a word. "*Outre?*"

"Yes, the Headmaster wanted me to interview with his Assistant Headmistress. They got in touch with me again by owl."

She shook her head. "No. How is that possible?"

I leaned back and took another stiff pull on my drink, "The owl caught up with me on a date. The young lady and I were walking on a street. The note that the owl dropped on my head was addressed to me at the street address where we were walking past at the moment the note hit my head."

She threw my arm down in disgust, "You are lying. You were just stringing me along to see how long I would go along with your cock and bull story."

I shook my head. She grabbed my arm again with amazing force, "How is that possible!"

I took another pull on my drink, allowing me to think. "I've told you that I think you are a smart young woman. How do you think it was possible? Use Sherlock Holmes' methods. Eliminate everything that's impossible and whatever is left—regardless how strange—must be true."

Her demeanor changed. She was laughing as though at some internal joke. Then she started naming possibilities. "The owl was trained. Someone was trailing you. He wrote the address and released the bird just as you reached the address."

I smiled. "Not bad. But it was night. We were walking briskly. The address was precise. It would be a very long shot at best. You have only one shot at getting it right if you were following me. Would you really risk it?"

She thought and then shook her head. Then she said, "The paper was electronic and the address was entered on a computer just as it hit your head."

I smirked. "Don't be silly. Such things don't exist—even now. That was a long time ago."

She was puzzled. I thought not just by the surface mystery but by how it could possibly have anything to do with Phil and Sally. The puzzlement shown in her eyes that seemed to be focused inwardly and the tilt of her head at an odd angle. She said, "OK. You know the solution. What is it?"

I shook my head. "Can't do that. You have to work it out for yourself. Otherwise, you'll not have a chance of believing it."

She lifted the wine glass and took a sip. Then she hefted it in her hand, seeming to consider throwing it at me. "It's impossible. There isn't anything left, Sherlock."

"Yes, there is. Think."

She set the wine glass down and stared at it, seeming to will the answer to appear in the glass. Finally, she shook her shoulders. It turned into a shudder that traveled the entire length of her body. "I give up. The only thing that's left is magic."

She gazed at me dumbly and then nodded slowly. "It is magic, isn't it? I nodded.

She shook her head and said, "That just can't be."

I said, "You need more proof, I see."

She didn't react, so I went on. "Think about this.

"When the earth was taken over by aliens. How do you think that they were defeated?"

She did something that I didn't expect. She grasped the table top with both hands and just shook her head violently and said, "NO!"

She seemed to regain control of herself and went on through gritted teeth, "I won't talk about that."

"I'm afraid you will have to if you want to be Maid of Honor."

She stared down into her drink and then began sobbing. The sobbing became more violent until her whole body shook forcefully.

The waitress came over to see if there anything she could help with. I shook my head and then had a second thought, "Could you bring a Dewars. Oh, and make it a double."

The waitress nodded and left.

The sobs had been silent but now were audible. With that, her body shook less. Her tear-streaked face showed no eye makeup tracks. I hadn't realized that she was not wearing makeup!

She started to apologize, but I said, "Have a drink of that Dewars. It will help."

She did and tried to say something but the sobs were re-starting. She looked like needing a hug, so I shifted to the chair next to her and hugged her. My body absorbed some of her shaking and after a while it all subsided.

She released her weak grip on me and I shifted to a different chair.

112

She had retrieved a handkerchief from her handbag and was drying her eyes. She took a good, big sip of the Dewars and said, "I'm sorry. I guess I still haven't gotten over . . . over being . . ."

I nodded. "I don't think anyone ever does."

"How do you manage?"

"That's a story that I'm going to hold for later. Do you want to stop for today?"

She took another drink and said, "No. But, please, let me tell my story now. I think it would help."

I nodded, and she began.

□
□□

For me, it started in a Starbucks. I was there with my new boy-friend, Donald.

He was a lawyer at the law office where we worked. On the first date, we went for coffee at lunch at the Starbucks in our office building. We enjoyed that enough that he took me out to dinner a couple of nights later.

The date was wonderful. We talked and talked the whole evening over the meal. I once saw the movie, "Dinner With Andre." It was just like that. We talked about each other.

We talked about our hardest times. He had enrolled in Oxford and just couldn't make the grade. He went back home, got a job in a law office as a paralegal, and just worked for a couple of years. He then enrolled in a less prestigious school (which he refused to name) and finished his undergraduate degree there.

Then he went to a law school and struggled through but ended up in the middle of his class. He then went back to his old law office and applied for a job. They offered him his old paralegal position!

He gritted his teeth and took it. He got the worst assignments! They sent him to courts that handled labor disputes to help the "real" lawyers. He did that for almost three years. Because he handled only one kind of case, he eventually got to be the law firm's specialist in that field. In the end, they sent him alone. He had actually become more expert in that niche field than the typical magistrate that he saw. He would advise them on the law. He got quite a reputation in the low courts where he went.

He was still technically a paralegal, but he was a lawyer and was fully qualified to handle all the assignments that he was given completely on his own.

I told him about my first date with a guy. He worked at the law firm that we both worked at. He was nice. We went out for coffee and had a good time. I stopped there.

He asked, "What was so awful about that. Did he try to get you into bed on the strength of that first 'date'?" He said the word date as though it hardly applied to having coffee with a guy.

"No. He was completely a gentleman."

"Well, then. Did he never ask you out again?"

"No. He asked me out to dinner."

"Well, then. Did that date go badly?"

"No, actually it was dreamy." I said that while cradling my chin in my cupped hands.

"Well, what in the world made it so awful?"

I almost cried at that point. I said, "It was the first date I ever had. I went all the way through private school and then through college without ever having a date."

Donald stared at me as though I were a unicorn. He said, "I don't understand. You're very attractive. You're smart. You work hard—you're really thorough. You've got a sense of humor. What is there not to like?!"

I did cry a little then and said, "Where were you when I was in school?!"

He smiled and gave me a wise-cracker answer that I'd probably have disliked under different circumstances. He said, "I was at Oxford like I said."

That crack was so unexpected that I couldn't help laughing. It brought me out of my funk and I actually found myself smiling again.

He went on. "Who was this bloke anyway. Is he still at our office? I'm happy he gave up on you, but I'd like to give him his comeuppance for dropping you after only two dates."

I could hardly keep from laughing again. I tried to be as dead-pan as possible as I said, "Oh, he's still at our office."

He said, "It was Rupert wasn't it? He was always a blighter with the women in our office."

I tried to keep a straight face as I said, "No. Not Rupert."

He was beginning to be really indignant. "Come, now. No protecting this . . . this . . . miserable moron. Who was . . ."

He wasn't able to finish his tirade because I broke out in boisterous laughter. "Oh, this is too rich. Too, too rich." A little fit of laughing struck me again. Then I said, "You ninny. It's you."

It took him a minute to take it in, but when he had, he said, "Well, I'll take care of this injustice right now.

"First, we're going out for coffee tomorrow at lunch. That's takes care of the next date.

114

"Second," With that, he stood quickly, bent across the small circular table and kissed me on the lips rapidly.

That quick kiss, that was hardly more than a peck, stayed with me the rest of the night burning my lips ferociously. When he dropped me off at my apartment at nearly midnight, we kissed again. It was a good kiss. It was really a great kiss, but I will never forget that first real kiss of desire as long as I live.

The next day we went to Starbucks for our next and last date.

We met at the Starbucks near the Harrods close to Hyde Park. We went after work. The place seemed quiet for that time of day, but there were a couple of people in line. We were the first to receive our coffees. We found a cozy corner with two armchairs with a low table between. We talked about work. It was very pleasant.

For a while it was pleasant. I noticed that Donald's eyelids were drooping, and I laughed internally that it must have been a long day for him. Then I realized that I was having a hard time keeping my eyes open. That was the last thought that I had for a long time.

I don't know how I realized that it had been a long time. There didn't seem to be any pause between closing my sleepy eyes at Starbucks and the blasted alarm clock pulling me up out of a deep, deep sleep. But there was a different sort of alarm going off in my head. Even before I was half awake, I knew that something was terribly wrong. I knew that a lot of time had passed.

My eyes opened and my fists wrung the last of the sleep out of my eyes. The bedroom in my apartment looked normal, but I seemed detached from everything. It was as though I were a fly on the wall observing someone else getting up in her apartment.

I was still not fully awake. I went to the bathroom and started my morning routine. Only it wasn't my routine. Then I got the real shock.

I looked in the mirror. I was wide awake now. My hair that I used to wear down to my midriff was now barely shoulder length. Then I remembered that the last thing I knew I'd been at Starbucks. I didn't cut my hair. I WASN'T CONTROLLING MY BODY!

My hands ran a brush briskly through my hair. I brushed my teeth quickly.

Then I screamed. Almost immediately, a strange voice in my head said, "Shhhh." gently, and I was gone.

When I awoke the next time, it was very slow. I didn't really know when I was awake. I noticed my hair, which was still short. I noticed my body that was different. It was strange. I was slimmer. I had noticeable muscles. After a while I realized why.

I was running every morning. I was running hard. When I stopped I was almost gasping for breath. But I'd run farther and faster than I'd ever run in my life.

Once, I'd gone to a shopping mall on a slow day. I'd parked in the mall's parking structure. I had come out with a small bag. The mall was never busy. That was one of the reasons that I liked it. But this day it was especially quiet.

As I walked from the mall to the parking structure, I thought I saw some movement out of the corner of my eye. I turned and saw a youth loitering outside the entrance to the mall.

I picked up my pace as I entered the structure. I tried not to appear worried. I turned a corner and broke into a run. It was as fast as I could manage. I rounded another corner and found stairs to the upper levels. My car was on the main level, but I looked around, didn't see anyone, and ducked into the stairs. I ran up two flights of stairs. I got out and broke into a run again to find another set of stairs.

I found more stairs and went in. I stopped and tried to calm down so I could think of something rational to do. I thought about calling someone on my cell phone, but I was afraid I'd just seem to be a silly woman afraid of her shadow.

I waited a while listening for the sound of a door opening on the stairwell where I was. It never did. I finally nerved up and went down the stairs to the main floor. I opened the door and glanced around quickly. No one was there. It took a while for me to find my car.

That was a very nervous time. I was ecstatic when I reached my car, verified that no one was hiding in it waiting for me, and drove off.

When I'd run in that parking structure, I ran as though my life depended on it. I was wearing flats, and I thought I was running pretty hard. That run was nothing compared to my daily runs each morning.

One day as I—or really that other voice—was dressing my body, I wanted so badly to weep that I tried saying something. It would have been, "Oh, what has happened to me?" I didn't utter a sound, but that strange voice seemed to have heard me.

She said, "Oh, you're still here?"

I tried to calm myself to say something non-threatening. "Yes, it's my

116

body you know."

The voice said with a tone that seemed to have some pride in it. "Don't you like what I've done with your body?" She gave my head a little shake, and my hair shimmered around my shoulders.

All I could do was ask, "Who are you?"

She seemed to puzzle that question a little. "I am a Soul. We live in our Hosts—like you."

I broke in, "You are a parasite!"

She seemed to think a minute. "We are in a symbiotic relationship. We gain a body. You benefit from our maintenance of that body and your environment."

Inside myself I felt anger growing again, "I'll trade places with you," I said bitterly, "I like my body the way it was, by the way. I like my hair long and my body a little plump. I'd rather hide my muscles. The curves are better than the hard lines you force on me."

She didn't say anything for a long time. We lived our separate lives—I in my invisible cell seemingly shut up in a nutshell and she in my body free to enjoy it as she wished.

I began grudgingly to admit that there were advantages to having her manage my body. My endurance and strength grew as we exercised together. My body was not my perfect image of myself, but she began to let my hair grow some.

When I realized that was happening, I asked her about it. She said, "I've decided that since we are doomed to share this body, you should have some say about it. Do you like the clothes we wear?"

I couldn't believe my ears. "Well, honestly, you wear very simple clothes that are not flattering at all. I am bored to tears when I see us in the mirror."

She considered that and said, "OK. Let's go shopping tomorrow."

I wondered what that meant. The next day, I found out. We went to a place that they called a "department store". That's what the sign said outside the building. We went in. There were simple display cases and racks for clothes. There were simple signs that announced departments— men's clothing, women's clothing, children's clothing, and so forth. There was no jewelry department. When I realized that my heart fell. I used to wear a bracelet that I'd bought before . . . well . . . before I lost my body. There was nothing here.

She noticed my dismay and asked what the problem was. I said, "I was hoping to find something to wear as an ornament. You know—earrings, necklace, bracelet."

She only said, "Why?"

"If you don't know why, I can never explain. Oh, well. I'll have to be satisfied with some clothes that are interesting."

We walked down the line of racks. All the dresses and blouses and skirts were perfectly grouped by size and color—nothing that you'd ever find in a real department store run by real people. I walked and walked looking for something. Anything.

I did find something. It was an outfit in black. It was a slit skirt, a simple top, pitch black, and a black jacket. I don't know how it escaped from the dull clothing mills of the Souls, but it was wonderful. It was silky. I'm sure it wasn't silk, but it felt like it was. The best part was that my Soul loved bright colors.

I asked her to take those off the shelf. She put them on me. The feeling of those silky clothes gliding over my skin would have made me weep for joy—if I'd been capable of weeping.

Instead, my Soul smiled with my lips and said, "This does feel so. . . so . . ."

I said, "The word you're looking for is silky."

Then the strangest thing happened. I felt something like a caress. I couldn't locate it. It felt like it was on my skin, but it wasn't. It was somewhere else.

After a minute, it stopped, and she said, "There! I've found it. You're right. The feeling is 'silky'. I see now why you like it so much."

I asked, "What was it that you were just doing?"

Casually she replied, "Oh, I was just glancing through your memory for that word, silky, and your associations with it."

I gasped or would have if I had control of my throat. She could look through my memory whenever she wanted to! Nothing was safe from her! As I absorbed the enormity of that I remembered something else that I'd heard her say before. "You said something about most . . ." I was afraid to ask the question, but I went ahead. "Most humans don't wake up after . . ." I didn't have a word that adequately expressed my disgust at what had happened to me at that Starbucks.

She cheerfully supplied the word, 'We call it insertion. Simple really. You just anesthetize the host and then cut a small slit below . . ." I stopped hearing what she was saying. I would have thrown up if I'd been in control of my stomach and throat. She finished up, "I could go into technical detail, but I doubt you want that."

Then she went back to the first point. "About two thirds of hosts never wake up. Then there's another 20% or so that don't wake after being 'shushed.' You're really quite special."

I mentally slumped. I would have screamed if I hadn't been afraid that she would "shush" me again, and I'd never wake up. I turned away from her. Of course, I couldn't actually turn anything. It just felt like I turned.

She was looking for a store assistant. She found one and asked for a bag to put our clothes in. The sales assistant brought one and asked her, "Do you want to wear your new clothes home?"

She asked me, "What about it? Shall we wear your new outfit?"

Fear and cold fury battled in my heart. If she thought that I was going to talk with her as though nothing had happened, she had a lot of thoughts coming.

She repeated the question a little louder, as though I couldn't hear every thought she directed at me. I guess some of it came out of her mouth.

The assistant asked, "Did you say something?"

"Oh, I'm just thinking out loud."

The assistant said, "Funny expression. I don't think I ever had a host where I 'thought out loud' before being here."

She directed a sharp thought at me, "Kay-Lee?" She rarely used my name, but when she did, it always came out with the accent on the second syllable and for some reason that I never discovered, she had trouble with the first syllable. She seemed unable to pronounce it correctly. It always came out "Kay." She never bothered to find out if she were saying it right.

The assistant was waiting patiently. My Soul, whose name came out something like The-Meaning-of-Speed, mumbled something about just wearing the new outfit. We left the department store. The rest of the day, she would say my name—sometimes softly and hesitantly and sometimes with determination. I never answered.

That night when she got ready for bed, she hung her clothes carefully, and we went through the usual routine. When we were in bed, she closed my eyes, and then said softly, "Kay-Lee, I love you."

It was a shock. How could someone who had tried to kill me—not once, but twice—possibly say something so, so stupid! If she thought that I'd ever speak to her again, she was crazier than she claimed we humans were.

.

□□ □
□□ □□

The next day we went into work as usual. The run in the morning was one in which she pushed herself harder than she ever had before. At work, she concentrated completely on work.

119

Her work was end-to-end inventory control. Her specialty was electronics. That day she needed all her concentration. There was a shortage of RFID chips developing. She tracked the shortage back the supply chain.

The first step was finding the suppliers of parts and materials. There were several raw materials. One of them, Germanium, was in short supply. It appeared that there were hundreds of manufacturers who needed the element. They were all electronics manufacturers. None of them were getting all the Germanium they wanted. There were dozens of factories refining Germanium. They all had shortages of the ores they used as raw materials. She began calling the mines where the ore was mined.

Even before she called, she knew there were three mines that were way behind schedule on their ore deliveries. Two of them had had cave-ins. The third had a bridge collapse that was the only way out of the mine to the shipping terminal.

She asked each if they thought that their problems were truly accidents in mines. The cave-ins were still being cleared but no one could say if the incidents were truly accidental. They all claimed to use the highest standards of mining.

After collecting her research, she sat for a while poring over it. She finally picked up her phone and called her boss. She asked for a meeting. Her request was granted.

We went to her office and entered directly. Her boss, asked what was happening with electronics manufacture.

Speedy answered, "There have been an unusual number of atypical accidents in the mines that supply a primary raw material—Germanium. You can see the statistics here. . ." She displayed a paper with a chart. "On mining accidents and the probability of these mines having accidents. The short story is it's small—very small."

Her boss asked, "So, you think there's another explanation?"

Speedy nodded. "It's wild hosts sabotaging critical industries."

Her boss just said, "Really?"

Speedy nodded again. Her boss sighed a long sigh. "There are some other signs of problems.

"Is there anything that you think you can do to help the situation?"

Speedy shook her head. The way she did it, I knew she was sad.

That night Speedy tried to start a conversation over dinner alone at our home. I was still determined to have my "back" turned to her.

Later when we went to bed, she again said, as she closed her eyes, "Kay-Lee, I love you."

She would get no satisfaction from me.

120

The days went on. The days turned to weeks. The weeks turned into a month, and we went on. Besides wishing me a good night with her love, some days she tried to talk with me.

One day at dinner, she actually carried on a conversation—at least half of one. She said, "I really like your black outfit. I've been wearing it a lot lately. . ." She paused for an answer.

Then she went on, "I think I'll have to replace it soon. It's beginning to show some wear. What do you think? . . ." Another pause.

"Would you like to try another color or do you really, really like black?" Her pause was longer. Then she tried a different tack.

"You know that I've been letting my . . . er . . . our hair grow longer. . . " Pause for comment.

"I think it might be nearly as long as it was before the inser. . ." She gasped and seemed stuck. She finished weakly, "Before we met."

She picked up again. "I'm really thinking of letting it grow until I can't stand how long it is. . . " Another pause.

"That could be quite a long time, because I really do like our hair long."

She seemed to have run out of steam. Later as she was doing the dishes, she said out loud, "I wish you'd talk to me."

My temper had cooled long ago, but there was still a slow simmer deep inside my gut. I wasn't going to give her any satisfaction for a long, long time—if ever.

We were sitting on the couch of our apartment watching TV. The final match of the Women's World Cup of Soccer was going. I'd rarely seen Speedy much excited, but the World Cup was different. We watched all the games that we could. Her boss had even let people take some time off for the knockout round.

It was the American women vs. the English. The game had actually been pretty good. The Americans scored first on something the commentators had called a bicycle kick in the box. I figured out that the box was the big box around the goal mouth. Why they called it a bicycle kick I really didn't get.

Anyway, the game had been pretty even from then on. There were two minutes of stoppage time at the end of the first half. The English scored on

121

a penalty kick in the first minute of stoppage time.

Penalties were really strange as played by the Souls. Everyone seemed to want to claim the fault when there was a foul called. The person who committed the foul was sure that she was guilty. The girl who was fouled was sure that it was inadvertent or not a real foul. On this one there was quite a lengthy argument between the referee and the girl who was fouled. I guess it was because the team that was fouled got to kick a shot with only the goalie to beat. I guess it seemed unfair for the team that was fouled to get such a big advantage.

If it had been a game with humans, the story would have been completely different. In this case, the penalty kick was good and the game was tied.

Half time featured commentary by four former women players—two from the Americans and two from us Brits. The commentary was deadly dull. You would have thought that they were commenting on a chess game.

That thought brought to mind the only time I saw commentary on a chess game. It was more exciting than this boring technical discussion.

The chess game was a tournament game a number of years ago. It was held in Paris. At the time, a fellow worker was a big chess fan. She tried to talk me into going to Paris for the knockout round of that tournament. I was never going to do that.

As a sort of compromise I agreed to go to the final match of the game. She was hot to go to that tournament because there was an up and coming Spanish woman chess player who was one of the favorites to win the tournament. When that player made it to the finals, Marilyn was really pressing to get me to go.

"We can take the Chunnel early. We can go direct to Paris. We'll get there an hour before the final game. It will be great fun!"

It didn't occur to me at the time, but I kind of think that Marilyn might have been gay. She insisted on paying for the trip, but I stood my ground. I just let her pay for the tournament tickets, which were pretty cheap.

Anyway, we arrived about half an hour before the game started. There was a big crowd standing around the table where the players were.

Marilyn cursed under her breath and said, "Shit, I wanted to see the woman play. She's a great player." She paused and added a little softer, "I hear she's a pretty blonde too."

But all was not lost. We went back to a large room with chairs set up in rows. There was a small stage. On it, there was a large chessboard on an easel. There were a couple of commentators. They moved the chess pieces as the moves came in from the game room. They then commented.

One of the two players was a woman who was in her early thirties.

She'd apparently been the protegee of an old French chess master. Her opponent was a sort of prodigy. He was largely self-taught. He was only fifteen years old. One of the commentators compared him to Bobby Fischer—whoever that was. I was glad to hear that he was English. Both commentators were excited about the players—especially the English kid. He'd apparently showed up out of nowhere a couple of years earlier at a chess tournament and been rising like a rocket.

The game had been really exciting from almost the beginning for the commentators and a lot of the crowd. Apparently, the game went an unusual way almost from the beginning. The commentators were talking about unexplored variations. The feeling in the room was electric. After a while, nearly every move brought a gasp or a shout from the crowd.

When the woman resigned there was wild applause in the room. That was an exciting game and exciting commentary although I really didn't understand a lot of it.

Of course, my friend was dejected, and we returned to London on the train that night in silence.

So, I knew what exciting commentary was like—how it could convert a game like chess into a real spectator sport. These soccer gals didn't have it.

Speedy was having popcorn—unbuttered, unsalted, about as boring as possible, of course.

Then something exciting did happen.

The commentators were interrupted by a news bulletin. Speedy sighed.

They switched to a pair of news anchors that I'd seen a number of times on the world news channel.

The woman actually looked dreadful. Her Telly makeup was awful. Maybe she didn't have any on. She was in the middle of the announcement. She was saying, "The explosion has been verified to be nuclear. It apparently happened inside a shuttle carrying about 250,000 Souls up to near Earth orbit where they were to be transferred to an interstellar ship."

At that point Speedy gasped, and my jaw dropped. We stared at the Telly. The newswoman was saying something like this, "We're about to show you video recorded from several different cameras. Anyone who is especially sensitive to suffering is cautioned that these scenes are very graphic."

Then there was a scene of a rocket on a launch pad taking off. The camera followed its ascent for several seconds. Then the screen went white. The next video was from a camera that was farther away. You could see a great deal of the launch facility including other launch pads. The rocket in the center of the picture rose gracefully for the same several seconds, and then there was a flash of white that filled the scene. It was followed by a brilliantly glowing sphere of fire rising. The picture disappeared after about twenty seconds.

Finally, the news woman said, "This last view is from twenty kilometers. Its low quality is due to it having been recorded by a street security camera."

At first, all you could see was a peaceful street scene. Then there was the exhaust of the rocket rising slowly into the skies. The rocket itself was hardly visible. Then a bright light flooded the scene for a second. Then, the fireball became visible. You could just make out a shock wave approaching the camera, knocking some buildings in the distance down. Finally, the shock wave hit the camera. It bounced around and apparently was knocked off its pole.

That was all that I saw. My view was destroyed by Speedy burying our face in our hands. She cried convulsively. Our shoulders shook. She was gasping between sobs.

I'd never seen her cry before. I hardly ever had seen her laugh, but definitely I'd never seen her cry. She wrapped her arms about me. I couldn't help myself. I actually had some control of our arms. I used it to rub her arms and back. I couldn't say anything. I'm not sure that she even realized that it was I who was trying to comfort her.

I eventually thought of something to say. "Tell me about it."

The shock of hearing my voice after such an extended silence seemed to bring her to the point of being able to speak. "Oh, Kay-Lee, this was your people, wasn't it?"

I said the first thing that came to my mind, "I sure hope so."

With that her sobs and crying began again. My mood changed instantly, "Oh, honey. It is going to be all right."

She tried rubbing the tears out of my eyes. "No it won't! You're going to force us to leave the planet, and you'll kill us and you'll laugh over our poor bodies."

I didn't know what to say. I knew people. There would definitely be people who would love to do all those things. Not too long ago, I'd have done them all joyfully.

My heart was rent apart by the sobs that resumed through my body. I still had control of my hands, so I caressed her and just said, "Now, now, now."

That seemed to comfort her a little. Then she realized that I was doing the caressing. That sent her into sobs again, "See! IT'S ALREADY

124

BEGUN!"

All that I could think to suggest was that we go to bed and try to get some sleep. She agreed and took control of our body. She looked at the tooth brush and floss in the bathroom and just muttered, "Oh, shit." We changed into the light pajamas that she liked and went to bed.

The next morning, she dragged us out of bed and didn't even bother to take us for a run. I was the only one to speak when we got up. I almost said, "Good morning" but a quick thought changed that to just "Morning." She was so downcast that I don't even think that she noticed.

At work, she sat at her desk and monitored production and delivery schedules. Nothing was very far off optimal. There were a few schedules that had gotten off the green and into the yellow. She'd ordinarily take a closer look at those if she had time. That day, she had time but didn't do it.

The mood in the lunch room was not so moody. There was a lot of talk about how quickly the security forces would track down the wild hosts and put the terrorism to an end.

She stood up and said, "You don't know what you're talking about. This is the end for us."

Someone asked her, "How do you know that? Do you have a wild host hidden somewhere that you talk to?" It was said in jest, but her throat choked up. The beginnings of tears formed in our eyes. She turned and ran out of the room.

That night we were both quiet, but when we went to bed, I said softly, "Love you."

I was surprised when she said, "Love you, too."

The days went by, and she slowly became less depressed. Nothing further had happened. We began talking again. Our exercise schedule resumed. We spent some time every evening before bed brushing our much longer hair. We went to a department store and "bought" a couple of new outfits—a black one to replace the threadbare original one and a bright red top to go with it.

We began having long talks before we went to bed. She wanted to know about my life before. I said, "You can just look and find out."

That caused her to stop. Finally, she said, "I don't understand how I feel about it. I used to do that all the time with other hosts before this planet. Somehow, I just can't do that now. It seems too much like an invasion of privacy."

I internally shook my head and thought to myself, "Just what do you

125

think you've been doing all this time, sis?" I found that I didn't think it with anger. The cold, slow burn in my gut had gone away.

One day we were sitting on our couch watching an old movie on DVD. It was an old Cary Grant movie, *An Affair to Remember*. By the end we were both sobbing uncontrollably.

That night when we were brushing our hair, something unusual happened. She released her control and let me control the hairbrush. Then, ever so gently, so gently that I at first didn't realize that she was doing it, she began rifling through the edge of my memories. It was like being very gently caressed, like her fingers running through my hair. My heart began beating uncontrollably. I felt myself becoming wet. I dropped the hairbrush and walked to the bed.

The next day, we were ecstatically happy. She could hardly concentrate on her job. We ran that night rather than in the morning. When we got home, we jumped into the shower and from the shower into bed. I think we missed dinner that night.

The next days were like that. Then one night we were sitting on the couch, ostensibly watching the Telly. Then something happened.

There was a blinding flash of light, and about half a minute later, the building shook. I was the first to recover. "Bloody Hell. Did the rebels bomb London?"

We ran to the window. There was still some residual light in the sky. We saw a small fireball rising in the general direction of Heathrow.

She brought our hand to her mouth and said, "Good God. Do we have to evacuate the city?"

The Telly quickly answered that question. We could hear the emergency announcement. It said something like this, "A shuttle was coming in to land at Heathrow Spaceport this evening when the remote pilot lost control of it. It turned upside down and drove into the tarmac at Heathrow. The resulting explosion was NOT, I repeat NOT, nuclear. There is no need for general evacuation of the London area.

"However, people within a one kilometer radius of Heathrow should evacuate overnight until fires and other hazards are cleared from the immediate area.

"There were no passengers on the shuttle, but it's believed that there were probably some people injured on Heathrow grounds and surrounding homes."

The announcement began looping. Speedy turned off the Telly and said, "That's it. We're done here. If the rebels can do that, we're lost."

I said hopefully, "You don't know that. It might have been an accident. They didn't say anything on the telly about rebels."

126

She shook our head, "Our shuttles never do that. It had to be . . . what did you call them . . . rebels?"

I was surprised that I could nod our head. I did.

There were no tears. I supposed that she'd cried the last of her tears when the rebels bombed Orly Spaceport. She looked around the room as though she'd never seen it before or as though she were looking for something. She said absently, "Of course, everything we have is yours."

I actually laughed. Were we a married couple splitting up belongings on the verge of a divorce? Then I sobered when I felt a tear in our eye. I said, "I'm sorry, Speedy. It's shock. After all that we've been through together, I can't believe that you're giving up on us now."

"It's done. Game over. Humans one, Souls nil."

I would have slapped her if she'd let me. "No, it's not over. Surely something can be done!"

She collapsed on the sofa. She let me pat her back. I used our voice to say, "Now, now, now. . ."

Eventually we went to bed.

Amazingly, things were pretty nearly normal at work the next day. No one seemed concerned. The newspaper reported the terms that Humans had given the Souls for surrender.

After a few days, Speedy's supervisor called her into her office. She was blunt, as usual. "The wild hosts are going to revive as many hosts as possible. I don't think there will be a lot, but we've got to start preparing to turn over production and distribution to them.

"I trust you more than anyone else in our group. You'll have the main responsibility for directing the turnover—if you'll do it."

Speedy answered, "Of course. Why do you even ask?"

She said, "You have some sort of relationship with your host, don't you?"

We turned bright red. I didn't think that was possible for Souls. None of them seemed to have a thimbleful of emotions. I had to rethink that. Speedy was different.

She said, "Yes, Kay-Lee and I are friends. What do the hosts call it?" She started to riffle through my memories. I quickly supplied the word, "BFFs". She said, "Oh, yes, BFFs."

Her supervisor said, "Yes, I suspected something like that. It doesn't happen with one in a thousand hosts. Do your best. That may make it harder for you."

Doing her job wasn't hard. As a matter of fact, it was easy. We felt no inhibitions at all. We were ecstatically happy for most of the time we had left. We took every minute we could to be alone together.

She wanted to see everything she could on the planet before she had to leave. She didn't spend a second that she didn't have to with her acquaintances. We made a list. It included the Louvre, cathedrals in Germany, the pyramids of Egypt, and Tokyo. There were others on the list, but we already had more than we could possibly see—even with suborbital shuttles that made it possible to make a trip to San Francisco a day trip.

As Souls began having to leave their hosts, her job became more and more difficult. She had less and less time away from the job. Of course, I was with her the whole time. Her supervisor probably didn't guess what would get in the way of her job the most.

The first item on our bucket list—the Louvre—almost did us in. We walked the halls, and it made her weep. At one point she sobbed. "I'll never be able to bring even a photo of this with me. I'll forget how wonderful it was. I'll forget what haunts Mona Lisa's smile. It will eventually all be lost—like tears in the rain."

I said, "I promise you, I'll never forget you!" Then I cried too. That night we just watched the lights of Paris from our hotel room window.

The next day she was looking in my memory for something from my childhood. Afterwards she said, "I found a day when you and you parents went to Hyde Park for a picnic. You were about fifteen or sixteen. You had your hair tied back with two blue ribbons. It flowed down almost to your knees. You were wearing a dress—black with pink polka dots. You were so cute."

I said, "I remember that day. My mom tied my hair back. I thought at the time that I looked so childish with the ribbons in my hair and the polka-dot dress. I think that was the last day that I wore my hair that way. Afterwards, it was always up in a big bun or just loose or in a pony tail."

That made me sad. In a way, it was the last day that I had anything of childhood left. As I thought of that day, I remembered seeing a strange old man with a beard that reached his waist at least. He was near the lake talking with a young man. It was funny to remember that.

A few months later we were standing in line waiting for what the Souls euphemistically call "extraction." We were both silent until the line had only one person between us and the end. She said, "Oh, Kay-Lee, I'll love you forever."

I nodded for real. "I know. Now stop, or I'll cry when it's our turn."

Of course, I cried anyway.

The last thing Speedy said to me was, "Don't cut your hair. I like to think of you like you were in that picnic in Hyde Park."

I nodded and tried to say "I promise" through the sobs that choked my throat.

Then it was our turn. I knelt down. I felt a cool pressure on the back of my neck. Then there was nothing. They had me stand. They'd put a band-aid on my neck and told me that I could remove it in a couple of hours.

"Can I see the Soul you took out of me?"

The nurse who was doing the extraction said I could. She was holding it in her gloved hand. I asked, "Can I touch it before you put it in the thermos."

She nodded but cautioned me, "We have an agreement with them. You mustn't try to harm it."

Tears came to my eyes for the millionth time. "I never would in life." I touched it ever so gently and bent to it, saying, "I promise."

Magic

She was exhausted by the narration of that story and all the emotions that went along with it.

I suggested that we might want to continue at a different time. She shook her head and said, "NO. I've dug into these memories, and I don't want to finish until I'm really finished. I will take another of that great whiskey."

I signaled to the barmaid. She brought another drink for both of us.

Haley said, "I still wonder about one thing. Speedy insisted on leaving the planet. I couldn't talk her into staying with me. Why didn't she? It broke my heart for her to leave, and I know she was very sad too. She didn't seem to have close friends and certainly no lovers among the Souls."

I decided that this was a good opening for what I wanted to say. "First, you surely must know how much the Souls are all rule-followers."

Haley nodded.

"Then you must know that she would never break a duty to her race. Staying would have broken one of those duties."

Haley took it in but shook her head. "I just don't see it."

Here was the critical point. "It was lucky for the both of you that she did leave."

Haley stared at me and asked truculently, "Why?"

I took a deep breath. "Neither of you would have survived more than a couple of weeks if she hadn't."

Her nostrils flared, and she almost shouted, "How do you know?"

I calmly said, "Here's the deal. It's something that we never wanted anyone to know—not humans, not the Souls, not even most wizards.

"We had an emergency backup plan."

She exclaimed, "What!"

130

"Yes, we wanted something just in case the Souls left a rear-guard that would slowly worm their way back into power."

She shook her head, apparently in confusion. "But you said yourself that they were rule-followers!"

"They are, but we didn't want to take chances. We had a special little spell in our hip pockets. It took a couple of weeks for us to cover the whole globe but we did. Any Soul within range would have been pulled violently toward the wizard. If it were in a mine shaft, it would be crushed on the ceiling of the mine. If it were in the sea, it would be dragged up into the air and collected. If it were in a person, it would be crushed by impact with the host's skull or ripped out of the human."

She seemed crushed. She finally said, "Then it didn't matter that she left, we'd have been separated no matter what?"

"That's right."

She absorbed that and took a long pull on her drink. Then something entered her eyes. Was it hope or something else? "Wait a minute. How do you know all this? Are you just feeding me a line to make me feel better?"

I couldn't help laughing. "Sorry, Haley. You just caught me by surprise. I know because I was the consultant that came up with the idea."

She stared at me first with incredulity and then with the beginnings of hate in her eyes. "How could you do that!"

"There was more than you and me and your Soul at stake. You know about how the Souls did business. They didn't care that the vast majority of their 'hosts' never woke like you did."

I was becoming a little bothered myself. "You know that most hosts normally never woke up even after extraction. You can't imagine how hard we worked so that almost everyone woke up after extraction. They were ready to leave the Earth without lifting a finger to wake the vast majority of hosts."

She chewed on that and took another sip of her drink. "You were actually part of the people who defeated the Souls?"

I nodded.

She looked me up and down and said, "Hard to believe."

I shrugged. "I know. I don't look like much."

She looked harder and said, "No, I don't believe that it was magic."

"But it was. What did you think made the Souls willing to go?"

She shrugged and said, "It was the nuclear bomb and shooting down that shuttle and . . . and . . ."

I smiled. "It's pretty thin isn't it. And I suppose you think that bombing that first shuttle was done by . . ."

"Well, by the US Navy. They had a submarine with nuclear missiles. It was a cruise missile, wasn't it?"

I shook my head. "Even we could shoot down cruise missiles. The Souls are so advanced that they'd laugh at a cruise missile. I was pretty sure that they'd have no problem shooting down ICBM's."

She frowned at me. "Well, then, Mr. Know-It-All what was it?"

"Magic. Wizards can disappear from one spot and appear at another at will. The nuclear weapon did come from the USS Ohio. But it was delivered by a brave French wizard who waited until the shuttle took off to 'disapparate' on-board with the weapon. He set the timer for a few seconds and disapparated off.

"The second shuttle was shot down by . . ."

She seemed much less confident as she suggested, "An interceptor?"

I shook my head. "A wizard wielding a very powerful wand. It was a record long shot."

She considered that. I went on, "But shooting down two shuttles wasn't what convinced the Souls to leave—by itself.

"The real reason was that they couldn't explain anything that was going on. There were more things than the public had any idea were happening. They were mostly fairly small things, but all were inexplicable, and all proved that the Souls were vulnerable. There were a couple of big deal things that I'm a little surprised that the two of you didn't notice.

"We took over the Soul worldwide TV network a couple of times with 'public service announcements'. I suppose you didn't notice them because they were rather late in the process. You and your Soul-mate were probably either working or making out when they happened. I'm sure that all her associates at work noticed. By that time, she was probably not talking with them much."

She gazed at me speculatively. "Were you directly involved in any of them?"

I took a deep breath. "Yes."

"Well, tell me about it."

I clamped my teeth but couldn't prevent a tear from rolling slowly down my cheek.

She insisted, "What? Could it be that bad?"

"Oh, it was an incident early on. It was hardly more than a skirmish. None of our people were killed or even seriously injured."

She urged me on.

I looked into her black-as-night eyes trying to decide how to tell it. I decided to approach it obliquely. I reached into my pocket and pulled out my purse. I held it up and casually opened it. I said, "I'm going to show you a little magic."

132

She let out a breath that I hadn't realized that she was holding. "Well, finally."

I nodded. "Yes, finally." I closed the purse again and handed it to her while saying negligently, "Open it."

She shrugged and made to draw the mouth of the purse open wider. Nothing happened. She squinted at it and put some real muscle into the effort. Nothing happened.

In disgust she said, "This is nothing but a conjurer's trick." She handed it back to me.

I negligently opened it. She grimaced and said, "Let me try that again."

I handed her the purse and she tried all sorts of ways to open it. She even tried pushing the bottom up through the opening. Nothing happened. Finally, she opened *her* purse and retrieved a paper clip. She held it up before her eyes and announced, "The universal tool." She then unbent the first outer loop.

She asked me, "Do you mind if I put a small hole in your purse?"

I shrugged, "Be my guest."

She tried that. The apparently soft fabric surface distorted but the "universal tool" didn't penetrate it. In obvious frustration she said, "I thought you said that you weren't a magician."

I said, "The proper word is wizard, and no, I'm not a wizard. However, it was a wizard who put a spell on that purse."

She said, "OK. You've proved your point. So what?"

I asked for my purse back. She gave it to me. I opened it. I then said, "There's something I want you to see." I reached in, took my Glock by the handle, and pulled it out a bit. Then I handed it to her and asked her to pull it out.

She didn't realize what it was that was protruding from my purse. She closed her fingers about it and drew it out. When she realized what it was she immediately dropped it to the table. She exclaimed, "Is that real?"

"Sure. It's not loaded and the safety is on, but yes, it's real."

She asked, "How is that in your purse?"

I misunderstood her question. "Oh, the magic spell on the purse makes the inside larger than the outside."

She scoffed. "Why didn't you bring out the purse to start with. That pretty much proves magic."

I shook a finger at her. "If I'd have done that, you'd have thought it was just a conjurer's trick to the end. With the preparation of what came before, you were open to reason."

She rolled her eyes. Then she asked in a voice heavy-laden with sarcasm, "So. Why are you carrying a gun around with you?"

I nodded. "Oh, that goes back a long way to when I first went to work at Hogwarts. I was pretty sure that I was in some danger from a group of wizards. I wanted something as protection."

"Did you ever use it to protect yourself?"

I thought a moment on how to answer that question. "Well, the only time that I really used it, that is fired it in a struggle, was during the war with the Souls. I carried that around for more than a decade without ever firing it. The reason that I showed it to you was that the one time that I have used it was during the skirmish I mentioned."

Haley asked, "Did you kill anyone then?"

"Most of the time in war, you never know if you've killed anyone. The heat of that skirmish was no different. I really tried to kill some Souls. Did I? I couldn't say for sure. When it was over, all the Souls but one were dead.

"Then I tried to interrogate that Soul. We had a powerful tool for interrogation. At least we thought it was powerful. It turned out not so much. In the end, I was angry."

A thought suddenly occurred to me. "Did you know that anger usually comes from fear?"

She shook her head no.

"Yes. I was terribly afraid that we would lose that war. Anyway, I decided that we couldn't let the Soul keep its memory of the skirmish and what it revealed about us. I decided to wipe its memory—completely."

That left Haley aghast. "How could you?"

I shrugged again. "Better living through Magic."

That angered her. "Don't be flip. What you did was hideous."

I nodded. "That's why I can't think of it without having second thoughts. That's why I have a hard time talking about it. I sometimes scour my memory to try to decide if there might have been another way."

My anguish must have affected her. She put her hand on my wrist. She didn't say anything but just remained silent for a while.

Then she changed the subject. "I just realized that I told you a very intimate story about myself. You haven't revealed anything near as intimate about yourself."

I chuckled. "The gun wasn't intimate?"

"You know what I mean. And make it a happy story. I'm tired of these gut wrenching memories from our past."

"OK. Let me think a minute." I did. I tried to think of an intimate memory that was purely happy. After several minutes I was still searching my memory. Then an idea occurred to me, "I'm having a hard time with a purely happy memory that's also intimate. How about a funny, intimate story?"

She twisted her head and eyed me suspiciously. "Are we talking funny ha ha or funny ironic?"

I said, "It's not ironic."

Then she said, "The funny thing isn't something to do with weird sex is it?"

I laughed at that. "No. As a matter of fact, strictly speaking, it doesn't have sex in it."

Still suspicious, she asked, "But it's intimate?"

I nodded.

"OK. Go ahead."

□

"Well, this goes back a long way. It was the second year that I was teaching at Hogwarts.

"Hogwarts has always had a Halloween party—on Halloween itself or the closest non-school night. People are invited to wear a costume, but it's not obligatory. More than half don't wear. Of the remaining ones, the vast majority either wear a non-magical costume or one that requires only very minor magic. You know, like the Tin Soldier or the Wicked Witch of the West from The Wizard of Oz. Practically nobody goes as Glinda, the Good Witch.

"Anyway, there's a small minority that use really advanced magic to create a costume. I remember one Halloween a professor spent the whole fall in his costume. But that's a different story entirely.

"There's a potion that changes you physically so that you are the image of someone else. It's pretty hard to make. Usually only professors can brew it, but one year, a first-year student succeeded in brewing it successfully.

"I don't know how it works, but you have to have a sample of hair or finger nail or something like that from the person you're going to imitate for it to work. Her only problem was that she accidentally got a cat hair rather than a human hair. The results were pretty distressing.

Haley jumped in. "I thought this was going to be a funny story."

"Yeh. Sorry, I got side-tracked. It all turned out well for the student.

"Anyway, my date for that party thought it would be fun if I went disguised as the assistant headmistress and that she should go as a guy."

Haley asked, "Isn't that dangerous?"

"Oh, no. It worked out all right. It is sort of disconcerting because the

135

potion actually changes your skin, your height, your hair—pretty much everything on the surface."

All Haley could say was, "Wow! What about your sex?"

"Right. Anyway, she had brought me a suit of clothes that would be appropriately sized for the Headmistress. We chose the Library to change in. It was closed that night, and it seemed like neutral ground for the prank.

"Now, when I started to change, some things happened that I wasn't expecting. For one thing, the assistant Headmistress had pretty long hair. It wasn't as long as yours, but it came down to the middle of her back. She almost always wore it in a tight bun at the back of her head. Another thing about the potion was that it screwed up my hormones. I had breasts that I was very aware of. Did I also have ovaries? I'm pretty sure not."

Haley interrupted. "Let me tell your story for a while."

"OK."

"You hair became that long, and it wasn't in a bun."

I nodded, "As a matter of fact, it was all over the place, disorderly, nothing like her hair."

Haley nodded. "Yes, so she had to help you with it—first to give it a good brush, probably slow and languorous."

I nodded. "She sat me down in front of a mirror that she'd brought and brushed all the tangles out. It was very . . . uh . . . "

"Stimulating. And, of course, you weren't wearing any makeup, so she just had to help you with your makeup."

I nodded.

"Right. She probably painted your face and applied lipstick ever so carefully—face to face."

"Yes, she did."

Haley laughed, "You know that she was trying to seduce you."

"Yeh, I figured that out by the time she started to pin my hair up."

"So, what happened?"

I stopped a minute to recall what had happened. "I decided that my only hope was to go to the party. I didn't stand a chance alone with my date. I just hoped that I could stay at the party until the potion started to wear off."

"How did that work?"

"Not too badly. We did stay to the end of the party, but by the end, I hadn't started to revert. Besides that we danced most of the night. She held me close through most of the dances. I was torn between trying to figure a way to get out without going to bed with . . . uh . . . him and to get him to spend the night with me. Of course, that would have been no problem at all. The other thing was that I was trying to figure a way to keep us in public areas until I did change.

"You know, pronouns keep getting in the way here. I never know how to refer to her and me when we were in disguise."

"Well, we were on our way up to the Library to retrieve our clothes. On the way, I kept wondering what it would be like to be made love to on a library table."

Haley squeezed the wrist that she'd never let go of and asked, "You didn't let him make love to you, did you?"

"Oh, on the way up to the Library I really wanted her to, but by the time we reached the Library I'd begun to change. That was it. The transformation is pretty awful, and you don't think of things like sex or seduction when you're transforming."

Haley seemed to be considering it. Then she asked, "Did she use a love potion on you in addition to whatever it was that transformed you into someone else? It just doesn't seem likely that looking like a woman would make you fall for the first man that came along."

That was an easy question for me. "I'm pretty sure that she didn't. In the first place, nearly all love potions work the same way. You can even buy one at Weasley's Wizard Weezes, a novelty shop.

"They have the same effects. Those include making the victim not so much a lover as an abject and willing slave to the other. They can't even entertain a negative thought about the object of their 'love'.

"Now, I've not seen someone who has taken that kind of a love potion, but I have heard descriptions from an eye witness. There's no way that I could have debated internally how to avoid making love to my date let alone actually carry out the plan if I'd taken that love potion.

"We actually had a student who devised his own love potion that was very different. That love potion seemed to induce a state that was almost indistinguishable from real love.

"I have seen someone who'd taken that love potion. She swore that she'd not taken a love potion. That isn't unusual, but what was unusual was that she gave rational explanations for her love and was actually able to keep herself away from her love voluntarily.

Haley asked, "Could she have given you that love potion?"

"No. That special love potion was only brewed long after the date I was telling you about. I think the original inventor didn't want a willing slave. He actually wanted someone who liked him to truly love him. I don't know whether he was successful or not, but I can tell you that unlike normal love potions that are fast acting and fast disappearing, this one seemed to have no end date."

Haley gasped, "Is the poor girl still in love with her poisoner?"

"No, he was quite willing to brew an antidote. You shouldn't think too badly of him. It was really an accident that she took it and fell in love with him."

Haley shook her head in disbelief, sending her hair shimmering. "How can that be?"

"It's a story for another time. At least, it's not a dark story like that other one." I smiled and then realized that that was not entirely true. So, I amended my statement, "At least, the main story isn't dark."

Haley's eyes widened. "Don't you have anything but dark stories?"

In amazement I declared, "Now, really, you just heard one that was not in the slightest dark."

Haley smirked, "You're right. It was funny and intimate. Wow."

We found ourselves gazing into each others eyes for a while. I don't know how long that "while" was, but I began to realize just what a fascinating woman Haley was.

Her smile shown like the moon and her eyes like the stars. She didn't say anything but somehow I thought that I knew everything that she had in her heart.

She said, "You know that I'm staying in this inn?"

I nodded silently. She stood, and I followed her lead. She started to walk to the exit from the dining room and turned half way back so that she was looking at me over her left shoulder. She'd pulled her hair all over her left shoulder while we were talking. When she walked away, it had shifted over her left shoulder and back as well. She was wearing a short skirt. From the perspective that I was viewing her I couldn't see what she was wearing. She appeared to be wearing nothing except her silky hair.

I was about to round the table to close with her when the bar maid came and cleared her throat. "Uh, sir. Since you seem about to leave, I was thinking that you might want to settle your tab."

I was stunned for a moment and then said, "Of course." I checked my pockets. I didn't have enough muggle cash to pay, so I opened my purse and found a credit card. I handed it to her, and she left.

I don't know what would have happened if that one moment of interruption hadn't occurred. It might have changed the course of my life.

Or something else might have happened to return me to sobriety. For I was inebriated and almost overwhelmed by the deep heart-to-heart talk that we'd had.

□□

I emotionally picked myself up off the floor and took the Tube to King's Cross where I'd agreed to meet Minerva.

When I arrived I found Minerva cross about how long it had taken me to arrive. It was already past dinner hour at Hogwarts. She said, "I suppose we should just go to the Cauldron to eat and debrief."

I didn't even object to disapparation. We arrived and claimed a table in an odd corner. We knew the menu so well that when Tom dropped by we just gave him drink and meal orders at once.

Minerva asked, "What in the world happened to you two?"

I tried to compose an answer that would make sense—both to her and to my senses. What I came up with was, "Well, I started out to explain to Ms. Haley about Magic by telling her a little of my history with Magic. I'd hardly begun when we discovered that my history with Magic intertwined with hers a lot more deeply than either of us realized."

Minerva turned a gimlet eye toward me and asked, "Well?"

"Well, she was a very rare person. During the Soul's occupation of Earth, she was a host to a Soul but was conscious during the vast majority of the time.

"Have you heard of the Stockholm Syndrome?"

Minerva frowned. "It has something to do with terrorism, doesn't it?"

"Yes, in a way. It's when a kidnapped person begins to have sympathy for the kidnapper."

"Well, you'd expect that in Sweden."

"No. No. You find it everywhere. You find it in the States. Have you ever heard of Patty Hearst?"

Minerva considered for a few ticks and asked, "Was she a terrorist?"

"No, she was a kidnap victim who came to completely support her kidnappers and help them in committing further crimes."

Minerva shook her head sadly. "You're not saying that that's what happened with Haley? She seems pretty normal."

I answered, "I don't think she ever committed anything that we would consider crimes, but she became close to her Soul."

Minerva laughed. "This isn't one of your bad puns?"

"No. She was actually mad at me for the part I played in kicking them off the planet."

She kicked me in the shins. That was something that hadn't happened in a long time. "I don't want to hear that you've persuaded our Maid of Honor to quit."

I'd forgotten just how much that hurt. "No. I won't tell you that," I quickly added, "because it's not true. But I do think that I should keep her at more than arms length until after Sally's married."

"That's fine with me. I think there are too many beautiful young women in the wedding party as it is." Then she asked, "Just how mad is she at you anyway?"

I then had to battle out just how much truth to tell. "When we were finished, I'm sure that she had forgiven me for freeing her from her captor. Although, I think the truth is that they were sort of co-dependent near the end. I think Haley's Soul wept at their parting as much as Haley did."

Minerva was surprised, "Did she really weep at their parting?"

I shrugged. "I think so. You know what Shakespeare has Hamlet say. 'I could be bounded in a nutshell and consider myself king of infinite space.' Haley was bounded in her skull unable to control even her body but considered herself queen of the world."

Minerva shuddered.

"Yeh. My sentiments exactly."

We finished our meal and returned to Hogwarts.

The Boys Club of Hogwarts

Back at Hogwarts the news of a wedding between the personal assistant of the Head and an American Auror sparked quite a bit of discussion. A week after we returned from the wedding dress meeting, I received an owl post from the Ministry of Magic Auror Office.

It came, as usual, at breakfast and landed in my cereal bowl. I was trying a healthy diet. I was having Cheerios and skim milk with half a grapefruit. The milk landed on the grapefruit and in my lap. So, I had sour milk in my grapefruit sections and a trip up to my bedroom for clean pants.

When I arrived and had changed, I decided to read the letter. It was from the Head of the Aurors. Apparently, they wanted to discuss some personnel changes. There was no more detail except for the date, time, and location of the meeting. The invitees weren't even mentioned.

As I was puzzling it out, Minerva came in. She asked, "What have you done now to rile up the owls?"

I simply asked, "Now? They've always been riled up over me. The only one that I've had a decent relationship with is yours."

She smiled and said, "Yes, I make it quite clear to her to respect you. What's the note?"

I handed it to her and asked, "What do you make of it?"

She puzzled over it and then said, "Well, to start with, the Head of the Auror Office doesn't make arrests, so I think you are safe from that hazard. . ."

I broke in. "Maybe they're preparing to award me the Order of Merlin, third class. I think that would be appropriate considering all the services I've rendered to wizard-kind over the years."

Minerva frowned. "You forget all the scrapes you've gotten into over the years.

"You have consulted with various groups in and out of government. I think they want your opinion on something. You'll notice that I'm not invited."

"But you wouldn't mind giving me a lift down there?" I said hopefully.

"Of course not. I don't have anything going the day after tomorrow. Sure. I could go shopping at Madame Malkins while you're chatting up the Aurors."

That was an occupation that I didn't mind her having—except that she sometimes got ideas about new clothes for me. I wasn't happy about that thought. However, I dared not suggest that she restrain her impulse to shop for me. There is no better way to set her on that course.

□

In the mean time, I received a delegation consisting of Dursley, Filch, and Professor Slughorn. They insisted that we had to repair to the Three Broomsticks. I knew that they wanted to talk about something over drinks. It was rare for us to go off campus for such meetings, so I was at some pains to get an explanation of the request.

It was Summer holiday, so we could go off campus pretty much any time we wanted. This day, we went during the lunch hour. The Broomsticks is fairly crowded at lunch time. We had to wait a bit, but we got a nice table in a quiet nook of the inn.

The barmaid took drink orders and asked if we were going to lunch there. There was an enthusiastic "yes" from the other three, which I joined. She provided us with menus and left to get our drinks. I asked, "OK. You've got me alone in a secluded spot. What is it you've got in mind?"

Filch immediately answered, "We're not all here yet. Let's wait for the fifth."

That was surprising to me, but I agreed to wait and just order. The bar maid returned with our drinks. I was surprised to see that there were five glasses. One was the largest mug I'd ever seen. With that, I began to get a hint as to who the fifth would be.

Before I could amaze everyone with my deduction, the fifth arrived. Hagrid walked up to the table and said, "Good, you've got my drink order already."

Slughorn shrugged. "Of course. You told us what you wanted already. Glad to help out."

I stood and extended my hand to Haggrid after he sat. That ensured that I could look at him eye to eye. He took my hand and shook it

142

vigorously. "Glad to see yer, Professor."

I smiled genially and said, "Same back at you, Professor." He had never gotten entirely used to being called Professor. He colored a bit and said, "Aw, yer don't have to be so official-like."

The bar maid had started taking our food orders. Apparently, everyone had their usual order already in mind—except me. I soon found myself pondering over the choice between Shepperd's pie and a chicken salad sandwich. I chose Shepperd's pie.

I opened the discussion. "As I was saying, now that you have me alone, go ahead and do your worst."

Filch gave it a shot, "Well, you see, Mr. Dursley and I were talking about . . . well . . . how we never get together on a reglar-like way. . . and . . . Mr. Dursley, why don't you explain?"

Dursley looked down at the floor and said, "Well, Professor Slughorn and I were talking one day while we were trying a new potion that had occurred to me. He mentioned that we haven't had any projects with you since I . . . well . . . you know, got into trouble with Ms. Pamela. And. . . Oh, why don't you explain it Professor?"

Slughorn looked around at us all and said, "You know that we really had a good time together that time after we got past the little misunderstanding about who owned the . . . uh . . . textbook in question. So, uh . . . You explained it the best when we were talking, Hagrid. Why don't you go ahead?"

I turned to Hagrid. He was my last hope to learn what no one seemed willing or able to explain. Hagrid cleared his throat. That sounded a little like a fog horn in the distance. Then he said, "We all want to get together and form a Boy's Club. We would go out once a week and have lunch and just . . . Oh, you know, shoot the bull."

I nodded knowingly. "I think that's a great idea. Why didn't you just say that?"

Dudley said, "Well, you know. It sort of sounds like something that a bunch of girls would do. Only they'd call it something like the Old Girls' Club or maybe the BFF Club or the Red Hat Society or something even more disgusting."

I had to laugh. "I think that the girls shouldn't get to have all the fun. We'll do guy things, like maybe go to a Quidditch Match or have a bachelor party for Phil."

Hagrid interrupted, "What's this BFF thing anyway? I hate acrobats."

Dudley said, "It's abbreviations. And BFF stands for Best Friends Forever or Best Female Friends."

Hagrid said, "Oh. That is disgusting. Of course, we're all friends, and we've been together forever, and I think you all are my best friends, but BFF? It's just so bad."

Everyone else nodded sagely.

The rest of the inaugural meeting of our lunch group, which was the way I liked to think of it, we talked about old times together. The first real act of the club was deciding to have a bachelor party for Phil. Then came the hard part, deciding who would organize it.

Slughorn asked, "Who has done one of these before?"

Dursley said, "Are you kidding?! My parents say I'm too young to get married. I don't know anyone who's gotten married—excepting yourself, Professor Wendt. And no one did a bachelor party for you."

I responded, "Yes. And why didn't anyone think of that?"

There were lots of people staring at the floor looking for a loose shoelace, I supposed. So, I let that drop, but I turned to Filch, "You've been around a long time. Even if you've never organized a bachelor party, surely you've attended a few, haven't you?"

He looked around the room looking for someone on whom to fix his gaze other than me, but failing, he looked at me and said, "You know, I never had any really close buddies—until I met Professor Dumbledore and Young Dursley here and yourself, of course. So, . . . uh . . . I guess I've never been to a bachelor party."

I looked to Hagrid. He simply gazed back and said, "Nope."

That left Slughorn. I turned my gaze to him. He shook his head.

I exclaimed, "How is it possible that with all your contacts and influential friends, you've never been to a bachelor party?!"

He had a kind of hang-dog look. He said, "I guess that when I was winning all those influential friends, I wasn't exactly winning real friends. I can get free Quidditch tickets and my letter printed in that filthy rag, *The Prophet* but never a simple invite to a friends' bachelor party."

I looked around at them and said, "I wouldn't have believed it, but I'm the only one here who's been to a bachelor party."

Dursley asked, "What happens at bachelor parties?"

"Well, the only one that I've ever been to was one held in honor of a cousin's wedding. I had heard about parties where they got the groom drunk and dumped somewhere buck naked." With the word "drunk", Filch's eyes lit up.

"That wasn't the kind of party that I attended. The organizers were tea-totalers. What we did was to take him out to the nicest restaurant in town, which was the Ponderosa. Then we kidnapped him, tied him up, blind-folded him, and took him to a remote cave where we dumped him."

Filch asked, "And nobody got drunk? What kind of a party was that?"

144

I shrugged. "I wasn't organizing the party. I just went along for the ride."

Filch said, "Well, being as you're the only one with experience, as it were, you should do the planning."

I shook my head in amazement—amazement that I'd let myself be talked into this project. "OK. What do we want to do at this party?"

Everyone made a suggestion. Slughorn said, "I like the idea of having dinner at a good restaurant. I know a French restaurant or two in France that are reasonably-priced, and we can get to easily."

Dursley said, "I like the idea of a practical joke at the end—like stunning him, taking his wand, and dumping him somewhere in Wales to find his way home."

Filch said, "I hear that they have a pretty girl jump out of a cake at bachelor parties. What would be really good would be having a Veela jump out of a cake!"

I started to object to the idea but Filch interrupted me. "Oh, come on Professor, you know a Veela or two."

I asked, "What are you talking about? I have never seen a Veela at closer range that a couple of hundred yards."

Filch drew himself up. "Professor, you do too. Bill Weasley's wife is a Veela. Seeing as how you're such good friends with the Weasleys, you should have no trouble getting Mrs. Weasley to jump out of a cake. We could invite him to the party too."

I shook my head in bewilderment. "How in the world did you get the idea that Mrs. Weasley is a Veela?"

Filch sort of shrugged and said, "Well, I hear tell that she has Veela blood in her anyway. Her Great Aunt on her father's side was a Veela or something like that."

"I don't know about that, but I can't imagine that Bill Weasley would let her jump out of a cake. If he ever heard you suggested that, I think he might stuff you into a cake."

Filch was still grumbling, "Well that Fleur was pretty enough to be a Veela. I tell you she had a lot of boys who couldn't take their eyes off her."

I turned to Hagrid. "Any ideas?"

Hagrid sort of drawled out his answer, "Well, professor, maybe we could invite him to be a member of our club."

Filch perked up again, and I had to admit that it wasn't a bad idea. That idea was a keeper.

After the meeting broke up, I found myself interrogated by Minerva about what half of the male contingent of teachers at Hogwarts had wanted with me.

"Well, they just wanted to get together weekly to try to figure out what you and your female friends do when you go out to lunch."

She guffawed at that. "Isn't it obvious? We talk about you men."

"I thought as much. Don't forget that you need to drop me off at the Ministry tomorrow morning."

She shook her head. "They still haven't told you what it's all about?"

"Nope."

"I suppose that you've been sworn to secrecy by the Head of the Aurors."

"No. He's just not told me anything."

"Well, maybe I could worm it out of you in some way. " With that, she wriggled a strap of her bra off her shoulder and said, "Oh! Oh! I seem to be partially in dishabille. Could someone help me?"

Of course, I helped her become even more in dishabille. But ultimately, you can't get blood out of a turnip or information out of a black hole despite what Stephen Hawking says.

The next morning, she insisted on my getting up at the same hour as she did. We had an unconscionably early breakfast in the Great Hall. We actually arrived before the house elves laid out the breakfast. Then we left for the Ministry by floo from the fireplace there in the Great Hall.

□
□□

We stopped at the reception desk to receive a visitor's badge. The receptionist commented that it had been a while since I'd last been there.

"Sure. I always seem to get in trouble when I visit here. Why should I come more often than I have to?"

Minerva hustled me up to the Auror's Office. On the way, we decided to meet at the Cauldron for lunch. I asked how I should get there.

She said, "Oh, there'll be someone who can take you there at lunch time. If nothing else, look up Mr. Weasley. Even Percy would do."

I got another visitor's badge at the Auror's Office. It had the ubiquitous Auror shield symbol on it. This time they also took a photo of me. It magically appeared on my badge.

I commented to the receptionist, "You guys are entering the 20th century I see."

The receptionist asked a surprised, "What?"

Minerva just leaned toward her and said, "Don't pay any attention. He likes to irritate me. You're just collateral damage."

The receptionist was expecting me if not my irrelevancies. She led me to a Conference Room that I'd been in before. She asked, "Would you like something to drink. The others should be along in a few minutes. We have pumpkin juice, water, tea, and the Minister of Magic just discovered something called "Coca-Cola". We have cans of that as well."

I nodded and said, "I think I'll just go with water with a little ice."

She motioned me to sit and filled a glass for me. Then she was about to leave the room. I interrupted her with a question, "Who else is attending this meeting?"

She smiled a mischievous smile and said, "I'm afraid I can't tell you."

"Can't or won't?"

The mischievous smile flashed briefly again, and she said, "Yes."

A few minutes after the hour, a man who appeared to be in his fifties with a neatly trimmed mustache and thinning hair entered the room. I got up and extended a hand.

He walked briskly over and shook it vigorously. "You must be Professor Wendt. I'm the head of the Auror Department, Jack Slate."

I nodded and said, "Yes, I am—Wendt, James Wendt.. Just who else is attending?"

"They'll be along shortly."

I guessed that they really didn't want me to know until I absolutely had to. I didn't have to wait long before I discovered. An Auror entered the room whom I did know. It was Ginny Weasley.

I stood, and we shook hands. "What was the big secret? I know you. Anyone else coming?"

Ginny said no. Slate said yes. I said, "Hmmm. This IS a secret meeting."

We all sat around one end of the conference table that easily would seat ten. I decided that just because it was a secret meeting, it didn't have to be unfriendly. I asked Ginny, "How's Harry?"

She perked up. "Oh, haven't you heard? He's been out of the country for a long time and hasn't returned yet."

"No, I hadn't. Hmmm. You know Sally Harker." Of course she did, but I wasn't sure how relations were between them. They had seemed to hit it off badly during the war of the Souls. I wanted to get the temperature of their relationship before talking about her.

Ginny said, "Sure. She's that pushy muggle, right?"

147

I nodded and decided to soft pedal things. But Ginny continued, "You know, it isn't often that I find other women who can be as mule-headed as I am sometimes. I like her."

I reversed course and said, "Then you'll be happy to know that she's getting married later this year herself."

Ginny smiled. "So, she's found someone who can tame the shrew? Good."

"I don't know what happens when their alone, but I know that he's as brave, strong, and smart as she is."

"Well, good for her!"

Just then I heard the door open and rose, turning as I did. I nearly fell over my chair. It was the Minister of Magic herself.

I blurted out, "Well what brings the wick . . . "

Pamela waited until I regained my equilibrium and hugged me. Ginny rubbed her hands together. Slate examined a spot on the ceiling. She sat down next to me. As she did, she finished my sentence for me, "Wicked Witch of the West? I have a close interest in what goes on in this meeting."

I looked from one to the other in the room. "OK. Would someone fill me in on what that interest is?"

Slate cleared his throat. "The thing is that it's . . . uh . . . sort of unprecedented. Maybe Ms. . . . " He never got to finish the sentence because Ginny spoke up.

"It's not all that complicated. The American Auror . . . uh . . . what do they call it. It's not Ministry."

Pamela supplied the word. "I think they call it a Bureau."

Ginny went on. "Thanks. Yes, the American Auror Bureau wants to exchange liaison Aurors. We've never done that before with any national Auror Ministry."

Pamela's knee bumped mine, which was an effective way to attract my attention. She said, "We know that you've worked with them a good bit the last couple of years. We thought you might have some back channel insight for us." Here she rested her hand on my arm momentarily as she said that.

This was not what I expected. I sat back on my heels and not just because of the knee action. I entered deep thought. I temporized with a couple of questions. "What have they told you about why they want to have a permanent liaison with you, and have they told you who their candidate is?"

Slate said, "Well, apparently, besides the war with the Souls, there was another dust-up that happened very recently. Part of the action happened here in England, although we had no idea it was going on. They say that they think that these sorts of things are happening frequently enough that we need to keep in constant contact.

"As to whom they want to send, his name is . . ." He was prevented from completing the sentence by the interference of Ginny, who said, "Phil Pearson."

Slate asked, "How did you know that? This was very hush-hush."

Ginny just looked inscrutable and asked, "Why did you invite me if not to provide key information?"

Slate just grimaced and went on, "Wendt, you don't happen to know anything about him do you? And do you know what this recent incident is all about?"

It was my turn to grimace. "Well, let me start with the incident. Yes, as a matter of fact, I do know something about it."

Ginny clucked her tongue and said, "Mr. Wendt to the rescue—again."

Slate looked at her quizzically, "What in the world do you mean, Ms. Weasley?"

"Oh, just that he always seems to be in the know about any topic that anyone comes up with. It does get boring after a while."

Pamela gazed over into my eyes and said, "Yes! Isn't it wonderful how that works!"

I gritted my teeth and prepared to talk about the recent incident. "OK. First, I have to say that I'm only going to give you a high level overview that doesn't break confidentiality requirements. You should have no problem getting details by going to the muggle English government and requesting the reports." I knew that what I was about to say would no doubt bring some sarcasm from Ginny, but I went ahead anyway. "There were several reports written. One was from the US National Science Foundation. One was from the Federal Bureau of Investigation. One was sponsored by the American Auror Bureau." I sort of lowered my voice and tried muffling it, "And one was written by me on behalf of British Witches who participated."

Ginny didn't miss the reference. She almost crowed, "Professor Wendt to the rescue again."

Pamela said, "Oh, Ms. Weasley, just restrain your enthusiasm."

I went on. "You are lucky to have a talented witch like Ms. Weasley."

Ginny looked at me with some amount of surprise and seemed to have something to say on her lips but didn't say anything.

I went on. "In any case, I can tell you the gist of my report. If you want details, request *A Report on the Appearance of Superluminal Flying Objects*. Don't expect details from me here, just the basic facts.

"There were four American soldiers who were assigned to Iraq. They sustained war-related injuries. They recovered extremely rapidly and individually walked out of the hospital without permission. They seem to have communicated in some way that nobody understands because they each seemed to have assignments. After they completed their assignments, they got together and built a . . . uh . . ." I had reached the sticking point. Did I name what they built or leave it to them to go get the reports and find out on their own?

Everyone was leaning in—even Ginny. Slate asked the obvious question. "What did they build?"

I took a big breath and answered, "A spaceship."

There was amazed silence for a full minute.

Pamela was the first to recover. She asked, "How could they possibly do that? What did they do with it?"

"The answer to the first question is easy. Nobody knows how they did it."

Slate was offended by the answer, "How could you not have at least gotten the plans from them!"

"Well, we didn't exactly 'get the plans from them'. They left them behind."

Ginny finally joined the conversation with her no nonsense attitude. "Let me get this straight. You have the plans?"

"Oh, yes."

"But you don't know how they built the spaceship?"

I looked around at them. "Well, that's not exactly true."

A smile broke over her face. "Well, now we're getting somewhere. So you could build another spaceship?"

In exasperation I said, "It sure seems like it, doesn't it. But I'm not so sure."

The exasperation transferred to her. "What do you mean, you're not so sure?"

"Well, for one thing, I don't know if anyone has tried. The second point is that we maybe could build it, but we don't have an operating manual. Even if we succeeded in building a copy, I'm pretty sure that we couldn't get it to take off. It might blow up or do nothing or maybe even do something we can't even imagine."

That set everyone back on their heels for a few minutes. Finally, Slate said, "The only other spaceships that weren't built by governments were those of the Souls. Are you sure that these people weren't hosts to Souls?"

I laughed. That didn't go over well with anyone. "OK. Sorry. It's just that I know a lot of facts about them that you don't know. No. They definitely weren't hosts to Souls."

150

Ginny said, "OK. I guess I can see why the American Aurors were worried enough about this to want to set up a permanent liaison. We've had two space-faring groups on Earth within a few years. Who knows what's next?"

I volunteered, "That's exactly the conclusion that one member of our team made at the end of the report."

Pamela admitted that was probably why the Americans were so anxious to have a permanent liaison. She went on, "Should we go along with the idea?"

We all looked at each other. Ginny asked, "Do we really have a choice?"

Slate seemed to take that as a given. He went on to his other question, "What do you know about this Pearson?"

Ginny started an answer to his question, "Don't you remember that he came over at the beginning of the war with the Souls? He was the one who kicked us off on that war."

Slate seemed to be taken aback by his failure of memory. "Is that the same Pearson?"

I interjected, "There is another?"

He didn't get the joke. He said, "There must be dozens in England alone."

I apologized. "Sorry. It was just a bad joke on my part."

He came back with a serious question, "Do you know anything more about him?"

Ginny just rolled her eyes.

I said, "Well, he was part of the team for that most recent incident."

Ginny threw up her hands and said, "What did I tell you?"

Slate ignored her and asked, "Has that most recent incident got a code name that we can use?"

I shrugged. "Sure. We ended up calling it the Legacy."

Pamela rested her right hand on my left thigh and asked innocently as she gazed up into my eyes, "Really? Why the Legacy?"

I twisted in an attempt to relieve myself of her hand—to no avail. I said, "Well, the root cause of the Legacy incident seems to have been an ancient race that died off more than ten billion years ago. It was their last legacy to intelligent races of the present."

I went back to the main question. "He is smart. He's published in some forensic magic journals.

"He's brave. He took some real risks in the war of the Souls trying to rescue an American military base that was eventually destroyed by the Souls.

"He's hard-working and thorough. He's got good judgment. I can't think of any prominent faults that he has."

Slate asked the air, "Why would his supervisor be willing to give him up?"

I said, "Well, I don't know that but I think I can tell you why he would be anxious to take the post."

With that Ginny took some sheets of parchment that she had been making notes on and threw them over her head in mute protest.

I went on, "He's getting married this year to a young woman who lives here in England, and who really likes her job. I think he's working a way for them to stay here AND keep his job."

Ginny stared at me and exclaimed, "It's Sally Harker, that muggle, isn't it? She's the one he's going to marry."

I could only nod.

Pamela asked smugly, "She used to work for you, didn't she?" With that she gave my thigh a squeeze.

I pulled my chair back, seemingly to look at her more directly, but actually to disengage that hand on my thigh. "Well, sometimes I wondered if it weren't I working for her."

Pamela smiled coyly and wondered, "What would it be like to have you under me—in the org chart?"

I said determinedly, "I don't think it would be comfortable for either."

She replied, "Oh, I can be a very accommodating employer."

As a last gasp, I said, "I'm already in love with my employer."

This conversation caused Ginny to smirk. Then she said, "Oh, I don't think that you could woo him from his current employment."

Slate seemed to be particularly dense or he just didn't want to go anywhere near this conversation. He took the lull as an opportunity to express the opinion that we'd achieved the goal of the meeting.

Pamela said, "For the moment. There may be more to come."

I said to myself, "God, I hope not."

We adjourned the meeting, and I hurriedly rose from my chair and made for the Conference Room door. Ginny was right behind me. After we were both out in the hall, she said, "Wendt, come down to my office for a cup of tea, will you?"

I nodded, and she rapidly strode down the hall and entered a door labeled Emergency Exit—No Re-entry. When we were both in the stairwell, I asked, "Are we going to exit the building?"

She sniggered, "No, the sign does not mean what it says. This is the quick way to get from one floor to another."

We exited on the next floor down. She led me to an impressive door to

152

an office that had a nameplate, Ms. Genevra Weasley, C. I. A.

I exclaimed, "CIA?"

She stared at me a second and said, "Sure, Chief Inspector, Auror."

I commented, "Well, to an American that means something very different. I see you've had a promotion or two since we first met."

She nodded. "The invasion of the Souls provided several of us opportunities to stand out. Come on in."

She held the door for me. Inside there was a nice desk that looked like mahogany and a small table that would seat four or up to six in a pinch. There were four chairs around it and a nice guest chair in red leather facing her desk. On a credenza there was a tea pot that began whistling shortly after we entered the room. She asked, "Like a cup'o?"

"Sure."

She conjured a couple of cups. The teapot flew over to our cups and filled them with steaming water. There was a small wooden box with a couple of varieties of tea bag. I selected one and put it in my cup to steep.

We each took a sip. Then she looked me straight in the eye with a no-nonsense gaze. "You'd better think about how you handle Madame Minister. She wasn't entirely kidding about working under her. Technically, you know, you are already."

I nodded, "Yeh. That had occurred to me after I made my comment. She, as the ex officio chairman of the Board of Directors of Hogwarts, is technically Minerva's boss, and therefore, she's my boss's boss."

Ginny raised her cup to her lips and looked over the rim at me reflectively. "You know that she has been under a lot of pressure the last couple of years--the war with the Souls, the restoration of order after their defeat, mending fences with the muggle governments has taken its toll. I think she's just beginning to get her sea legs back. This flirtation with you is the last vestige of her recovery. When she's fully back—and that won't be long—she'll either drop you or come after you like a Seeker after the Snitch."

I growled, "Just what do you think she might do?"

"Well, if I were she. . . "

She leaned back reflectively. I thought, "Thank goodness she is not Ginny, or Ginny is not she or whatever."

"Well, I guess there are two attack surfaces. She could do a frontal attack. That would be to give Minerva a choice—give you up voluntarily and keep her job as Headmistress or lose her job. She might even threaten to take over running the school herself so that you literally . . . or . . . maybe it's figuratively would be under her."

I shook my head in disbelief, "Do you really believe she might do that?"

"Don't forget the lengths that Fudge pursued to get rid of Dumbledore and my darling Harry. The only thing that he was after was power. She is a woman scorned." She hesitated as though trying to remember something. Then she went on, "What was it that Shakespeare said about a woman scorned?"

I grunted, "Something about Hell having no fury as . . . and so on."

A sly smile crossed her lips as she went on. "But I don't think that you have to worry about that."

I answered, "Thank goodness. It would kill Minerva to have to give up Hogwarts."

She chuckled. "Are you so sure that it would be Hogwarts that she'd give up?" After a heart-stopping moment she said, "Just kidding."

It's rather hard to tell with Ginny when she's kidding and when not. I asked her, "Why do you think that she wouldn't go that route?"

"Oh, several reasons. Little miss Minister wouldn't want anyone to think that she'd had to blackmail you out of Minerva's arms. It might cause a scandal that would get her removed from office. But the most important reason. . ." Here she hesitated for effect. "Is that she would like to outsmart Minerva."

I sniffed. "I see. Same scenario only the direct victim would be me. She blackmails me. The threat is that she'll fire Minerva if I don't leave her."

Ginny shook her head decidedly. "No. No. The blackmail would be that if you don't become her lover secretly, she'll fire Minerva."

I mumbled mostly to myself, "Well, Stanley, here's another fine mess you've gotten us into."

Ginny has pretty acute hearing. She asked, "Who's this Stanley?"

I chuckled. "Oh, it's just an old saying from a movie, a comedy, featuring a couple of blunderers who are always in trouble.

"Have you got any ideas about how to discourage the Minister?"

She just shook her head.

I asked, "What if I just am an awful lover?"

She stared at me and said, "That doesn't even deserve an answer."

I took a sip of my tea and discovered that it had cooled. Ginny noticed and pointed her wand at the cup and said, "*Caliente.*" It was immediately steaming.

I absent-mindedly thanked her.

She shook her head and said, "I guess you're just screwed."

That just struck me as terribly funny. I actually almost lost my breath and couldn't answer Ginny's slightly worried glance. When I did recover my breath, I told her, "Oh, it's just such a perfect summing up of the situation that I couldn't help laughing."

Then I had an idea. "Ginny, how would you handle the situation if you were in my place?"

She leaned back and seemed to be relishing thinking about the situation. What she finally answered was delivered with a perfectly serious deadpan expression. "I guess I'd just curse her. You know, something that would put her in St. Mongo's for a month or so. It'd be hard to trace back to me. With George to help me, I'm sure I could come up with something."

I had to admit that was not a bad thought. "Would you hire yourself out for that assignment if it came to that?"

She smiled a wicked smile. "I might just do it for free."

She then changed the subject completely. "Oh, by the way, how did you make out with that MMOH?"

My mouth must have dropped. Ginny repeated, "Oh, you know, muggle Maid of Honor. How did you make out with her? Did she have a cow when you told her about Magic?"

I thought about how to answer her. I decided on short and sweet. "Oh, she took it pretty well. She'd been through quite a lot in the war with the Souls. It might be better to ask how she made out with me. I was kind of shocked by the story she had to tell. I suppose there are a lot like it, we just don't hear about them because we don't know a whole lot of muggles."

She sort of ended the discussion by saying to me, "Well, good luck with the MOM. If you get in over your head, give me a shout. Maybe we can work something out."

I asked her, "What is it anyway with women and acronyms or as Filch would say, acrobats."

A puzzled look crossed her face. "Why, it's obvious. They're just shortcuts that everyone understands."

I stared at her and said, "Or don't you mean that they're a way to exclude those who don't understand?"

She hummed and said reflectively, "Might be."

I thanked her and started to leave. Ginny called me back. "Would you like a lift to the Cauldron?"

I decided I'd take her up on her offer.

We walked down the emergency exit stairs to the Atrium floor and to the floo's. I asked her about the ID badges that I had.

She said, "I'll take them back."

She held out her hand to me. I took it. We entered a floo, and Ginny cursed, "Damn. I forgot to get some floo powder." She dragged me back to the entrance. She said, "Be a dear and grab some powder."

155

I asked, "Will that work?"

She smiled. "We'll never know if we don't try."

So, I took a handful, and she dragged me back into the floo. I threw it down on command.

She spoke our destination, but nothing happened. She shrugged and said, "Be a dear again and get another handful."

"Are we going to keep doing this until it works?"

She laughed, "No, silly. Just hand it to me."

I did, she spoke the destination as she threw in down, and we came out of the floo in the Cauldron.

I commented, "I don't know how you witches stand that every day."

She was still holding my hand. She laughed and said, "Oh, you can get used to anything given enough time."

I nodded. She didn't move right away. Eventually she released my hand and walked back into the floo, forgetting powder again. She slapped her head and said, "I don't know what's come over me. I never forget this. She laughed nervously and went back into the floo. This time she really did disappear.

Tom came by and asked if I wanted a table for lunch. I think he really was just reminding me to give him *pourboire* for the use of the floo. He looked a little surprised when I told him that Minerva and I would like a table. He showed me to a table and took my drink order.

Within ten or fifteen minutes Minerva did show up and we had lunch. She wanted to know what the deal was with the Aurors. I gave her a 50,000 foot view, excluding only the overly affectionate behavior of the Minister of Magic.

Halloween or Christmas?

Back at Hogwarts, the school year started uneventfully. There was the usual sorting of first years into Houses. There were no beginning of year warnings about anything unusual in the announcements. Of course, there was still the warning about the Forbidden Forest.

My classes were now well laid out. I'd been through all levels at least twice by this time. I occasionally changed the reading list. That occasioned changes to lesson plans. And, of course, there were always minor changes depending on how quickly we got through the material. I would have killed for a laptop and office software to make those changes easier and faster.

Then one day in the second week, as I was leaving breakfast in the Great Hall, Sally came up to me and grabbed my arm, "Not so fast, cowboy. I need to talk to you a minute."

I shrugged. "Sure. What's up?"

"We're having a wedding planning meeting on the weekend. I'd like you to come."

I scratched my chin and considered the possibilities. "Why would you need me? Goodness knows that both you and Phil are serious adults."

She hemmed and hawed, looked at the floor, and said, "It's not either of us. The Maid of Honor has to be there, of course. We'd like to have the meeting here. It would be more convenient for nearly everyone. It's just that the MOH is still a little nervous about wizards and witches and would be more comfortable if another muggle were there."

I rolled my eyes and said, "Oh, come on. She's an adult, too."

Sally pulled rank on me. "Now, I don't want to have to take this up with Minerva."

"Oh, I suppose so. What time is the meeting?"

Sally punched me in the shoulder and laughed. "I knew you'd be a good sport. We're meeting Saturday for dinner in the Great Hall, and then we'll go to the Teacher's Lounge for the meeting."

"Let's just make it short and sweet." I hesitated, afraid to ask the next question. "Just what is the agenda?"

Sally smiled radiantly as she said, "Oh, it's all fun. Choosing deadlines for the invitations to go out, wedding shower, the rehearsal, and of course, the wedding itself. We have to pick a spot for the rehearsal dinner, too."

I gaped at her. "Do you mean to tell me that you don't know when the wedding is going to be?!"

"Yeh, I think I mentioned that."

I thought to myself, "This could go on all night and until dawn." I said, "That might be something that you could kind of narrow in on before the meeting."

Sally, still radiant, said, "Oh, we've got two main dates that we're choosing between."

"Would you care to share them?"

She shook her head. "I don't want to prejudice you." She then went off, almost skipping.

□

That Saturday I was in my office grading some papers when a knock on the door interrupted my train of thought.

"Come."

The door opened, I looked up, and I discovered Sally. I glanced at my watch and asked, "It's only 3 PM. It can't be time for dinner already?"

She nodded vigorously and said, "It's just one little favor I have to ask."

I had a bad feeling about it, but I said, "OK. Shoot."

She looked down at her feet and said, "Would you mind picking up Haley?"

My jaw dropped. "Why don't you? And how in the world can I pick up Haley?"

She answered the first, "I've got to set up the Teacher's Lounge for the party. Also, you wouldn't have to pick her up alone. Ginny has volunteered to give you a hand."

"Is she coming here to pick me up?"

Sally glanced down quickly and then said, "Well, as a matter of fact, she ought to be arriving any time now."

158

She had hardly said that when there was a swoosh in the fireplace of my office, and Ginny walked out in a cloud of soot. She coughed once and asked, "Am I too early?" as she used the scourgio spell to sweep the dust from her clothes.

Sally shook her head and said, "No. Just about right."

Ginny said, "Great. Come on." She extended her hand to me.

I said, "Don't forget the floo powder."

She shook her head. "Are you never going to let me forget that little incident?"

"I don't know. Are you ever going to stop taking me places by floo?"

She shook her head. "Minerva always said that you are prejudiced against magical travel."

I reluctantly held out my hand as I rose from my desk. "Where are we going?"

"A wizard bar in Soho and then to Paddington Station."

I had reached her by then. She took my hand, and we entered the fireplace. She didn't forget to take some floo powder. We stepped out into a bar that was undeniably a magical bar. Besides wizards, there were several goblins, a half-giant like Haggrid, and what must have been a Veela. I couldn't get much of a view of her because she was surrounded by a crowd. I did get the occasional glimpse of her shimmering platinum hair.

Ginny snapped her fingers in front of my face and said, "Come on. We've got to have a drink and get out of here."

I reluctantly turned my head and commented, "I can't believe the establishment allows Veela in here. It must cut down on their trade."

We sat at the bar. Ginny ordered a half-pint of ale. I had a shot of whiskey. It was better than Filch's but not by much. I asked Ginny, "Why come here rather than the Cauldron?"

"Oh, I get bored with the Cauldron. This place has a more interesting clientele."

She hadn't drunk much of her ale, and I'd only had a sip of my whiskey when she took my hand and looked me in the eye, "Don't you think it's time?"

I assumed that she meant to leave, but she wasn't standing. I said, "Yes, I suppose so. I couldn't understand why we had to start off so early from Hogwarts."

She smiled. "I suppose you're right. We could finish our drinks without rushing."

We sat and drank. Then she turned to me again and said, "What do you think Haley sees in you?"

I had a swallow in my mouth that ended up sprayed across the bar.

159

Luckily, the bartender wasn't in the line of fire.

I asked, "What do you mean?"

She said slyly, "I talked to her when we arranged timing for this. She was really insistent on your being the muggle to accompany her."

I gulped, "Well, it's sort of bad luck."

"How could that be? I mean besides its being bad luck if Minerva ever found out—for you."

"Well, I was telling her about magic. She had a hard time believing me, so I told her about how the war with the Souls was actually won."

"I don't get it."

"I'm not done telling you. I had hardly got started explaining how only magic allowed us to win, when she broke down."

Ginny stared at me in disbelief. I said, "Have you ever heard of PTSD?"

She shook her head.

"Well, you may not have heard of it, but you've seen it from the war with Riddle. I think Neville's parents had an extreme case of it. It happens after people have been in an extremely traumatic experience. Frequently, they never escape the effects. Years—even decades—later they can relive the experience and suffer just as if it had just happened."

Ginny thought about that a minute. Then she asked, "But I never met a muggle who seemed to have that."

I nodded. "You're right. The vast majority of muggles were possessed by Souls and never were conscious during that possession. For them possession was like being under anesthesia."

Ginny asked, "Like what?"

I rolled my eyes. I was never going to get anywhere at this rate. But I soldiered on. "OK. Sometimes muggle doctors have to do something that would ordinarily be very painful for the patient. There is a standard way of getting around that—anesthesia." I could see that Ginny wanted to ask another question, but I refused to let her. I hurried on, "Anesthesia renders the person unconscious. As a matter of fact, they are so far gone that they have no sense of time passing whatever. That's what being possessed by Souls was like for the vast majority of muggles.

"But a couple of people out of every thousand were actually awake part of the time that they were possessed. For those people, the experience was very traumatic.

"I've not tried to follow those people to see if they all have PTSD, but I'd bet a knut against a lot of donuts that almost all of them do."

Ginny said, "OK. So she had this PTSD thingee and broke down when you started to tell her about how we beat the Souls. I get that. But how does that make you so desirable?"

I took another pull on the whiskey which didn't taste quite so bad. Ginny called for refills for us. I went on, "After she broke down, she talked about her experiences. This might not have been the first time she'd done that, but I just bet that she'd never told anyone the full story before."

Ginny nodded, "So, you were the sympathetic ear that listened. I suppose you didn't blame her for any of her problems."

"Of course not."

She had rested her hand on my arm. "I can see how that would be very attractive in a man." We sat there for a while silently. Then she repeated, "Very attractive."

I said, "We've got to go don't we?"

She seemed to come to. "Right." She rose and had already taken my hand.

I interrupted her, "I've still got to pay for our drinks." I opened my purse and found only a bunch of one galleon coins and a couple of twenties. I put one of the twenties down and said to myself, "Well, if I ever come back here, I'll have a rep as a great tipper."

She let my hand go but immediately retook it when I'd finished fiddling with my purse.

I asked, "I suppose we're disapparating to Paddington?"

She seemed to be distracted. She said, "Oh. Oh. You're right. I'll do it as soon as we leave the bar."

I laughed. "I hope you weren't expecting me to do that."

She laughed nervously and said, "No, no. Never. I guess I was sort of expecting . . . Oh, well."

Then my stomach turned inside out, and we ended in the women's loo in Paddington. I didn't realize that immediately, but I didn't waste time leaving the loo as soon as I did. When Ginny had gotten out, I asked her, "Where are we supposed to meet Haley?"

With an absolutely straight face, she said, "Track 9 and ¾."

"You didn't tell her that."

"I did."

"What did she say?"

"Right."

I doubted that, but we headed for Track 9, figuring we'd find her somewhere around there. As we approached Track 9, it became apparent where she was. She'd dragged a bench between the two tracks about three fourths of the way to Track 10. As we approached her, she rose and came toward us.

When we were separated by about a meter or so, she closed the

161

distance quickly and threw her arms around me. The hug brought her face next to the side of my head opposite Ginny. She whispered, "I love you", into my ear. It was impossible for me not to hear, but very unlikely anyone else would—even Ginny with her excellent hearing.

Ginny said, "I see we're all really chummy. Let's go to the ladies' loo."

Haley objected. "I don't have to use it."

Ginny smiled, "We all have to use it. It's the best place nearby to disapparate from. I'll go in and stay until the coast is clear. Then I'll signal the two of you to come in."

That pleased Haley. She said, "Oh. Good idea. We'll be waiting out here."

Ginny went in, and Haley sidled closer and placed a hand on my arm. She asked, "Oh, what have you been doing? I wondered if I'd ever see you again."

I didn't have a good answer, so I said, "Oh, the beginning of the year is always very busy."

She nodded wisely and seemed to take that as gospel. I guess it was pretty much true, but that wasn't why I hadn't seen her again.

By this time, somebody had just come out of the ladies' loo. Ginny poked her head out and signaled us to come in. We did. When we got in, Ginny said, "Quick! Into a stall—all of us." We picked a handicap stall because it was larger. Even so, it was pretty crowded.

Haley instinctively took my hand. Ginny took hers and then took mine. Haley immediately objected. "Why do you have to take HIS hand?"

Ginny smiled a wicked smile and said, "The one on the end of the chain is in the most danger."

Haley's mouth opened in a large "O". Then she said, "Yes, yes. Do it."

Ginny took my hand and squeezed it visibly. Then, without warning, she sent us into hyperspace or wherever it is you go when you disapparate. It was so unexpected that even I was taken by surprise. We came out in the open. I was close to vomiting, and I'd disapparated any number of times without heaving. I don't know how Haley held it in. Her face was as green as one of Minerva's dresses. She actually looked like she was a going to be very sick, but somehow it didn't happen.

As a matter of fact, a moment later, she made light of it, "I see what you mean James about magical means of motion."

Ginny looked at her and said, "James, is it?" Then she turned toward me and said, "Well, Jimmie, would you lead us to the castle?"

I could tell that she was angry, so I decided to keep an eye on her through the rest of the night. We were about half-way between

Hoggsmeade and Hogwarts. I led the way down the trail towards Hogwarts. On the way, I did a little travelogue, pointing out the Forbidden Forest, the trail back to Hoggsmeade, the largest magical community in England, and of course, the loch, which was just coming into view.

Ginny just glared at me. I was glad that I was getting the attention away from Haley, but I didn't quite get why Ginny was so mad.

We rounded a corner as we worked our way up the high hill where Hogwarts was built, and had a rather nice prospect. We could see the lake, the castle, the Forest, and Haggrid's house. The view stopped me dead in my tracks.

Haley misunderstood my stopping. She said, "It's a wonderful view. I'll wager that many a couple has stopped here for the view."

"Is that why you stopped? Did you once bring a young lady here?" She was smiling in some sort of triumph—as though she had deduced a deep secret of my heart.

What stopped me was that I had realized that the spot where we stood was where, on a very dark night, I had gone to my knees to steady my hand that was holding the Glock—the same one that was still in my purse. I'd been trying to get off a clean shot at Snape. The tableau was burned into my memory—Haggrid's home aflame, Fang whining maddeningly, Snape and Potter in a one-sided duel. It wasn't until this very moment that I realized that that had been the last time that I'd seen Snape in life. A tear tried to form in my eye, and I couldn't reply to the question that Haley was asking.

"Ah, I see that I must be right. You and some lady friend were enjoying a sunset here or maybe a moonrise? How romantic with the castle above and the lake below!"

I choked down my tear and managed to say. "It's romantic in the original sense of the word. It's a dark story that should not be told in the daylight of a happy day."

She put her hand on my arm and said, "I know about that kind of story."

I looked up at her and wanted to do something—maybe it was to slap her, maybe it was to shout an obscenity at her. I did neither.

Ginny snapped off, "How is it that I've never heard that dark story?"

My anger transferred to her. She realized it. She backed down and said, "Sorry."

We walked the rest of the way up the hill to the castle in silence. We went directly to the Great Hall. I immediately regretted not telling Haley about the ceiling. It was too late. She glanced up and gasped, "Is there no ceiling on this room!"

Ginny was quicker than I. She immediately answered, "Oh, it's just a little bit of magic. It's transparent."

It was not quite time for dinner. There were a few students who were drifting in. Ginny's mood had changed somewhat, perhaps by being in a place that had had so much happiness for her. She implored us, "Come! Let's sit with Gryffindor."

Haley looked the question at me. I answered, "Hogwarts is a residential school. Students are sorted into dormitories called 'houses' when they first arrive here. There are four."

Ginny jumped in. "There's Gryffindor, the best of the lot. We all sit at this row of tables. Next to us is Ravenclaw next the wall. On the other side is Slytherin and next the far wall is Hufflepuff."

She'd chosen a seat at the end nearest the main entrance to the Great Hall. I sat opposite her, and Haley sat next to me and skooched next to me as closely as she could. While she was doing that, she asked, "What's the basis for sorting kids into 'houses'?"

Ginny said, "Oh, it's based on their characteristics. There's a magic hat that sits on their heads and decides what house gets each kid."

I added, "The Gryffindors are known for courage. The Ravenclaws for smarts. The Slytherin, for . . . uh . . ."

Ginny supplied the word for me, "For being stinkers."

I nodded and went on, "The Huffelpuffs are known for devotion to duty."

Ginny said, "In Gryffindor, we say that the Ravenclaws are thinkers, the Slytherin are stinkers, the Hufflepuff are doers, and the Gryffindors are darers."

Then she asked Haley, "Which house would you be?"

Haley asked, "Tell me which you two were."

Ginny said, "I was a Gryffindor as you should already know. Wendt never went to Hogwarts."

I said, "Oh, there's no question. If I had attended here, I'd have been a Ravenclaw, although I did spend almost a year in the Gryffindor dorm."

Haley beamed. "Then there's no question. I'd be a Ravenclaw."

Ginny seemed to be firing up a reply when a couple of sixth and seventh year students approached our table. They greeted Ginny with a hug and started asking her question such as "What brings you here today?"

Haley looked a question at me. I said, "Oh, those are Gryffindor girls. I think they must have been here with Ginny when they were first or second year students."

Haley looked a little downcast. "They're all so pretty. Do you have them in classes?"

"Oh, I've had all of them in a class or two over the years. Only the blonde is in my upper literature class this term."

She looked at me hard. "Don't you think she's too, too gorgeous?"

I shrugged. 'No. Officially, I can't offer an opinion—to anyone."

Haley's knee touched mine. I grimaced and wished the meal would get started. Actually it was hardly a moment later when Minerva showed up and brought the growing crowd to silence. She reminded everyone that it was the custom at the evening meal to take a moment of silence in thanks for the blessing of our lives and for those who had died to make that life worth living.

When we turned our attention back to our table, we discovered that the house elves had transported tureens of soup, baskets of breads and rolls, and bowls of salad onto the tables. Haley gaped at the sudden appearance of the food. I explained, "The kitchens are below the Great Hall. There are servants there—house elves—who know food and its preparation like no one else does."

She got the idea. "And they magically transported it onto our tables."

I saw Ginny preparing a retort. I tried to give her a telepathic signal by expression on my face to can it. Miraculously, she did.

Haley thought the soup was marvelous and the bread heavenly. She had some salad and declared that she was full. Ginny rolled her eyes and said, "You shouldn't fill up on bread and salad. We still have the main courses, not to mention desert."

Her eyes seemed to bulge from her head. "You're kidding! Just to be able to have meals here is a slice of heaven." Then she added, "And that doesn't take into account the company that you have." With that she bumped her knee into mine again.

Ginny said, "Yeh. You probably could eat up the company."

Haley giggled.

□□

The meal did end. Haley did get at least a taste of one of the main courses —chicken cordon bleu. She also had a little desert.

Ginny reminded us that we were here a-purpose. We needed to go up to the Teacher's Lounge to join our co-conspirators to decide on a date for the wedding and other things.

As we ascended the long staircases Haley asked, "How is it that you don't have elevators here? Wizards have elevators, don't they?"

Ginny almost sneered, "Of course, we do." However she didn't expand on that.

I said, "My theory is that Hogwarts doesn't have elevators because

165

they aren't needed. The youth that attend Hogwarts are able-bodied. The elder teachers can get around with the help of magic."

Ginny asked me, "Where does that leave you?"

I said, "I guess one day I'll not be able to make it to my classroom and that will be the end of my career."

Haley looked at me as though I were serious. "I'm sure someone would gladly volunteer to help you!"

Ginny rolled her eyes again, but she didn't say what she must have been thinking, "I wonder who would volunteer?"

We entered the Teacher's Lounge and found that Sally was putting finishing touches on decorations that included pink cupid-shaped doilies at places. There were heart-shaped name tags at each place. Sally commented, "You see where you are to sit by your name tag."

I sighed. I wondered if I would be made fun of if I refused to wear my name tag. I picked it up and found that there was a piece of spell-o-tape on the back. It was not a big surprise that Haley was seated next to me.

Ginny took the initiative to change the name tag on the other side of me and exchanged it with the one at her place. She promptly sat. I knew that it would take a dragon to drag her onto another seat.

Minerva was not part of the wedding party, so she wasn't present. The rest of the wedding party was except that the parents of the bride and groom weren't. Phil's were in the States and couldn't get away. Sally's had declared that she was an adult and could plan on her own. I was there as the escort of the Maid of Honor, of course.

There were all the bridesmaids—Haley, Sinistra, Luna Lovegood, and a Ministry witch whom Sally had to communicate with a great deal, a Laura Lambert. The groomsmen were mostly not there because they were from the States. but a delegate had been sent for the meeting, Matt Beery. He wasn't the best man, but apparently everyone trusted him to represent them fairly.

Sally took her seat and noticed Ginny next to me. "There seems to be a mistake here. I thought that Luna was next to you, Professor Wendt."

Ginny answered for me, "I just sat where my name tag was. She pointed at it above her left breast."

Sally just shrugged. "OK. There is a full agenda, but the most important thing and the only one that absolutely has to be completed today is settling on a date.

"Phil and I have discussed this at some length and there are two dates that are acceptable to both of us—Halloween weekend and Christmas. The floor is open for discussion."

Aurora leaped into the fray immediately. "I suggest Halloween. The two of you must be anxious to have the deed done. The sooner the better."

Luna, looking at no one in particular, seemed to say to the ceiling, "Doesn't Aurora like to play practical jokes on Professor Wendt on Halloween?"

Haley whispered in my ear, "That Aurora woman has designs on you."

I whispered back, "Came to nothing. We're both married now."

Aurora snapped back, "Everyone plays practical jokes on Halloween."

Luna said lackadaisically, "I don't."

The Ministry witch said, "Halloween is awfully close, it will be hard to get the invitations out and the reception planned and the band booked and so many other details settled by then."

Phil said, "Sal and I have been looking into those already. We've got a band identified for each event. We can book either if we move first thing on Monday."

Sally added, "This meeting is good for getting ideas for the reception and making assignments."

Luna said, "I don't think there's anything so dreamy as a wedding at Christmas."

Matt said, "It would be easier for the groomsmen to get off around Christmas."

Ginny poked me in the side and said, "Mr. Saves-the-Day, why don't you tell us the ideal time?"

I was beginning to remember how awful planning my own wedding had been. I said, "I suppose that the only reason we're having this discussion is that each of you two want a different date."

Nobody said anything—a sure sign that I'd hit the nail on the head. I went on, "Why don't you just tell us which date each of you wants. Then we can choose up sides—bride or groom."

I don't think anyone really liked my suggestion, but in the end everyone agreed that it was probably the best way. It turned out that Phil was in favor of Halloween, and Sally preferred Christmas. Then each gave their arguments. Phil's boiled down to just wanting to be married as soon as possible.

Sally was in a way more romantic—in Haley's sense of romantic. She said, "Don't think that I'm not anxious to be married, but I want it to be a special ceremony—not rushed. I've seen a Christmas wedding at Hogwarts."

At that moment, I knew the wedding she was talking about. It was Minerva's and mine. It was a beautiful time of year at Hogwarts. The castle is decorated. There's a giant fir tree in the Great Hall. The ghosts wear Dickens era costumes. How they manage that, I don't know. There's snow everywhere. It makes the whole area look like a winter wonderland (whatever that is).

Sally was going on. "The snow makes even the ugly parts of Hogwarts and Hogsmeade special.

"There's a long holiday—perfect for a honeymoon. The kids, most of whom just think weddings are a nuisance, are gone. We probably would invite a few of the older ones who would appreciate it to stay."

She had me sold. But then, my marriage had happened at Christmas at Hogwarts.

After she'd finished, we went around the room polling the wedding party. Matt, speaking for all the groomsmen voted for Halloween. The bridesmaids were split. Haley was enthusiastically in favor of Christmas. Even Aurora was in favor of Christmas. That surprised me. But amazingly, Luna was in favor of Halloween.

Ginny insisted that she deserved a vote. Her argument was that she'd already contributed considerably to the wedding by putting up with Haley and me. She said, "No offense intended, Haley."

Haley exhibited her angelic smile and said, "None taken." I thought, "Why don't you apologize to me?"

Since the vote seemed safe or maybe irremediable to everyone, no one really objected. Ginny voted for Christmas. Then she surprised us all. "Wendt deserve a vote too."

Then there were objections. The partisans on both sides saw a danger or help for their position. Among others, I voiced my objections, "Look, my vote can only confirm the majority or cause a deadlock. I can't do anything useful."

Ginny disagreed. "No. You can do some good. And besides that, you have had to put up with Haley even more than I have. You deserve a vote."

I whispered to her, "Here's another fine mess you've gotten us into."

Haley was waiting for some sort of comment from me. What I came up with was, "I've been helping out for the sake of Sally. She deserves it."

Haley sighed deeply. Apparently, I could do no wrong in her eyes. I decided that I had to vote my true conscience rather than make things easier for everyone, so I voted for Christmas. "Well, now we're in a fine mess. Anyone have any good ideas?"

Amazing, someone did. Phil stood and said definitely. "I've decided that I have to vote for Christmas. Wendt is right. Sally does deserve to have the wedding she wants most."

There was another deep sigh from Haley.

The rest of the evening went downhill from there. The next topic was the color theme of the wedding. There was a lengthy debate about the virtues of organdy versus rose petal blush and passion red and fire engine red (that was my suggestion). We took a break after an hour or so of that for biology and food. The guys grouped together. Matt suggested that we'd done all the damage that we could. We should adjourn to the nearest pub and let the ladies wrangle over colors and whatever else they thought was important. He was close to swaying Phil.

I interrupted. "Look. I'm a veteran of these things. Phil, you will be in so much trouble if you bail out at this point that you'll regret it until your first wedding anniversary."

He admitted the justice of the point. Matt was still in favor of him and my leaving post haste. My response was that we would be the worst sort of cowards if we left Phil in his hour of need. He needed us for moral support and to put a damper on the worst excesses of feminine enthusiasm. Matt gave in. We all returned to the conference.

At one point in the evening, I felt something brush my arm. I thought it might be an insect until I looked over to Haley and saw that she was doing something with her long silky hair. She was pulling it into a sort of ponytail over her head. Then I realized that she was winding it into a sort of bun on top of her head. I was transfixed by the way that her hair which had hung below her hips was now constrained in a small twist on top of her head. It had all happened in a few second's time.

She noticed that I was watching the operation. Her angelic smile changed into one of a different nature that seemed to say, "You could watch that in a more intimate setting if you wanted to."

The depths to which this conference proceeded is not fit for general male consumption. Suffice it to say that we stuck it out to the hideous end. At the end, we had to endure a debate over what lucky niece would be the flower girl.

Even worse was the debate over what unlucky nephew would be the ring-bearer. I had the irreverent image at that moment of the poor fellow standing at the crack of doom with Smeagol bearing down on him.

That caused me to actually laugh. The ladies wanted to know what was so funny in such a serious decision. I looked around from face to face trying to decide whether I should be honest. When I saw the serious look on Haley's face, I knew that discretion was definitely the better part of valor. I simply relied on Sir Thomas Moore's dictum—whatever may be done by smiling, you may count on me to do. I smiled a smile that I hoped conveyed embarrassment and a little good humor. That carried the day.

It was after midnight when we finally finished. Matt implored me to join him and Phil in finding a pub somewhere in disapparation range to which we could retreat. Reluctantly, I had to say, "I'm committed to taking the MOH home—with Ginny."

That was generally regarded as an inadequate answer—even after I revealed what MOH stood for. Ginny seemed to be on the side of the guys but she was stuck too.

The three of us—Ginny, Haley, and I—walked out the main entrance and down the hill to our disapparation point. Haley was sure that she needed some support on the hill even after Ginny lit her wand so brightly that the path was lit like daytime. So, she held my arm as we worked our way down the hill.

At the point that we'd stopped before, she pulled my arm and said, "The evening's so beautiful. Let's stop for a few minutes to admire the view." Then she sighed deeply.

It was very pretty. The moon was a crescent, setting near the lake. The castle was dimly visible behind us. Even Haggrid's house was invested with charm by the thin moonlight.

Haley commented, "I wish we could just stay here forever." She accompanied that with a squeeze on my arm, which she was still holding.

I was pretty sure that "we" didn't include Ginny.

Ginny came close and placed a hand on my shoulder. After a moment, she said, "Are we in astronomy class? We've got to get going."

I was pretty sure that Ginny didn't much care if the "we" included Haley or not.

Haley sighed and said, "Oh, I suppose we have to." She grasped my arm even more firmly as though afraid that Ginny would pull even that from her.

We reached the spot that we'd disapparated to earlier. Ginny said to no one in particular, "Back to Paddington?"

Haley put real pressure on my arm. "No! Please take me to my home." Then she quickly added in a very clear voice the address of her apartment. Then she quickly added, "My cell is . . .." She had a small piece of paper that she stuffed into one of my jean's pockets. I was pretty sure what was written on it.

Then we all took hands, and we arrived at Haley's apartment building not much the worse for wear. She started to invite us (me?) up for coffee, but Ginny made it clear that she would not be available to take me back to Hogwarts except at that very moment. That gave me an opportunity to walk out gracefully.

Haley unlocked the outer door of the building. Ginny and I walked away. She asked me, "So, again, what does she see in you?"

I looked at her in amazement. "I've not the slightest. If you can't tell me, then no one can."

"All I've got to say is that you're both lucky that Minerva wasn't invited. Haley is an idiot. If she fancies you, I could tell her how to go about it, and it sure wasn't her way."

"Well, it's lucky that you don't fancy me then."

We'd reached an alley and walked in. She reached her hand out. I took it, and we landed someplace that I didn't recognize. I was feeling sick as a dog. She kept my hand and said, "Are you all right?"

I managed to croak, "Sure." I looked up into her eyes and saw the image of compassion.

She said, "I missed my destination. Let's try again, and I'm sure it will go better."

"Well if it doesn't, you won't have to worry because I'll be dead." She laughed. We disapparated again. It did go better. She squeezed my hand that she was still holding and said, "Good bye."

Then I looked around and found myself at the edge of Hogwarts grounds at the main gate. Now, why couldn't we have done that the first time?

The Halloween Wedding

The next couple of weeks were uneventful for me. What the happy couple was doing, I had no idea and frankly didn't want an idea. That extended to Haley, Ginny, Aurora, and everyone else.

About two weeks before Halloween, there was a knock on the door of my office. I glanced at the calendar and realized that it was time for Aurora to come up with one of her crazy schemes for Halloween.

I decided to pretend that I wasn't home. I sat very still and made not the slightest sound. Then I heard a voice that I was pretty sure was Aurora's say, "OK, Wendt, I'm coming in ready or not. I hope you're decent."

I heard her use the *allo amora* spell. It was totally unnecessary. I never lock my door except when I'm using my office as my apartment. That hasn't happened in a long time. Before it was finished, I said, "Just come on in. I don't keep it locked."

She walked directly to my desk, took my old red leather chair, and said, "I suppose you know why I'm here."

"Sure. Only a dolt wouldn't know. You're here to make a dolt of me at the Halloween party."

She shook her head and tsked her tongue. "Now, you know better than that. All of my ideas are quite intelligent."

I laughed, "Being intelligent hasn't kept them from getting me in trouble."

Aurora leaned forward and said, "This will be great! Even you will agree."

I silently considered my options. I could ask her to leave, but I'd not hear the end of it. If I listened to this harebrained scheme, I could at least point out its problems. She'd be back with "fixes", but I could keep the

172

discussions going until Halloween was past.

She waited patiently as I thought. Perhaps she was thinking about the same things. I decided to let her present her proposal. "Go ahead. What have you got?"

She clapped her hands together—not a good sign. "Well, it's really simple. It's an obvious extension of the meeting about Sally's wedding."

"Uh-oh," I thought.

She was going on. "Well, why couldn't we let Phil have his Halloween wedding?"

I dropped my head to my desk and started pounding it against the mahogany surface.

Aurora shook her head sending her long black hair cascading around her shoulders. "No. No. It's not that bad. I don't mean have a real wedding. I mean just that we disguise ourselves as Sally and Phil. We'd dress in wedding dress and tux. That's all. It would be fun!"

Yes, to a mad-woman it would be fun. I didn't dignify that assertion with an answer.

Aurora leaned back and said, "Just tell me what's wrong with that idea."

An inspiration hit me. "Well, that does sound all right. . . "

Aurora shook her head up and down triumphantly and said, "Just what I told you."

Then I went on. "I don't see why you and your hubby don't do it. If it's such a good idea, why do you need me?"

That stopped her for a moment. Then she said, "Well, Nicky has this silly principle about not attending the Halloween party."

"And why do you suppose that is?"

"Well, he says something about the example you set of getting into trouble every time you attend."

I smiled. "Well, there you have it. We don't call him the boy genius for nothing. My reason in a nutshell."

She sat back and considered that. She thought a while and then said, "Well, if I could get him to attend, would you re-consider?"

I thought. "Re-consider is the only thing I will promise."

She leaped up and retreated to the door rapidly. I wondered if the quick response was to prevent me from re-considering my re-consideration. But it was too late. She had already left my office.

For the next few days I felt pretty good about my escape. But then I began to realize that she might just get Brahms to come to the party. Then what would I do? Just coming wouldn't commit him to follow Aurora's stupid scheme. I decided that I needed a fall-back position just in case.

□

So, that night as Minerva and I were in her apartment behind her office, doing a little canoodling, I mentioned that Halloween was getting close.

She struggled upright despite my best efforts to keep her in my arms. When she was up, she said, "It's that Aurora, isn't it? What crazy scheme is she peddling this time?"

"It is pretty batty. She wants to disguise herself as Sally in a wedding dress and me as Phil in a tuxedo."

She looked at me warily. "You did turn her down cold, didn't you?"

I raised my hand in a Boy Scout pledge, "On my honor, yes."

She was no less wary. "But . . ."

"Well, I thought it might be good to have a fall-back position, you know, just in case."

Her visage was even more wary. "Just in case?"

"Well, you know, she's pretty wily."

Minerva rolled her eyes. "Yes. Wily. Ok. I suppose I ought to at least know what your fall-back is."

I had her intrigued. So, I boiled the fall-back to a single sentence to start negotiations, "If one couple is good, wouldn't two be better?"

□□

There was a student in my office consulting with me. I call it consulting rather than tutoring or having detention or receiving a makeup assignment because it was actually a consultation.

She was a second year. She looked younger. I thought she'd found the wrong classroom when she'd shown up for my third year literature class. But it turned out that I'd been wrong. She was in the right class and for the right reason.

Her muggle private school had identified her as a gifted student. Their assessment had pegged her as good for my third year class. Minerva had seen the assessment but hadn't shared it with me—yet. She was a very bright young lady. Her name was Cecelia Watson Brewster.

When she'd come in, I again thought that she'd found the wrong office. She was one of my best students in third year. Her papers were models of simple direct exposition. She had the declarative sentence mastered. She could see meaning in some of the readings that we did that sixth years routinely missed.

But, as usual with her, I was wrong when I asked her, "Aren't you in

174

the wrong office?"

"No, Professor Wendt."

She was short for her age, which led people to underestimate her. I was constantly struggling to avoid that. "Well, then, what can I do for you?"

She was as straight-forward in her speech as she was in her prose. "I'd like you to start up the wizard chess club that you used to run."

I gasped in surprise. "What! How do you know about that?" I thought that no one missed that club. Surely no one she was friends with was around when it was going.

She smiled at her own cleverness, "Oh, my Dad is a big Quidditch fan."

If she thought that was an explanation, she greatly overestimated my intelligence. "And . . ."

"You must realize that you have a reputation for . . . "

"Knowing everything?"

She nodded.

"Well, let's just pretend that I don't know everything."

She gave me a cute smile. I supposed it was the preface for making it embarrassingly clear why I should have known. She began, "Well, do you remember the 1995 Quidditch World Cup?"

"Sure, I attended the final game." Then a bell began to ring in my head.

She charged along. "My dad followed the Tri-Wizard Tournament avidly."

I chimed in on the "Tri-Wizard Tournament". I continued, "So, he read all the coverage about the players, including Cedric."

She rushed in. "Including Cedric's other interests—Quidditch and Chess!"

She was right. I might have worked it out on my own given enough time. I asked her the obvious next question, "Why do you want the chess club re-upped?"

She was really intense as she said, "I really, really like chess."

It was a good reason. "Are you good at it?"

Her face turned crimson, and she examined the floor as if she'd just dropped her lunch money. I supplied the gap in the conversation. "I see that you think you're pretty good."

She just nodded.

"OK. Then let's play a game."

I reached into the drawer above my Dewar's drawer and rummaged a little until I found the travel set that I always took along when Cedric and I went to tournaments. I rarely used it, but I always had it—just in case. It consisted of a soft fabric board and a small set of wooden carved players. The "board" had drawstrings woven through the edge of the board that could be drawn tight and tied. It would then contain the pieces. They were large enough that they weren't inconvenient to hold and move. It was very nice.

I opened it up enough to retrieve two pawns—one of each color. I moved my hands behind my back and exchanged the pieces from hand to hand enough that I lost track of where white was. I then displayed my closed fists to Cecily and said, "Pick one."

She didn't hesitate taking my left hand. I opened it to reveal the white and at the same time opened my other hand revealing the black.

I tossed the rest of the set to Cecily. She caught it deftly. I said, "Set up the board, please."

While she did that, I went to my bookshelf and found a book. I picked it up and opened the book to a random page. The previous owner had covered it with a nice plastic slip cover that was not transparent. I had to take a deep breath to hold back a tear. I stayed at the bookshelf until I thought I was safe.

Cecily had been getting impatient. She cleared her throat.

I nodded and walked back to my desk. When I arrived, I discovered she had moved. I opened the book to the index and found "Nimzo-Indian." I turned to the page indicated and glanced at my first move. I made it.

The game was what I would call leisurely. Cecily considered her moves for a moment or two and made them. I looked up the response in the Nimzo-Indian and made it. I made my moves a little faster than she did. We went down one of the standard lines for about eight or ten moves. Then she diverged.

I knew it would happen eventually. My intent was to keep playing on my own until the end was obvious. So, the game pace changed. I slowed down, and Cecily sped up. We went on for about half a dozen moves or so, and then she forced an exchange of her knight for one of my pawns. I thought for quite a while after that move.

Eventually, I decided that since I didn't have the slightest understanding of how that move could be useful to Cecily, I lay my king down.

Cecily's reaction was immediate and violent. She almost screamed, "You can't do that!"

I quite reasonably said, "I think I just did."

"No, NO, NO! That's not fair. The game was just getting interesting."

"Look, Ms. Brewster. I have real work to do. I'm in over my depth in this game, and I just don't have time to be entertaining."

She apparently realized that she'd overstepped the bounds with her outburst. She calmed down and said, "I'm sorry, Professor. I know that wasn't called for. I've just not had any real competition for a long time until now. Won't you please finish the game with me?"

I sighed. "All right, I just don't have time now."

She got up to go and headed for the door. But she stopped half way there. She turned and asked, "What was the book you were reading?"

I stared at her. "Have you ever heard of the *MCO*?"

"The what?"

I laughed, "Sorry. When I was mentoring Cedric, everyone we met knew the *MCO*, that is, *Modern Chess Openings*. It's probably the most popular book among serious chess players."

As she started to turn again, I had an idea. "Wait a minute, Ms. Brewster. Even if I don't re-start the chess club, I can still help you. Come here a second."

She came back to the desk and sat in the old red leather chair. I handed her the book. "Here. A present from me."

Her eyes bugged out. She opened it to a random page. As she thumbed through a few pages, she gasped, "It's full of your notes. You can't give this to me."

"Sure I can. In the first place, they aren't my notes. They're Cedric's. I gave him this book as a present. Now, I'm giving it to you."

She flipped to the first page and read the inscriptions aloud, "Cedric, Best wishes for your career wherever it goes. J. Wendt." And then she read, "James, we know that Cedric would want you to have this to remember him. Thanks for everything you did for him, Reina Diggery." She stood looking at it and then said, "Are you really sure that you want to give this up?"

"Sure. I've got lots of Cedric's handwriting. Come over here." I went to the bookshelf and pulled a loose leaf notebook off a shelf. I opened it to a page that I'd looked at a lot myself. I said, "Here is a sample."

She glanced at it and then looked closer. "This is an essay on *Huckleberry Finn*."

"Yes, have you read it?"

As she scanned down the page of closely-written parchment, she said, "Yes. I borrowed it from the school library of my muggle school.

"My parents were careful about what I read. They wanted to know what it was about.

"I told them it was about a couple of teenagers who ran away from home in Oxford, built a raft, and floated down the Thames. Along the way, they picked up a runaway house elf."

I asked, "And they believed you?"

"Oh, my dad started reading it. He quickly picked up on the fact that it was the Mississippi not the Thames, and it was a black slave not a house elf. He actually read the whole book. At the end, I think he had a different attitude toward house elves.

"We never had a house elf, but we knew a couple of well-to-do families who did have a house elf. My mum was always uncomfortable when we visited them after that."

She handed the binder back to me and picked up the *MCO* that she'd placed on my desk. She looked at the inscriptions again and asked me if I would write an inscription for her.

I agreed and wrote an inscription. She read the inscription aloud, "For Cecily, In all the things you do, you may win or you may lose, but you can always act with dignity. Best wishes, J. Wendt"

She thanked me.

Just then there was a knock at the door. The door opened immediately and Aurora entered. I went to my desk and scooped up the chess board, catching the pieces in it. The few that were off the board, I quickly retrieved and stuffed in the bag.

Aurora apologized for interrupting. I said, "We were just finishing."

Cecily said, "Don't think you can get out of it. I'll be back to finish. I've memorized the position we were in." Then, she went through the open door.

Aurora raised her eyebrows. She said, "I'm sure this is totally innocent."

I just frowned at her and asked her why she'd come.

She took the red leather chair and said, "Now, you know perfectly well why I came."

I took my seat and asked her if she wanted something to drink.

She said, "I don't need any more stimulation, because . . ."

I finished the sentence for her, "You somehow convinced Brahms to come to the Halloween party."

She smiled broadly, "Well, now we come to it. How about my idea for disguises?"

I had decided that I was going to go along with her—at least in planning. I didn't want her to think that I'd given in too easily though. I said, "But you've not got him to go along with your disguise?"

She shrugged, "No. He's still pretty stubborn. All that he'll agree to is coming to the party. Eventually he'll go along."

I leaned on my left arm and looked at her searchingly. I eventually said, "It's an interesting idea, and I can't see any flaws in it."

She perked up, "Then, you're in?"

I was still playing hard to get. "I've not completely decided. How can I trust you after all our history at the Halloween parties?"

She reacted in a way that I never expected. She said, "After all the things that we've been through the last couple of years, do you really think that I'd just play practical jokes?"

She seemed serious, but I wasn't sure. That uncertainty must have shown through. She leaned forward, put both hands on my desk open upward almost in supplication, and said, "Really. After the battle with the Souls I've been thinking hard about my little jokes. Life is too short to live without humor, but it's also too short to hurt people."

I nodded. "OK. I'll go along with you. I'll need the sizes of his tuxedo."

She sighed in apparent relief. "Good, but you don't need to worry about the tuxedo. I'll supply that."

I rubbed my chin as though considering. "Still, I'd like to know it anyway."

"Oh, if you must. But, I'm still providing the tux."

"That's fine."

She seemed surprised. She asked for something to drink.

I reached into my desk's lower left drawer. Inside I found two clean glasses and a bottle of Dewars. As I poured two glasses, she just nodded. I gave her one, and I took the other. It was early in the day for a drink, but somehow her changed mood seemed to justify one.

We drank in silence.

She got up and left without comment.

□
□□

Later that evening I was talking in bed with Minerva. I told her about Aurora's meeting with me. She commented, "Good. We'll get you a tux of the proper size."

I added, "I think I'd like a nice color. Maybe midnight blue."

Halloween Comes Early This Year

I was sitting in the Great Hall after everyone had left dinner for the evening. I was contemplating the beautiful night sky through the transparent roof of the Great Hall. The lights magically dimmed when there were few people in the room. There were a few clouds in the sky. The rest of the sky was very dark and quite beautifully bestrewn with stars.

As I sat and contemplated the strange incomprehensibilities of the universe, my thoughts were interrupted by a tap on the shoulder, "Professor Wendt, Professor Wendt."

I looked around and saw that it was Cecily. When she had my attention, she asked, "Can we finish that game?"

I had almost succeeded in forgetting that. I couldn't prevent a grimace crossing my face. Then I restored my usual impassive visage. "Yes, if you insist on seeing me humiliated."

She was insistent both that we should complete the game, and that I would be a good opponent. I had no other commitments for the evening. I felt that I had to accept the inevitable, so I said, "OK. Let's go to my office. But mind you, if the game is finished or not, you have to leave in time to reach your house before curfew begins."

She agreed, and she strode along at a good pace. I kept pace with her. My long practice with Minerva made that easy. When we reached my office, I opened the drawer with the board and pieces and tossed it out on the desk. She opened it quickly and laid out the position efficiently. I couldn't swear that it was the same position, but it was at least close. After she placed the final piece she nodded to herself satisfied that it was correct.

She said, "My move." With that she moved her piece, and the clock was running. Of course, I hadn't used a chess clock, but I felt like I should play a near blitz game—both to finish the horror show quickly and to get Cecily on her way to her house. At that moment, I realized that I didn't know which house it was.

I asked her.

She seemed surprised, "Don't you know what houses all of your students come from?"

I smiled. "I do my best to avoid knowing where my students are from, and in case I do learn, I do my best to forget it quickly. I want to be fair with everyone."

"But you're a teacher. You're fair with everyone."

I smiled, "That's because I work hard to be fair. I avoid learning anyone's house as much as possible. It's not always possible."

She said, "I'm from Ravenclaw. Doesn't that break your rule?"

I chuckled, "Oh, I'm already prejudiced toward you. It doesn't matter."

She said, "Cedric was from Huffelpuff."

I nodded.

Cecily adopted my speed-up style, and I survived longer than I expected. After a while though, I was defeated by a discovered mate. I supposed it was better than having to tip one's king.

She used the victory to press her point. "You see, I'm good. You should start up the chess club again!"

I gazed at her for a few minutes as I thought about the results of agreeing to take the role of her chess mentor. I decided to postpone a decision. "Well, for now, you take that *MCO* and study. I'll think. It was very hard losing Cedric. I don't know if I want to take another chance."

She opened her mouth to say something and then stopped. She got up to go. But she did ask me, "Are you really prejudiced about me?"

"I shouldn't tell you this, but I think you are one of the best students I've ever taught." I waggled my forefinger at her and said, "Don't let that go to your head. And don't let this victory go to your head. Beating me is about as hard a beating a wet noodle."

She left my office.

□

The day of Halloween was Saturday, so we had the Halloween party that night. Aurora's plan was that she and I meet after dinner in the library.

My plan was different. That evening after dinner in the Great Hall, I scampered up to Minerva's office and our apartment. When I arrived, she was already taking Polyjuice Potion to assume her disguise. She had set aside a cup. I asked her, "How are things going?"

As she answered, her visage and form changed. Her answer was that everything was going according to plan. She had her dress laid out and ready to don as soon as she had completed her change.

I said, "I'm on my way up to the Library. See you soon."

I arrived and found that Aurora had already taken her dose. She explained, "We're running late. Got to move." She was changing in a carrel.

I smiled. "Don't worry. I'll take mine and change as quickly as I can. You go on down, and I'll join you momentito." She scampered off. I followed her shortly, going back to the Headmistress's office. There I took Aurora's potion for me. It was just as drastic for me as for her. Phil's body was taller and thinner than mine. It was easy taking off my robes. Donning the tux was not challenging, but it seemed way too slim for me. Of course, it wasn't. The hardest thing was tying my bow tie. I'm decent at it, but it took me more time to get it right than everything else did.

When we both transformed and dressed appropriately, we left for the Great Hall where the party had already started. We left the tux that Aurora had for me in the office. We reached the Great Hall as the band was warming up. The Great Hall had been transformed to a ballroom with tables on the edges loaded high with drinks, food, and party favors such as crackers.

There were a few people already there, mostly first, second, and third years. One of the last people that I expected to see was there—Cecily. I'd have said hello to her were it not that that would not be in character for the person I was pretending to be.

The bolder third years came by and asked who I was. I, of course, answered, "Phillip Pearson, an Auror."

One of them asked if I were a Yank. I quite honestly answered that I certainly was.

He then said, "There's no mistake with that accent of yours."

I nodded and Minerva hurried me on. By this time, there were a lot more students arriving as well as teachers. The band had fired up with a song that would have done any heavy metal group credit. It then became impossible to talk for a while.

That was OK, because questions were sure to come soon. The second wedding couple had arrived. I was sure it was the real Phil and Sally because he was wearing a deep green tux. It was too loud to talk, but as soon as they saw us, they nodded in our direction.

Finally, the third wedding couple arrived. It featured the faux Sally in a traditional wedding dress and the faux Phil in a normal black tux. Unlike previous events like this, it was easy to tell who was who. The real Sally wore a wedding dress with a short veil and no train. MY Sally wore a gray wedding dress that was entirely appropriate for a re-marriage.

The other faux Sally wore an average length veil. She and her "fiancée" arrived shortly before the band switched to a set with mainly slow romantic music. Thank goodness throughout the entire night there wasn't a single Celestine Warbucks song played. They took to the dance floor as did the other wedding couples.

At a break between sets, Aurora and her partner joined us at the refreshment table. I had a glass of Coca-Cola and ice. Minerva was drinking pumpkin juice.

Aurora asked us how we enjoyed the evening. Minerva said, "Oh, it's such a romantic evening. I can hardly wait for my wedding."

Aurora regarded us suspiciously and asked, "How do I know you are the real couple?"

By this time the third couple, the real couple, arrived. I asked Sally, "OK. Sally number three, Sally number 2 wants to know how you would prove that you and Phil number three are the real Sally and Phil, assuming that you are."

She smiled and said, "Well, since everyone else are false Sally's and Phil's, I'm pretty sure that I'm the only one with a real fiancée. I think it's very easy." With that she put her arms around Phil, drew him close, and gave him a torrid, open mouth kiss.

Before she'd finished, Minerva said, "Well, that's easy." She repeated the operation with me. Of course, I fully co-operated.

That had taken Aurora so much by surprise that she simply stood there gawking. But her partner had learned from our experience. As soon as our kisses were complete, he performed the most passionate of all the kisses.

It was hard to tell if Aurora were completely co-operating or not. When the smooch was finished, she pulled back from the fake Phil and exclaimed, "Who are you and what have you done with Wendt?"

He simply smiled.

She then slapped his face and ran from the room.

I said, "That seemed like a completely acceptable kiss. Did you bite her lip?"

He shrugged and asked the other two Sally's if they would like to dance.

Sally # 3 accepted. Phil # 3 asked my Sally for a dance. She accepted. That left me without a partner.

However, as the other two Phils entered the dance floor, a young lady approached and asked me for a dance.

I smiled and said, "Cecily, I'd be honored to. That is, provided that you understand that you can't get me to start up a chess class by giving me the favor of a dance or even two with you."

She giggled and said, "Of course not professor. I was right then that you're Professor Wendt."

It was a strain dancing with her because she was so much shorter than even I am. We were almost at arm's length. The dance was a slow dance. The next was another hard rock special. We both fumbled along at more than arm's length.

When that dance was finished, she was as red as a beet. It wasn't due to extreme exertion either. She thanked me and sort of shuffled backwards. One of the good things about that dance was that she would probably be embarrassed to come to my office until after Christmas.

All of the wedding party resumed dancing with our normal partners. The Phil of Aurora hung around for a while and eventually left before the end of the party. I had a couple of dances with the real Sally before the night was over.

She said, "It's amazing. As long as we've known each other that we've never danced before."

I smiled. "Well, I expect to have the occasional dance after you and Phil are married."

She concurred.

□□

The next day, I slept in with Minerva. That sort of evening sort of gets the party juices flowing. We had a two-person party after we got back to our rooms.

I missed breakfast and decided I'd be at the Great Hall to greet the first hot dishes up from the kitchens when lunch was served. So, I was sitting at my place before anyone else—even Minerva—arrived.

The next people to show up were a sort of delegation. The leader of the delegation was Filch. He walked directly up to me and said, "We've decided that we need an emergency meeting of the Old Boys Club. It's lunch time. Let's go to the clubhouse for a meeting."

I wasn't quite sure which "clubhouse" we were referring to, but it soon became obvious when we left the Great Hall and Filch led us off in the direction of the main entrance to Hogwarts. We were bound for the Three Broomsticks.

We arrived and were a little early for the lunch trade there. We had our pick of tables. Filch chose one near the fireplace. It was a bit nippy out and it was good to have the fire nearby.

As soon as we were seated, Filch asked the question that I had expected, "What in the world happened at the party?"

Slughorn nodded and said, "I mean to say. It's obvious that you and Aurora were disguised as Phil and Sally, but who were the other Phil's and Sally's."

Dursley nodded too and added the question, "Why did she slap you? If she wasn't hoping to sneak a little snog in why in the world did she go to all the trouble of disguises?"

I couldn't help laughing. That seemed to cause a lot of consternation in the group. "OK. I'll tell all.

"First, you're right that the slapper last night was Aurora. But you want to know how we got to that point.

"As you know, every Halloween she wants to go to the dance with me in disguise. She usually gets the better of me in every way. This time, I decided to turn the tables completely on her."

I hesitated and considered what I would say, "Before I give you details, you have to swear on Old Boy's Club honor that you won't tell anyone else what I tell you."

Dudley asked, "Not an unbreakable oath?"

I nodded. "No."

Everyone assented to that condition, so I went on. "This year, as usual, Aurora came with a harebrained idea. She thought that it would be fun to go to the party as Sally and Phil dressed for their wedding.

"Of course, I refused—as I always do. She's used to that and can usually work around my refusal. This time, I decided that I would prepare to seem to co-operate while preparing a few surprises for her.

"After some consultation with Minerva, we had developed a stratagem. I would agree to go disguised as Phil Pearson. That agreement would be completely genuine. However, I would actually go with Minerva. She would be disguised as Sally."

Dudley immediately asked, "But surely Aurora would realize that you weren't going with her." He hesitated and then said, "Unless . . ."

Slughorn picked it up. "Unless, you had someone who would use Polyjuice Potion to disguise himself as you in your Phil personna."

I nodded. Then Filch's eyes lit up as though he had an electric shock go through his body. "Oh. Oh. I think I see it. Phil would go disguised as you. Brilliant! Then Aurora would give him Polyjuice potion to disguise him as himself!"

I said, "That's a good idea. I kind of wish I'd thought of it myself. But I had a different idea.

"Minerva and I had the idea of having the Boy Genius disguised as Phil. We would switch places at some point in the evening."

185

Dudley slapped his head. "Of course, then it would be perfectly natural for him to give his wife that spectacular kiss. I suppose you planned that."

I had to say, "Another good idea that didn't occur to me. It actually came up naturally. And it was Aurora's suggestion—sort of. She wanted to figure out who was the real couple. Sally, that genius, thought of kissing her boyfriend passionately. It was perfect. Then I could kiss my wife passionately. The B.G. picked up on the idea immediately. You probably couldn't tell from where you were watching, but he gave her a kiss that should have been reserved for the bedroom."

Filch laughed so hard that he slapped his knee trying to get control of himself. When he had some control, he said, "Aurora, that old gal, must have thought you were trying to . . . trying to . . . seduce her. That really turned the tables on her. God, I wish I'd been closer. That slap must have echoed in his ears for a while."

I was laughing myself. "Yeh. I wish you could have seen the look on her face. I bet she was swearing to herself that she'd never play another practical joke in her life."

Dudley shook his head. "What I wouldn't give to tell that story to *The Prophet*."

Slughorn said, "I still have some contacts in *The Prophet*. If you really wanted . . ."

I shook my head. "I said that what I tell you here doesn't leave here. I meant it. Aurora gave me some hard times in the past, but I think she really didn't mean this to go badly for anyone."

Dudley said, "What I wouldn't give to be a fly on the wall when the two of them made up!"

It was a very entertaining lunch.

The next month or so was pretty quiet. The wedding party continued planning and executing. They sent out invitations. Of course, everyone who were teachers or staff were invited. I don't know if everyone accepted the invitations, but I didn't hear about anyone who didn't.

I was not directly involved in any of the work. From that point on, everything that required the MOH was done at muggle locations. A lot of it happened at Sally's mom's home in Southampton. So, my presence wasn't requested—at least, as far as I knew.

I'm Dreaming of a White Wedding

The month of December was progressing satisfyingly toward the Christmas holiday. I took a short weekend vacation—with Minerva's help in London. One of my main objectives was finding an internet cafe where I could get online to place some Christmas present orders for family and friends back in the States.

Minerva and I took the floo network to the Cauldron fairly early in the morning. After having a cup of tea (with a substantial tip) we went to an internet cafe that I'd found several months before. Minerva, as usual, complained that the "cafe" didn't serve anything other than tea and coffee and some snack bars. Oh, yes, there were computers.

With all the online sources for gifts, it had become relatively easy for me to buy gifts and have them delivered—especially if I wasn't that particular about price. I mostly frequented the Penney online catalog as I had used the Penney paper catalog years before. The addition of Amazon to the online catalogers expanded the scope of my gifts to include books and nick-knacks.

Minerva dearly wanted to go to Diagon Alley for gift shopping for her gifts. I tried to get her to do that, saying that we could meet outside the Cauldron. She didn't trust me to find my way there all by myself. I decided to try something strange. I'd order a dress for her. Yes, a muggle dress. She sometimes wears them. Dudley had sent an owl to Madame Malkin for me to get her dress size.

Madame Malkin is pretty sharp. She deduced that I didn't want the size to order something for Minerva from her. Her return owl was prompt and only asked from whom I was ordering.

My return owl told her that it was to come from JCPenney, a store in the States. That made her less worried. I bet that she was sure that Minerva would be dissatisfied with it.

It was hard ordering her dress without her noticing. I kept flipping around from one item to another and gathering information about dresses in little snatches. Then when I added it to the shopping cart, I had Minerva get me another tea. By the time she got back, I'd placed my order, including all delivery instructions. "Well, Minerva, let's go to Diagon Alley."

When I got there, I sent Minerva on into Diagon Alley with instructions that I'd follow soon. I just wanted to shop for her by myself.

After she left, I went straight to the bar and ordered a coffee. Then I signaled to Tom, the owner of the Cauldron. He came over. "What can I do, Prof?"

"I'm sending a gift for Minerva to your address. Would you accept it?"

Tom chuckled with that wheezy laugh that no one else I know uses. Then he said, "Sure. A secret, eh?"

"Yeh."

"How is it coming—owl? Messenger?"

"Uh. . . UPS."

Tom squinted and said, "Ups? Never heard of that. What is it?"

I said, "I know that you have an 'official' British address. It's where you receive some things that only come from muggle sources."

Tom smiled. "I thought nobody knew about that."

"Well, I found out who supplies Dewars whiskey for you. They shared your address with me."

Tom shrugged. "OK. I'll hold it for Christmas, right?"

I nodded. Then I went into Diagon Alley. I wandered around a little. It had been a long time since I'd been there. It hadn't changed a lot. Mr. Olivander's was still there as always. I wandered in.

"Well, Mr. Olivander, got anything new for a witch?"

He smiled at me. "You are desperate for a good Christmas present?" He stroked his chin. "I don't know . . ." Then he glanced around his shop. "Hmmm. Does you wife have a wand-finder?"

I stared at him. "What in the world is that?"

"Oh, it's something invented by Mr. George Weasley. It fits on the handle end of the wand. When the wand's separated by more than a couple of feet from its master or mistress, it lights up and pulses."

I thought a minute. "Sort of utilitarian for Minerva, but who knows? She might like it. . . Sure, I'll take it." He wrapped it well enough for a Christmas present. I appreciated that. After paying for it, I left Olivander's shop, expressing thanks for his help.

Outside, I found that I didn't have anything else to do. I walked around waiting for Minerva to show up. I stuck my head in Flourish and Blotts. I can waste any arbitrary amount of time in a bookstore. That would be the first place that Minerva would look when she finished her shopping.

I decided to see what Flourish's small record section had. There was a display advert for the latest Celestine Warbuck's Christmas album.

That is where Minerva found me. "I see you're developing new musical tastes."

I frowned at her. "The day that I buy a Celestine Warbuck album is the day that it's time for you to point my Glock at my head and pull the trigger."

Minerva chuckled. Then she suggested a late lunch at the Cauldron. I always agree to that.

Later, we returned to the castle. I headed for my office to work on final exams. Minerva went to her office.

□

I got out old exams and started modifying them to fit this year's classes. As I was working through them, making notes, there was a knock on my door.

"Come."

The door opened. I looked up and found Cecily there. She walked in and asked if she could sit.

I pointed at the red leather chair. "Of course." She needed no further urging. She sat.

"Professor Wendt, we haven't finished talking about the chess club."

I leaned toward her, "I won't start it until next term—if I start it."

She leaned forward as well, "But what do you think about me?"

"I think you're a very good player. You're probably too good for me to judge."

She took a deep breath. She held it for quite a while before asking, "How about Cedric? Am I as good as Cedric?"

Now I was taking the deep breath and unconsciously holding it. "OK. I honestly don't know. You were both good when I first met you. You were both really beyond my ability. From whom did you learn?"

"Oh, my dad taught me the moves. We just played. For a couple of years he could always beat me, but of course, he didn't. Then for a year or so it was. . . Oh, what did dad call it. . ." She spent some time remembering. Then she said, "No quarter asked, none given."

"And after that?"

She hesitated again as if trying to decide just how much to reveal. She said, "After that, he asked for quarter, I gave.

"It was a pawn at first. Then it was two pawns. Then it was a knight. When we reached a bishop, we stopped giving quarter. We just played even. I always won.

"He knew when I was letting up. I just played straight, and he played straight."

She stopped talking. I thought and said, "Then finally, he didn't know when you were letting up."

She looked to the floor for an answer and just nodded.

I commented, "Most people think they're smarter than their parents when they're teenagers. You actually are. Don't get a swelled head. It's only in one very narrow field."

She shook her head and seemed close to tears. "I know. It's just that. . ."

We were silent for a while. Then she made her real request. "I know that you helped Cedric a lot. It wasn't by being a better chess player than he was. It was by helping him play in tournaments and things."

I knew we were heading in this direction. I hadn't done enough thinking about this. "OK. Here's the thing. The first priority is to get your parents to agree to my being your mentor. That's not trivial. Cedric's family was against it at first. I had to win them over."

"That wasn't the only thing. It was easy because he was a boy."

She jumped up, "I knew it. Just because I'm a girl, people don't think I'm worth the trouble."

I put my head in my hands, trying to think how to explain it. I stood and paced. I was amazed at how patient she was. I wished I could offer her a real drink. That would let me have one too. I sat down again.

"Here's the thing. Yes, it is because you're a girl." Her nostrils flared as I said that. Still, she listened.

"But because you're a girl, I can't do things that I could do with a boy. I could take Cedric to tournaments. It was just he and I most of the time. We'd share a hotel room. You're smart. You can see the problem surely."

"Sure, people might think that you were going to . . . oh . . . I don't know how to say it."

I smiled, "The usual way to say it is 'to take advantage of you.'"

She threw her hands up, "But we can stay in separate rooms. My Dad can come along. It's not that hard."

I almost got up to think on my feet again. "The problem is convincing your Dad that I'm not in it to exploit you." I watched her face show puzzlement. Then she asked, "Is there anyone who would really think that about you?"

190

I smiled. "If there is one person in the world who might think that, I've got to assume that everyone would."

I stood and said, "I want to think this over. It was a big commitment working with Cedric, and it was very hard the way it ended. I've got to decide if I want to go through that again."

"Well, it won't end that way with me. The Dark Lord isn't around any more. I'll work hard. I really will. I'll do whatever you say."

I still stood. I wondered if she would get the hint. Apparently, she wouldn't. I walked to the door. "I'll think about it—seriously—but over the holiday. We can talk again after school starts up." I opened the door, and she finally got the hint.

She stood, walked to the door, went through, and turned for one last plea, "If you don't, it would just be so, so . . . unfair."

I said, "Ms. Brewster, have a good holiday. I'll see you next term."

□□

I was sitting in Minerva's office with her. She said, "It's going to be a busy weekend, don't you think?"

"Oh, yes. Friday—the end of term banquet. Then Saturday is the Yule Ball. Sunday is the rehearsal dinner. Monday is IT."

Minerva said, "You know that the whole wedding party has decided to come here on Saturday for the parties."

"Is the old gal up to so much partying?"

Minerva's eyebrows went up, and she asked, "Are you talking about me?"

"Oh, oh. I was talking about the old gal, Hogwarts or really, the house elves."

It started the next day—Friday.

□
□□

Friday morning I finished grading exams. After lunch, I sat in the Great Hall contemplating the skies. There was a mixture of broken clouds and clear space. I didn't think I'd ever had so much partying in one stretch in my life.

I went out for a walk. There were walking trails around the castle. I decided to walk off the nervousness that was growing somewhere in my gut.

I arrived back at the castle in time to avoid being the last in for the end

191

of term banquet. Minerva gave her end of term speech before dinner began.

The main points were that tomorrow morning the Hogwarts express would be leaving bright and early at 9 AM. Anyone who didn't leave at that time would be able to attend the Yule Ball and then leave on the Hogwarts Express the next day. The very few students who were invited to the wedding could remain.

Ordinarily, this banquet would be a big deal. It's one of the meals that the house elves outdo themselves along with the beginning of term banquet, the Halloween banquet, and the Yule banquet. Of course, this year had additional events—the rehearsal dinner and the reception for Sally's wedding. Four of them were happening in a row, and this was the first. It was very good, but it just didn't seem that special.

I sat at the head table as usual. There were no special guests. Even Phil Pearson didn't make the dinner.

After dinner, Minerva had an announcement that was for the Head Table only. It was a reminder that the staff assignments for the Yule party were posted in the Teacher's Lounge.

In bed that night, both Minerva and I wanted to get a good night's rest in preparation for the procession of big days coming up. Of course, neither of us had a good night's rest.

The next day both of us were up not so very bright but very early. We dragged through getting up and dressing and easily made it to the Great Hall shortly before the house elves served up breakfast.

For most students, the breakfast before the Express left for London was hasty and informal if it happened at all. Minerva gave her usual wish to all present for a Happy Christmas, and that was it.

I had a light breakfast. I needed to save some room for the feast tonight. Afterwards, I ambled up to the Teacher's Lounge to just be sure about my assignments today. I arrived and began to shuffle through the pages of assignments. When I reached my page, I found the usual things.

I was supposed to be responsible for supervising the food table for part of the evening. There had been enough monkeying with the food in past years that we needed volunteers for that. I was supposed to keep a tally of who left on the Express and when. I'd have to get down to the station pretty quickly to collect that from the heads of the houses.

There was paying the band. I guess Minerva figured that I must know how to manage money because I had a lot of gold in my vault.

Then I noticed that there was one more thing. It was, "Escort MOH to

Hogwarts with help of Ginny Weasley and introduce to staff." I had to get down to the train station, but just as soon as I got back, I'd look up Minerva or more likely Sally to see what this was about.

The Express had arrived last night and was close to boarding when I saw it in the distance. I'd not arrive in time to check students off on my list, but the heads of house would be keeping their own tally.

By the time I got there, I'd already started ticking names off on my list. I didn't know everyone, but it was important to have a second set of eyes picking up names.

The last ones boarded, and the train was fewer than ten minutes late getting started. It wouldn't start until the heads of houses and I gave the OK.

The five of us huddled and compared lists. My list had missed about ten whom I would have recognized that were on the others' lists, and I had seven whose faces I didn't know. I accepted the ten that the heads had noted. I also accepted the seven names that I hadn't known.

By that time, the conductor came to us with his count of heads actually on the train. His count was one fewer than ours. We thought and thought about the extra name that we couldn't identify. The conductor looked over my unified list and nodded. "Yes, It's the 6th year, Avril Lescoud. She decided to stay for the Yule Ball. I saw her change her mind and leave. She was one of the early ones on.

So, we gave the go-ahead for the Express to depart. They were about a quarter hour behind schedule, but they could easily make that up on the route.

I took my list and headed back for the castle.

I'd decided that it must be Sally who'd requested that I escort Haley to Hogwarts. I began thinking of places that she might be. I started in the Great Hall. I had no luck there. I tried the Teacher's Lounge. I went outside to the courtyard. I even went to my office, thinking she might be looking for me.

Finally, in desperation, I went to Minerva's outer office, where Sally held court. There she sat behind her desk. By this time, what with running all over the castle, I had worked up a sweat. She took a look at me and calmly asked, "Is there something I can do for you?"

"Well, besides being somewhere that I can find you, could you please take me off this escort duty for your MOH? Ginny can handle it perfectly well. I don't add any value. I have better things to do."

Her visage turned stern. "You know perfectly well that Haley doesn't feel totally comfortable around magic." She hesitated and added, "Or Ginny yet. She hasn't had the ten plus years that you've had navigating the tricky waters here."

"Yeh. Well, you haven't either, and you get along just fine, thank you."

Her face turned even sterner. I growled, "OK. OK. I'll give her the grand tour. She'll know the castle like the back of her hand when I'm finished."

Sally asked, "I don't know what it is with you and Haley. She's a perfectly charming young woman."

I growled again, "Right. I guess I've gotten used to women who are not quite so charming and are a bit more assertive, present company included."

Sally nodded, "Why, thank you."

"Anything that may be done by growling, you may depend on me to do."

So, I steeled myself for the ordeal of being with her. Of course, the problem was that Haley was very charming, and it was easy to fall into pleasant conversation with her. Thus, even walking the halls of Hogwarts was dangerous.

The assignment to escort Haley was not supposed to start until 3 PM. I could probably waste time on a tour of Hogwarts and staff until dinner time. Then I was off duty.

□□
□□ □

I was just finishing up lunch when I happened to glance down at the Gryffindor table and noticed the flaming red hair that had to be Ginny's. I was sipping on some tea and almost choked.

I got hold of myself and realized that she'd just come a bit early so that she could enjoy the renowned cuisine of the Hogwarts house elves. I sighed a sigh of relief and turned my attention back to the *Times* crossword for the weekend. I wondered as I puzzled over a particularly difficult clue if I'd ever filled in more than a quarter of that weekend puzzle. I knew that there were people who ate that puzzle for breakfast. I thought they must be aliens.

I had just decided to move on to the next clue when I heard a voice that I'd come to recognize as well as I knew Minerva's. "Professor Wendt, are you ready to pick up your escort?"

I looked up with a grim expression on my face. "No, I'm not. The schedule calls for that to happen at 3 PM."

"Oh, don't be a spoil sport. I've got some duties for the afternoon besides ferrying you and Little Miss Perfect around. Let's get going."

194

I sighed. It was going to be a long, hard afternoon with me having to be on constant guard the whole time.

I asked, "The floo, I suppose."

She said, "Sure, we're burning daylight, Professor."

I got up and accompanied Ginny to the Great Hall floo connection. She took my hand and with her other grabbed some floo powder. With a green flare, we arrived in the same pub we'd been in the last time.

Thankfully, all I had to do was put some coin on the bar and we were out the door. I took her hand again, and we spun our way to Haley's apartment building. This time, though, she was standing outside.

I asked Ginny, "Did you tell her we'd be here early?"

Ginny just shook her head.

I then asked Haley, "I suppose it's just luck that you happened to be out here with your overnight case."

Her smile would have incinerated a lump of lead. "Oh, no. I was just too, too excited to wait around inside my apartment until you arrived."

Ginny turned her back to Haley and made a gagging pantomime with a finger down her throat.

I smiled feebly and chose not to ask her how long she'd been out waiting for us. We walked to a side street, and we repeated the exercise of everyone taking everyone else's hand. We arrived just outside the gate of Hogwarts.

We walked into the castle, and I began my guided tour. As we went, we occasionally ran into a member of the staff, whom I introduced as we went. I told Ginny, "Well, I know my way around, so you can go do your pressing assignments."

She just smiled slyly and said, "Oh, I'll just tag along for a bit."

I decided that we'd start at the lowest level and work our way up. Of course, I didn't know the passcode for Slytherin, so I only mentioned the house name in passing. Haley took my arm as I said the name, "That sounds so . . . oh . . . sinister."

Ginny took my other arm.

On the next level, we approached Filch's office. I knocked on the door and asked if anyone were home. Filch invited me in. It turned out that the three musketeers were there. In addition to Filch were Slughorn and Dudley. So I introduced them. I also commented, "They seem to be together so much lately that I'm thinking of nicknaming them the . . . "

Haley finished for me, "The Three Musketeers. What do you all teach?"

Filch said, "Slughorn teaches potions. I'm the chief facility Engineer. Mr. Dursley here is my apprentice, but he and Professor Slughorn have written a book in their spare time."

Haley looked the question at me. I replied, "Oh, yes. Mr. Dursley and Professor Slughorn might just be the world's greatest authorities on potions."

Filch added, "And he's MY apprentice."

Haley asked, "Potions. You mean like poultices and love potions?"

Filch agreed, "Yes, siree, ma'am. Mr. Dudley here invented the love potion to end all love potions. Right, Professor?"

Slughorn agreed.

She just nodded. We went on up to the main level, passing Minerva's office. As we did, I said, "You know Minerva and Sally, of course."

We then went up a level, dropping by the Charms Professor, Flitwig. We stopped for a few minutes at the hospital wing. We passed my office.

I wasn't going to say anything but Ginny said, "This is Professor Wendt's office. He has a small apartment behind it. That's where you'll stay when you're here. He, of course, will be in the Headmistress's quarters."

Haley brightened up. "Why don't we go in for a minute so I can get used to it."

I thought, "used to it," you'd think that she was planning on staying for a long time.

I unlocked the door and handed the key to Haley. Her hand closed around it, squeezing my hand for a moment. "There's not much to see. This is my office. I led them through to my apartment. "The usual—a bed, dresser, WC, nothing else. . . Oh, I do keep a change of clothes here just in case I'm working really late and just spend the night here. It happens very rarely."

Haley smiled at that.

After leaving my office, we came to a parting of the ways. "We could go up to the astronomy tower, but you already know the Astronomy Professor, Sinistra. We'll go to the other 2nd tower at the opposite end of the building." I chuckled. "Really, the opposite in every way—the Divination tower headed by Professor Trelawny."

When we'd finished the tour, it was just past 3 PM. I was beginning to wonder if there were anything else that we could do to kill time. I didn't have to. Haley said, "I'm fascinated by castles. This whirlwind tour of yours has been fun, but I'd like to take a leisurely tour of my own. I'm a big girl and can find my way around on my own."

That was a real surprise. I nodded approval and said, "Good. Well, just make sure you find your way to the Great Hall for the Yule feast by 6 PM."

She smiled her sunny smile and said, "Don't worry. I wouldn't miss it for the world." With that, she turned and trotted down the stairs.

Ginny and I turned toward each other. She asked the question that was on my mind. "What in the world do you make of that?"

"I don't know. Let's do some brainstorming. What's the worst thing that she could get into?"

Ginny looked down away from me. "I don't know. She's not a witch, so it's hard to see her getting anything that requires magic to go bad." She hesitated some and then added, "Hagrid's not got any blast-ended scrouts around. Hogwarts is a whole lot less dangerous since your wife took control."

I had the feeling that she wasn't entirely on-board with that, but that was not my problem now.

I couldn't think of anything with which she could in trouble. I said, "Of course, potions can always be dangerous to anyone including muggles, but Slughorn is on top of all that. I'm sure he keeps his lab locked whenever he's not there."

Since we couldn't think of anything that could go wrong, I decided to go to Minerva's office. I knew the passwords, so I could get in and hunker down.

I spent the next couple of hours worrying about what might happen the next couple of days. At 5:30 PM I decided that I couldn't wait any longer. I walked down to the Great Hall. I discovered that I was not the first to arrive. There were a number of students and Ginny. She was sitting at the Gryffindor table. I decided to join her.

"No sign of our ward?" I asked.

She patted the spot on the bench next to her and said, "Well, at least we can talk while we're waiting."

Of course, there turned out to be not so much to discuss. Ginny quickly turned the conversation to the Yule Ball. "What are you going to wear?"

"Me? I guess I'm going to wear my dress robes." I thought a moment. "I have a new pair of shoes," I said hopefully.

She seemed unimpressed

I asked, "Well, then, what are you going to wear?"

She smiled and touched my arm. "I've got a new set of pink dress robes that I've been saving for a special occasion."

"Don't you think they'll clash with your hair."

She smiled slyly. "That's the beauty of it, I'm hoping it will attract attention." Her smile broadened. "What do you think?"

I didn't have to attempt that question because Minerva showed up spot on 6 PM. She walked up to the podium and announced, "We will take a moment of silence to remember our lost friends." We did.

Then she said, "Now, as Professor Dumbledore would have said, 'Tuck in.'"

Just then Haley showed up and sat down opposite me. She appeared to already be wearing her party dress. It was a dark sea green. She asked me, "What do you think?" She stood and pirouetted nicely. Her long silky black hair shimmered as it flared out with her turn.

I said, "Very nice."

Ginny just sniffed in derision.

Haley's smile didn't falter in the least. She sat and rested her chin on her hands. That didn't last long because platters of food materialized on all the tables as did glasses and pitchers of various beverages.

I picked up a carafe of hot tea and asked, "Hot tea anyone?"

Ginny refused with thanks. She wanted pumpkin juice. Haley accepted the hot tea with thanks. We passed food and had a superlative meal. The food was too good to do much talking.

At one point, Haley offered to warm up our tea cups. I nodded. She poured some additional tea in our cups. She seemed a bit clumsy and spilled some outside my cup. She sopped it up with a napkin.

We finished the meal at our leisure. Haley had begun gaily talking about the party. It was mostly silly and giddy, but as she went along, I discovered that what she said was not so much silly or giddy as it was clever and fun to listen to. I couldn't reproduce any of it, because I soon was not paying that much attention to what she was saying, but rather noticing how expressive her fine eyes were.

I barely noticed Ginny rolling her eyes at the beginning. The amazing thing was that I was getting in the spirit. I was beginning to talk with her about her ideas of how romantic the evening was, how the cloudy sky visible through the ceiling was enchanting, how I was sure this would be the most wonderful evening.

I think that Ginny was becoming disgusted. She said something about having to go to the ladies' WC to throw up.

I discovered that Haley's hand had closed on mine. Somehow that didn't seem strange in the least. Before we knew it, the meal was over and the platters of food were disappearing. That brought me to life.

I told Haley, "I've got to check with the band. I have to be sure that we're clear about the contract and how much they're being paid."

Haley was overawed. "Really! Oh, can I come along and listen?"

"Sure. It'll be boring. You'll wish you had stayed here."

She shook her head in that fascinating way that made her hair shimmer. "Nothing with you would be boring."

That stupid enthusiasm should have driven me crazy, but then I was just eating it up. We went up to the stage. The band had begun setting up. I found the leader, and we talked through the plan for the night. She was planning one fewer set than we had agreed to.

We went back and forth a little, and I finally offered, "Look. Play all the sets that you AGREED to and you'll get paid what you AGREED to. . . plus maybe a little if we like your performance."

She wasn't really happy, but she bought into the deal. Haley was ecstatic. "Oh that was wonderful!"

I could see in her eyes that it was wonderful, but maybe not as wonderful as she was.

By this time the Great Hall was pretty well set up for the Yule Ball. The food tables were set up. I had to take the first watch keeping an eye on them. I gazed into her wonderful deep eyes and said, "Another even more boring duty. I have to watch the food tables to be sure that no pranks get played—boring."

She gazed back into my eyes with wonder. "Oh, could I stand guard too? I think it would be just fab."

The amazing thing was that I thought that was fabulous too. How could I be so, so, so silly? I didn't know, but I couldn't help myself.

We spent the whole hour that I was supposed to be on duty staring mainly into each other's eyes. My replacement came on duty, and neither of us noticed until Flitwick tapped me on the back.

Thus interrupted, I noticed that the band had been playing. They were playing something slow. I couldn't help myself. I suggested that we dance. She agreed enthusiastically, and we were on the dance floor.

You may wonder what Minerva was doing all this time. I had no idea, and I didn't care a whit. I learned much later that she was entertaining our guests who had arrived early for the wedding. She assumed way too correctly that I was entertaining the MOH.

Suddenly, there was a tap, or maybe it was more like a pounding on my shoulder. I looked around to find Ginny Weasley thumping me with the business end of her wand. I looked a question at her—not a very polite question.

She said, "I'm cutting in."

I said, "No, you are not."

She was insistent as only Weasleys can be insistent. But Haley came to the rescue. "I suppose I can't hog you for the entire evening. Go ahead.

199

I'll be over at the refreshment table getting something to drink. I'm pretty hot."

Ginny swiveled into position, and as we began dancing said, "I'll bet she is hot. But what in the world are you doing dancing with her all night?"

I dropped back to think for a second. What was I doing dancing with her? Then I realized that I'd never been so happy in my life as when she was in my arms. I answered honestly. "At the beginning I thought I was just escorting the MOH as requested. But now. . . I'm not so sure."

I must have gotten a far-away look in my eyes because Ginny snapped a finger in front of my face. "Earth calling Wendt. Where were you just now?"

Again, honesty was the only answer, "You've got me."

She was dumbfounded. Eventually she asked, "You don't fancy Ms. Poetzl do you?"

The answer that immediately struck me was one that I didn't want to make—that, yes, I did fancy her.

My uncertainty must have given me away. "You do, don't you?"

I tried near-honesty this time, "I don't know."

By this time the band had finished the set. Ginny pulled my head close to hers and whispered, "You'd bloody better not be."

Of course, I knew that she was totally capable of making any threat good. We walked off the dance floor and in the general direction of the refreshments.

Haley approached us as we were coming toward her. She was holding two glasses. She handed one to me and with her freed hand looped her arm through my free arm. She then dragged me off while saying, "It's about time that you gave him up." I'm glad I didn't see the look on Ginny's face.

I was perfectly willing to be drawn off by Haley, but I wanted to know where we were going. She replied, "Oh, we're going to complete the tour of the castle that you never finished for me."

I was puzzled for a moment. There were a few places that we'd not gone. She made clear our destination quickly. "Oh, how could you forget the Astronomy Tower?"

I was fascinated. "Why you clever girl! What a wonderful idea. We can watch the moon and the stars in the comfort of the Astronomy classroom rather than the cold outdoors. The best thing is that no one will be up there other than us."

"I thought you'd like my idea," she said coquettishly.

We seemed to glide up the flight after flight of stairs effortlessly. When we reached the top, I led her to the balcony that overlooked the castle, the lake, the vast empyrean realm of space. The moon was nearing the horizon.

I sat her down on the floor and sat behind her with my arms around her waist. I lifted an arm to point out a constellation here then one there. My heart burned within me. I could finally not hold back what I'd been longing to say for most of the time we'd been in the Astronomy Tower. "Haley, I love you with all my heart."

She turned in my arms away from the beauties of the heavens and gazed into my eyes. "I do, too. Do you know why you love me?"

I took the question completely literally and said what was in my heart, "You are the most beautiful woman I've ever known. You hair drives me crazy. It's length, it's sheen, the way it flows when you shake you head, the feel of it on my arms as I hold you, its smell that fills to overflowing my senses.

"Your eyes that twinkle more brightly than the strongest stars are always in my eyes. Your perfect figure that fits so neatly into my arms is incomparable. Your . . ."

She interrupted me, "No, silly. I mean do you know what happened to you to make you love me?"

With those words I had a revelation. Of course, I knew why I was so not-desperately in love with her. That was it. I wasn't desperate. I was confident in my love. I didn't doubt it in the least. If she'd walked away from me and never returned, I'd still love her, and the thought of her would fill me with joy.

I realized then how awful what she had done was. I tried to put as much indictment into my question as I could, "How could you do that?"

Instead, it came out as though I'd said, "What a clever girl you are to think of such a wonderful idea."

She threw her arms around me and we kissed enthusiastically and then again more casually—as though in the knowledge that we had all the time in the world to enjoy each other's lips and bodies. When we finished with the kiss, I repeated the question with a different emphasis, "Just how did you manage to get hold of the Real love potion?"

She smiled, and my heart filled with joy at the sight. Then she began telling me. I'll leave out all my expressions of admiration and joy at her brilliant ideas and so on. You might actually finish the story if I held back my exuberance.

After I left you and Ginny this afternoon. . . By the way, what is it with Ginny? You'd think she thought she owned you. Anyway, after I left, I hurried down to Filch's office, hoping to find somebody there. It turns out that only Dursley was there.

When I knocked on the door, he invited me in. He was very polite. I could have beat around the bush, but I just didn't have the time. I asked him, "Would you tell me about your love potion? How does it work?"

He was a typical male. He wanted to brag about his great invention. He swiveled his chair around and said, "Well, here's the deal. I don't really know how it works, but I think there isn't a magician alive who knows 'the how' of magic. But I do know a few things.

"First, this potion is life-long or at least it lasts for nearly a year. We did an experiment with it. After that time, the love was every bit as powerful as at the beginning.

"Second, the potion is odorless, color-less, taste-less, and is pretty darn indistinguishable from plain water."

I interrupted. "How do you know it wasn't just water?"

"Well, for one thing, I brewed it myself—uh with some assistance from a student.

"Anyway, another thing about it is that the love it produces is a whole lot more like real love than what the other potions produce."

I asked hopefully, "What do you mean?"

"Well, most potions just induce hopeless infatuation. The subjects . . . er . . . people become sort of like slaves to your will. This potion leaves their will pretty much alone. They want to please you, but they can decide what they will do separate from you will. It's really strange and hard to describe."

He stopped and seemed deep in thought. Then he said, "Here. I actually have a sample that was left from the original potion. Let me show you."

He then unlocked a drawer of his desk, reached in, and found a small bottle.

He actually handed it to me. I held it up to the light. He was right. I would have no idea it was anything other than water. I started to unstopper it.

He shouted, "NO!" Then he added more calmly. "Believe me, the first experiment was more of an accident. I hated myself for months while we eventually undid it. I don't want another accident."

I couldn't help smiling as I said, "Believe me, I would never use it accidentally." Then I handed it back to him. I added a question, "How many doses are in the bottle?"

He shrugged. "I don't know. At least one. But, I'm pretty sure that you could get two or maybe even three out of that bottle."

I nodded knowingly. Then I said, "See you at dinner."

I left the office. But I didn't go far. I stayed close to the office but out of sight around a corner. There was a broom closet nearby that I could duck into if someone got close.

It was a long wait. My watch told me it wasn't much more than a half hour, but it seemed an eternity to me. Finally, I heard the door to Dursley's office open. I peaked around the corner and saw him leave and head up the stairs. After releasing my breath—which I'd been holding the whole time until he disappeared from view, I went back to the office.

I pulled a hairpin out of my hair and started to work on the lock. It was a long bitter struggle with that lock. Every creak and groan of the door, the lock, the stairs behind me scared me out of my wits. Finally after working on it for close to a half-hour, I sat back on the floor and almost cried. Then I had an idea that should have occurred to me from the beginning. I decided to see if the door was even locked.

With great trepidation, I grasped the doorknob and twisted. It turned effortlessly and soundlessly. Then I did cry. After I did some cursing, I closed the door behind me and went directly to the desk. This time, I tried the drawer. It was locked.

I sat and began working on the lock with my hairpin. It gave way almost immediately. I actually laughed out loud. In a different life I could have been a burglar.

I opened the drawer and immediately spotted the bottle. It was the only one in the drawer. I picked it up and held it up to the light. It seemed impossible that I was this close to your life-long love. I quickly put it in my purse after being sure it was tightly stoppered.

I went back to your room and changed for dinner. I made sure to bring THE bottle. During dinner, when I freshened your tea and mine, I freshened yours with half of the love potion and the other half I added to mine.

Then, I started having the most delightful evening of my life. Being with you is always refreshing, bracing, filled with good humor, and even, at some times, love. Now we have been in heaven together. I can't imagine that heaven could bring more happiness or cause my heart to burn with desire more than it does now. If it did, I couldn't survive it.

□□ □□
□□ □□

I couldn't resist praising her and delighting in her in a thousand ways during the story. It is not an adequate summation, but what I had to say was summed up in what I said when she finished. "You are such a wonderfully clever girl! How can I possibly be lucky enough to love you? And to give each of us the potion is a stroke of genius that I would never in a million years have thought to do. You deserve all the love I have to give you and far more!"

Her eyes shone like diamonds. Instead of saying anything, she pulled me to her and we kissed. My hands flew over her body, caressing every part of her that I could possibly reach.

Then, suddenly, she stiffened in my arms. I started to move, but then I was struck by what had to be a *petrificus totalis* spell. I had experienced that on several occasions. I didn't have to imagine what she was feeling and thinking. I'd been there before.

I was experienced enough with that particular spell that I wasn't worried at all by it. I knew it would be released eventually, but I was beset by the most terrible fear for what Haley must be thinking. The terrors of being incapacitated without any idea why or how it happened is deadly fearful. I wanted more than I could express to whisper in her ear that was so close to my lips that she shouldn't worry. We would be released, and then we could comfort and caress each other. I couldn't do that.

I turned my mind to trying to deduce who had done this to us. The only person whom I could think of was Ginny. She had been acting very possessive of me. She would like to put an end to our love-making, and this was a perfect way to do it.

I wondered how long it would be before she released us. The time slipped by so slowly that I had no idea how long we'd been frozen. Eventually, the sky began to brighten. I knew that we were approaching mid-morning. Was Ginny ever going to release us?

It did eventually happen. The sky was full daylight. I was sure that Ginny wouldn't ruin Sally's wedding and having her MOH go missing would definitely cast a pall on the wedding.

I felt her body slacken just before mine did. She drew me closer and whispered, "What in God's name happened?"

I quickly said, "You're OK. Nothing bad happened."

I hadn't seen her yet, but I was so sure that it was Ginny that I just said, "Why, Ginny?"

I could feel Haley's body stiffen and was sure that she was about to exclaim something. Before she could do that I heard Ginny say, "Well, you never give up do you Mr. Wendt, the Hero. Yes, it was I."

She addressed Haley, "Well, Missy, you can just let go of your Hero and back away."

Haley did. That gave me an opportunity to turn my head. I saw her sitting cross-legged behind us about a meter away. She was holding her wand pointed directly at Haley. I felt the adrenaline coursing through my body. I also knew that she'd have me frozen before I had cut the distance between us by half. I temporized, "What do you want?"

She said negligently, "Oh, nothing hard. I brought a little elixir for the two of you. You just have to drink it. Bottoms up."

Haley snarled, "What makes you think that you can get me to drink it?"

Ginny was still speaking negligently, "Oh, I don't have to convince you to drink it. If you won't, I'll stun your ass and pour it down your throat."

Haley gasped. She knew Ginny enough to know that she was perfectly capable and willing to do just that.

Trying to buy some time, I asked, "Just how did you know it was Dursley's love potion?"

Ginny actually laughed, "Oh, that was easy as pie. You don't think that your disappearance from the Great Hall went unnoticed, do you? The hardest thing was figuring out where you went. Even that wasn't very hard. You weren't really trying to cover your trail. When I figured out that you were up here, I just walked up. You were so much absorbed with your play that I came almost as close to you as I am now."

She directed her attention to Haley. "And you, Missy, co-operated by telling your boy-friend just what you'd done. When I was convinced that you were telling the truth, I just stunned the both of you.

"Of course, I had to look up Dursley or Slughorn and get them to brew the antidote. They were pretty tired after partying, but I can be persuasive when I want to. I found them both, and we went to the room of requirement."

Haley asked, "What?" in spite of herself.

Ginny explained, "That was another place that didn't make it on the tour. Of course, you can't blame Wendt for that. You have to be magic to get in. Anyway, the two of them had a bloody potions lab set up in there that you wouldn't believe. They did a great job.

"And here I am with that very antidote. Now, all you have to do is take your medicine, and we'll be able to go down to join the others for the wedding.

"Oh, by the way, if you do something like accidentally spilling the antidote, I'll just stun you and, like I said, bottoms up. Now, who's going to be first?"

Haley and I looked at each other. It was like Minerva and me. We know each other so well that we usually know what the other will say or do. We just nodded in complete unspoken agreement.

Haley and I spoke in unison, "We'll take it together."

Ginny shuddered and said, "Spooky." She stopped in mid-sentence and then said, "Almost like Fred and George. It's almost a shame to break the two of you up. Now, just turn around so that I'll have an undisturbed minute to pour your doses."

We did. She took my hand and said, "I'll always love you."

I said, "You know that I always liked you. That will never change."

Ginny said, "Really touching. Your glasses are ready. Turn very slowly and drink them down."

We picked up the glasses. Again, we didn't have to say a word. I extended my glass to her lips, and she did the same for me. We gazed into each other's eyes for a ten count, and then we swallowed.

I don't know if I was expecting anything particular to happen. At first, I didn't think anything had happened. Then I realized that I was hungry. That convinced me that it was done. I tried to identify what had happened about my feelings for Haley. I couldn't put my finger on anything.

Then I noticed that I didn't have that heaven-on-earth happiness that had seemed to suffuse everything before. I looked over to Ginny. I couldn't even work up any hatred for her.

Haley touched my cheek with a hand and asked, "Are you all right?"

I turned back to her. "Sure. How about you?"

She stared at me and then said, "Heaven is gone."

I nodded. "We've probably seen too much of heaven. We may never be satisfied with Earth again."

Ginny just sniffed and said, "Well, you've managed to miss breakfast AND lunch. You'd better get ready for the wedding rehearsal. It's only three hours away. I think I can trust the two of you with yourselves. You're never going to get the dynamic duo to brew you another taste of that elixir of love again."

She stood, turned, and walked.

Haley said, "You know, I am hungry."

"Well, I can do something about that. There's another spot that we missed on the tour."

Haley asked, "Really? The kitchens?"

I smiled. "You bet. We'll go down. But you've got to promise me one thing before we go?"

She laughed. "I would promise you ANYthing that you asked."

"Well, this might be easy, might not. The people who run the kitchen are house elves."

She looked at me suspiciously. "Is there something . . . uh . . . wrong with them?"

"No. No. It's just that they are very short, mostly wear things that no one could possibly mistake for clothes, and are . . . well, let's be honest . . . are ugly as sin."

She smiled. "Kind of sounds like my cousin, Esther."

"Oh, I'm not kidding. You've got to steel yourself and promise me that you will act as if you'd just been invited to tour the kitchen of a French Cordon Bleu, because you kind of have been."

She nodded slowly. "OK. I get it. It's an honor to visit their kitchen. I have to be on my best behavior. Right?"

I nodded.

We'd been walking down stairs all this time. She looked like she'd been putting her game face on the whole time.

I had to chuckle, "Well, maybe I've over-prepared you. Just be yourself and remember that you're in someone else's kitchen."

"You've got it!" she said enthusiastically.

We reached the kitchen doors. I threw one open and invited her to enter. She did. Almost immediately, the sous-chef appeared and asked, "Can I be helping you, Professor and Ma'am?"

I said, "We missed breakfast and lunch. I was wondering if you could fix us a little something to hold us over until the rehearsal dinner?"

He frowned and looked down at the floor in concentration. "Oh, I am really not having anything good." He thought a little more. "I have some left over tomato basil soup that I could warm a little, and I could make chicken salad sandwiches. We is trying hard to do our best for Miss Sally's dinner."

Haley enthusiastically said, "Oh, that would be more than we deserve. That's wonderful!"

He went off to work on our request. After he was out of earshot Haley said, "Oh, I can't help it. It was wonderful being in love with you and having that love returned to me. If we had only met a couple of years ago, would we be married now?"

I sighed deeply and was thankful that it couldn't happen. Then I thought a bit more. Time travel was possible. Of course, there weren't any time turners left. But someone had made them. Was that knowledge—how to make a time turner still around?

Haley noticed that I was abstracted and asked me what I was thinking about. I was momentarily stymied trying to decide whether to talk about time travel. She pressed me to know what I was thinking about.

I sighed again and decided to tell her. She would be a pain until I did. "OK. Here's the thing. Do you know that time travel is possible?"

She laughed. "You mean in science fiction?"

I shook my head, "No. I mean in real life. The physics people I know tell me that there's nothing in the laws of physics that prevents time travel."

Her eyes bugged out and she asked, "Really!"

"I'm afraid so. I even know a couple of people who've done it. But here's the catch. They travel a few hours into the past. It gets more and more likely that you'll do something disastrous the farther back in time you go. Going back in time years, you're virtually certain to break something—badly."

She stared off into the distance and said, "Oh, what I wouldn't give to just spend one day with you in—oh, say in 2001."

I shook my head. "To be honest with you an experiment like that might be fun. But here's the thing. Time travel doesn't work that way. You go back, and you have to live every day from then forward—forever. If you went back to 2001, there would be the other earlier you wandering around at the same time as you for years."

She just said, "Oh."

Just then the sous-chef arrived with two warm bowls of tomato basil soup and then a platter with several chicken salad sandwiches on it. I said a brief grace, and we dug in thankfully.

The sous-chef returned in a few minutes with two plates of salad. Haley looked up at him and marveled, "Oh, this soup is heavenly." She had a thought, "I really mean it. It is really like being in heaven. I know. I've been there."

The sous-chef didn't know quite how to take it, so I translated, "She means that she really likes the soup."

He bowed and said, "We are being pleased that you like our food." Then he left.

After she'd finished a sandwich and most of her soup, she looked at me again and said, "You can't imagine how much I wish we were. . .uh . . . together. Having you and living here would be more than one person could endure—in a good way." She hastened to add that last comment.

It was clear that we were done with lunch. I said as much. I also said that we needed to clean up and dress for the rehearsal. Haley replied, "Oh, can't we spend just a little more time here?"

"No. I can't believe that the MOH doesn't want to be with the bride."

She looked at me cross-eyed. "You know far better than that. But I suppose you're right." She stood and made to leave. Then she turned and said, "Oh, just one more thing. You'll save some dances for me at the reception, right?"

I nodded. She practically skipped off. Then someone tapped me on the back. I turned and found Kretur. I said, "It's good to see you. What's up?"

Kretur stared at the floor. Finally, he said, "Are you and the Headmistress . . . uh . . . are you having the good . . . uh . . . days. . . uh . . ."

I took him by the shoulder. That wasn't easy. I had to get down on my knees. I said, "Kretur, I don't know what you've seen or heard but Min. . . that is, the headmistress and I are fine. Really."

Kretur looked up at me. That was really strange for a house elf. He just said one word, "Real?"

I said, "As real as days are long and hard for house elves."

He looked at me. "They are not being long and 'ard at 'ogwarts for 'ouse elves."

I had to laugh, "What? Is the Headmistress making you take a day off every week?"

Kretur almost laughed himself. "Hard. We is having to take a week vacation once a year."

I shrugged. "Sorry. Things are good with the Headmistress, but I can't help you with that."

Kretur shrugged and walked away.

I headed for the Hard Headmistress's Office.

The dress rehearsal went off well—as far as I know. Since I had no part in the wedding, I stayed away from the rehearsal. As a matter of fact, I stayed holed up in the apartment behind the Headmistress's Office.

I went down to the kitchen for dinner. I found the Old Boys Club there having dinner. Dursley asked me why I wasn't with the Headmistress at the rehearsal dinner.

I answered, "Well, I really don't have a role in the wedding. Minerva's only there as a representative of the school."

Dursley smelled a rat, I think. He asked, "But surely, you could go as the husband of the Head? Why didn't you do that, anyway?"

I rolled my eyes and said, "Look, I don't have any role in this wedding, but I've spent far more time helping with it than most of the people who are in it. I've had it up to here." I then put the palm of my hand above my eye level.

Filch assumed a crafty look and said, "Well, if you've not got anything else to do, why don't we declare an impromptu meeting of the

Old Boy's Club at the Three Broomsticks."

I smiled and agreed. "Sure. Frankly, I wouldn't mind picking up the tab for the evening. After all, why should the wedding party have all the fun tonight?"

That offer was soundly approved by all. Apparently, only Hagrid had gone to the rehearsal dinner. I deputized Filch to go collect him for our impromptu meeting. It took him a while to retrieve Hagrid. I guess the cuisine was fully up to the house elves' standards in the Great Hall. When Haggrid appeared, he was with Pearson and his best men.

It was dawning on me that this was actually a bachelor party for Pearson. He was treated grandly. We drank toast after toast to him. Pearson's friends made toasts that I never remembered, but the OBC all had toasts that were memorable.

Slughorn started off, "Phil, you are the luckiest man in the world. Take it from someone who never had a love in his life—except for one young lady when I was a student. Her father forbade us to marry. I never saw her again. I tried substituting influential friends for that love. It left me the loneliest man in the world.

"You are a fool if you don't appreciate the love of the good woman that you have."

Dursley stood and said, "Phil, you are the luckiest man in the world. I had to watch the love of my life poisoned—almost to death. She is across the ocean. I never get to see her. Your Sally is always near."

I rose and said, "Phil, you are the luckiest man in the world because you are committing yourself to one of the most brilliant, attractive, hard-working, determined ladies that you could find on the shores of this fair land.

"Take it from a man who worked with her under the most trying of circumstances that she will stand beside you with good humor and dedication when no other will. She had the courage to face the worst that the Deatheaters, the Ghosts, and I could throw at her.

"She has had her heart broken once by an unnamed Deatheater who killed the love of her life—Fred Weasley. Let me assure you that every man in this room would stand in line for the chance to avenge her if you ever disappoint her.

"Remember that all of us see her practically every day of the year. We will know if she is unhappy. We will know if she is disappointed. We will know if you have been less than honest with her.

"If there is any justice in the world, you two will be the happiest, most joyful, most generous couple on the face of the earth—possibly excluding Minerva and me."

Filch rose unsteadily and said, "Phil P., the most luckiest man in the world. I lived in the same castle with my love for more than sixty years before I had the courage to ask her for a date. You will be living a date for the rest of your life with this most beauteously young woman, may it be long and extuperating.

"I give you all, Phil Pearson!"

There was general applause and calls for another round of libations.

Dursley stood at one point and said, "We are now approaching the witching hour. We all know what must be done now." He drew his wand as did Slughorn. At that point, I froze and fell forward onto the table.

It was really dark when I regained consciousness. Also, I was wearing a heavy coat. As the numbness left my limbs, I experimented with moving them. I hit something that made a noise. It said, "Here's another fine mess you've gotten us into, Stan." It was Phil.

I asked, "You know about Laurel and Hardy?"

"Sure, everyone in America does."

I said, "I suppose that this is a little prank that our 'friends' have played on us. Let's do an inventory to find out what resources we have." I felt in my pockets and was happy to find that I had my purse. Also, there were a nice pair of gloves in the pockets of the coat that I was wearing.

Phil said, "No wand. No nothing. I understand why I'm here—sort of. Why are you here?"

I sighed, "I suppose that I'm here because without a wand, probably in a muggle world, you're pretty helpless. I'm supposed to help us get back to Hogwarts. OK. Can you disapparate?"

He chuckled mirthlessly, "Without a wand?"

"OK. How about using the floo system?"

"I can do that."

"OK. So we need to find the closest floo connection."

"Yeh. I suppose there's nothing to that!"

I thought—for a while. Phil was getting a little impatient. He interrupted my thoughts. "Well?"

"Do you mind walking in the moonlight? We're lucky to have a nearly full moon."

He had stood and was looking around. "No, I suppose not. What do you think of . . . Ow! Hello! What's this!"

I stood and looked around. He'd run into some sort of sign. He said, "Well, it looks like we're on the outskirts of the fair hamlet of Sharpenhoe. Do you think we might knock on someone's door?"

I made a grimace that I'm sure Phil couldn't see. "I just don't know about that. If you wanted to do that, I'd think we'd be better off waiting until there's light in the sky."

"Well, I'm not going to stand around waiting for light in the sky while I'm freezing to death. Let's start walking. I suppose it doesn't matter which way."

I'd been looking around too. I said, "Look off there in that direction."

He verbally shrugged, "So?"

"There's light in the sky. That means there's a town over that way. We should try walking toward the light."

So, we started off. Phil grumbled, "How do we know that the road that we're on doesn't bend up ahead and go somewhere else?"

"No way of knowing."

We went slowly because, even though there was a good bit of moonlight, there was also a hedgerow next to the road. We'd stumbled off into it more than once in our hurry. At one point, we struck a fork in the road. The road to the right, Sundon Road, seemed to be making straight for the light, so we took it. It wasn't long before it took a turn that sent us away from the light. We had a little argument there.

Phil said, "Why don't we go back and take the other fork?"

"Look, with winding country roads we can be second guessing ourselves all the time. Let's just keep going."

He was still not happy. It was hard to blame him. While we were walking, we were actually fairly comfortable in our coats. It was not fun, though, walking in the seeming endless dark. We hit a couple of more forks in the road and took the one that sent us toward the light at each turn. It was becoming clear that we constantly getting closer.

After the last turn, Phil exclaimed, "Hello! Is that a street lamp in the distance?" That raised our spirits. The problem was that it also got Phil to wondering what we would do when we reached the town square.

I said, "Well, there are several possibilities." I'd been thinking about them as we'd walked. "My main goal is to get us to London. A secondary goal would be to get to somewhere that you know there's a floo connection. How we get there depends a lot on what town this is that we're approaching."

Apparently, Phil wasn't satisfied with a general answer like that. He said, "Go on. Don't leave me hanging!"

212

"OK. There are several possibilities. The best would be that we're close to London and that there's a rail connection to London. In that case we'd just buy tickets and ride the rail to London. If we're unlucky and we're not in a town with a rail connection to London, then we might be able to hire a cab to take us to the nearest place with a rail connection."

Phil interrupted me. "Wait a minute. I don't have any muggle money."

I smiled. "But I do. Our 'friends' left me with my purse."

"Have you looked in it? They might have 'helped' us a little more by leaving you with only galleons."

I was still smiling. "Don't think that for a minute. My purse can't be opened by anyone but me. It's made of mokeskin."

"Neat. I should get one myself."

By this time, we'd passed the street lamp and saw that the cross streets were becoming more common.

Phil asked, "What if we're too far from a rail connection or can't find a cab to take us there?"

I smiled. "You can almost always find a cabby to take you anywhere you want if you offer them enough galleons. Anyway, if we reach London, we can definitely find a cabby to take us to the Cauldron, or at least, close to the Cauldron."

"Sounds good in theory. I just hope it actually works."

By this time, we'd reached a point where we could see a rail line. This time, it was I who exclaimed, "Hello! Hello. Hello. What do we have here?"

Phil said, "I guess it's your precious rail line. I hope you're right about finding a station."

It was still quite dark, but my watch said that it was getting close to six AM. There was beginning to be street traffic. It was still pitch dark. As we walked, we sometimes lost sight of the rail line, but we never were far from it. Finally, I saw the famous British rail symbol on a sign that had an arrow. I exclaimed, "This is it. We're close."

Phil was mystified but followed my lead. We took a roundabout route but eventually found ourselves outside Luton station. He exclaimed, "It seems like magic—how you got us here. But I'll not complain."

Inside the station, there was more magic. Phil had never ridden British Rail before. When I bought fare cards for us, he said, "How is it that these muggle things need these plastic cards? How do they work?"

"Well, let's get on board a train bound for London and then we can discuss technology. By the way, where do you want to eat? We could grab something when we get off the train or we could wait for the Cauldron, or I suppose that we could even wait for Hogwarts."

Phil harrumphed. "I wouldn't count my fried eggs before they're hatched or whatever. Let's just get to London first."

He picked up pretty quickly on how to use the fare card. He only fumbled once or twice inserting it into the automatic turnstile. At this hour, there were a few people waiting trackside for the next train to London. I looked at our fellow passengers and commented, "All we need is a briefcase each, and we could be average commuters."

"Speak for yourself, muggle."

It turned out that he wasn't that interested in how the fare cards worked. He was very interested in where we would exit the train. When he saw that Kings Cross was on the line, he picked that with no room for argument. By the time we reached the outskirts of London, the train was packed. We got up to let a pair of little old ladies have seats. He had a little trouble after that with acceleration around curves and at stops. At the first serious jerk he would have hit the floor if I hadn't been standing next to him. He'd obviously never ridden a mass transit rail system before.

At King's Cross, he insisted in walking past 9 ¾. I argued, "Why go past the Express track. We couldn't possibly take the Express even if it were running today. We'd miss your wedding by several hours."

He just frowned and said, "I've been stuck in the land of the muggles so long that I just wanted some proof that I wasn't permanently exiled from the realm of magic."

He insisted on dragging me onto track 9 ¾. I was getting seriously hungry. I wasn't interested in this sight-seeing. I dragged him out to the street where we eventually found an available cab. It was past eight at this point, and the streets were packed. We crawled along the roads until we reached the Cauldron.

When I had the cabbie stop, he asked, "What you want here? There's nothing?"

I just gave him a good tip, and we got out. Phil grabbed me by the forearm and we ran up to the door into the Cauldron. Inside, we were greeted by Tom. "Well, look what the hypogryph drug in. I heard that the two of you might be showing up sometime this morning. Do you fancy some breakfast?"

I exclaimed, "Yes!"

Phil exclaimed, "No!"

Tom said, "Breakfast it is." He showed us to a table and took our order. I had two eggs sunny-side up and toast. Phil had fried eggs, muffins, bacon, etc.

Our order came pretty quickly. Once we had some food and warmth inside us, we were a good bit more companionable. I commented to Phil,

"See. Now that you've gotten around a good English breakfast, the whole world looks a lot more pleasant."

His mouth was full of food, but the sound that came out of his mouth was not grumpy. He still was not entirely happy. When it was time to go, he said, "You know, I ought to leave you here, stranded the way I was. I'm convinced this was your idea."

"Oh, come on. You'll look back on this as a fond memory-maker."

He grunted, but he did take me along in the floo. We came out in the Great Hall. Breakfast had just finished. The rest of the OBC were sitting on the Huffelpuff bench nearest the hearth. Slughorn said, "We had a pool going as to when you would return. I had nine-thirty. Pay up, gents."

I said, "Just for curiosity's sake, what time did each of you have?"

Dursley said, "I had seven-thirty. Haggrid had eight."

Filch broke in, "I had eight-thirty."

I said, "I don't know about Phil, but I'm going to catch up on sleep." With that, I left the happy group and headed for the Headmistress's quarters.

I had hardly awakened from a nap and was changing into my dress robes when Minerva bustled in, "Do you know that the MOH is moping around, and we can hardly get her into her dress. I thought you were supposed to keep her entertained."

I said, "There is only so much that mere flesh and blood can accomplish. Believe me, I have gone far beyond the call of duty to keep her happy."

"Well, maybe it wasn't such a good idea to throw two such unwilling people together for even just one day. When she arrived, you had to wear sun glasses. Her smile was that bright. One day. One Day! The next day, she could hardly put a smile on her face."

I just shrugged.

We got changed. Neither of us were in the wedding party, so we could take our time. Minerva had been very busy with the wedding but only as the proprietor of the wedding and reception venue. Since all the planning and most of the execution was done, she could relax now.

We ambled down to the Great Hall, which had been transformed by having the benches aligned like pews in a church. The raised stage had drapes of very fine gauze. It looked like the stage was floating in the clouds. Even the floor looked like cloud tops. The clear sky visible through the transparent ceiling completed the illusion.

I commented, "A veritable scene from heaven."

Minerva said, "A fitting beginning for a life together, wouldn't you say?"

I thought about our life together. "Well, our life hasn't exactly been heaven, but heaven seems always in reach."

She nodded and rested her head on my shoulder.

We had arrived almost an hour early. No one else was in the Great Hall, but before long people began arriving. A string quartet played somewhere beyond the gauze.

People began seriously arriving then. We were sitting on the bride's side. The other side was pretty sparse and would be. It's a long way from the West Coast of the US to here.

The wedding proceeded much as usual. The bride and groom had their little idiosyncrasies catered to—music and words said to bless the union.

After the wedding was complete, and the bride and groom had recessed out the main doors of the Great Hall, the house elves arrived to set up the Great Hall for the reception.

It took forever for the photographers to finish with the wedding party. There were two—one with magical equipment and the other with the latest mechanical film cameras. It had been hard finding a photographer who didn't have some electronics in his cameras.

The head table was on the stage but at one point, there was a call for toasts. After the wedding party finished, a general call was made.

I stepped up and took the podium. "I have only one thing left to toast. That is the fact that Sally finally has to stop calling me boss. There actually was a time in the deep recesses of history when I really was her boss. That time is far in the past, but she has never stopped calling me boss.

"Well, now I gladly yield that title to the groom." I turned to him and said, "With that release of responsibility I add that if you are smart you will never call yourself the boss. Here's to the end of my realm as 'boss'." I then drank from my champagne glass as all others did.

I returned to my seat and tucked in.

As the meal was ending, the band set up. Before too long, the round of formal dances began—the bride and groom, the mother of the bride and the groom, and on and on. Finally, general dancing began.

As I finished a dance with Aurora, a familiar voice said, "I've come to claim my dances."

I smiled and took her in my arms. As we began to dance, she asked, "How did I look?"

I nodded, "Sally and I go back a long, long way. I love her. However, she was not the most beautiful woman on the stage just now."

Haley perked up a bit, "And just who was?"

"Don't be coy, even without your glasses you know that you were—as we say in the States—by a country mile."

She sniffed.

"Really. That raises a question. How is it that you've not at least got a serious boy friend?"

She was silent for a long time. Eventually she said, "Do you think that you can love more than one person at a time?"

I had to think a bit too, "Are we talking in generalities or about someone in particular?"

"Do you think that I can love more than one person at the same time?"

That threw me for a loop. I thought she was asking about whether I could love more than one woman at a time. "I don't know. You are a mystery to me. You've been through so much, and you've surprised me so often that I just don't know."

She replied, "I don't know either, but until that happens, I won't have a serious boy friend."

Then she threw me another curve ball, "Wendt, do you think I'll ever be back here?"

She had had her head on my shoulder. I pulled back and looked at her directly. "Have you burned your bridges with Sally by being sulky at her wedding?"

She laughed,."Oh, no. Sally thought I was just sad because I wasn't getting married, too. It's ironic. She swore she'd find someone for me."

"Well, then. I'm sure you could invite yourself here once in a while—especially in the summer."

We were still dancing while gazing at each other. She asked, "Do you want me to?"

After a long while I said, "You are cruel."

"No more than you."

I said, "I would like you to be around every now and then."

"Me too. Every now and then." Then she added the question, "Even if we're not lovers?"

"Even if we're not lovers."

The rest of the evening we spent silently dancing—sometimes with each other.

After the evening was over, Minerva asked me, "I see you were trying to cheer up Haley. It didn't seem to be working."

"No, I don't think it did."

She laughed, "You don't know the first thing about women."

"I guess I don't."

217

The End?

About the Author

 William Wilkin lived in a small Southern Ohio town until he began his college career. He has a Bachelor's degree in Physics from The Ohio State University and a Master's degree in Physics from The University of Chicago.He has a career in corporate Information Technology.and currently lives in Nashville, TN.

He enjoys music, both "serious" and "classic Rock". He reads classic Detective fiction and Science Fiction & Fantasy as well as trying to stay current in Physics.

He began writing seriously about 2005. He has a blog, in-mid-world, where he writes about Science Fiction & Fantasy and remotely related topics.